ROO THE DAY

ELLEN RIGGS

BOUGHT-THE-FARM
MYSTERIES

FREE PREQUEL

Rescuing this pup could bring Ivy
a whole new life... if it doesn't kill
her first.

Discover how big city executive Ivy meets Keats, her crime-solving sheepdog, in A Dog with Two Tales. Ivy Galloway doesn't know how desperate she is to escape the big city and her soul-sucking corporate career until she meets a sheepdog in need of rescue, too.

This short prequel to the laugh-out-loud Bought-the-Farm Mystery series is a page-turner for lovers of animals, humor and spunky amateur sleuths. Go to **ellenriggs.com/opt-in** and join Ellen Riggs' author newsletter to get this FREE prequel.

Roo the Day

ISBN 978-1-998742-15-8 D2D Paperback
ISBN 978-1-990613-58-6 eBook
ISBN 978-1-990613-59-3 Book
ISBN 978-1-990613-60-9 AudioBook
ASIN B0CRCTBCVL Kindle
ASIN 1990613594 Paperback

Publisher: Ellen Riggs
www.ellenriggs.com
2512231250D2D

CHAPTER ONE

I was picked last.

Despite everything that had happened in the last two years, from animal rescue to facing down cold-blooded killers, I was picked last.

"Ivy, let it go." My best friend, Jilly Blackwood, gave my arm a reassuring pat as we walked across the grass. "I didn't get picked at all. Daisy didn't, either."

"You two wanted to sit this out, whereas I got picked after everyone else. Outrageous!"

Jilly wasn't taking outrage for an answer. "You know your mom would have been picked last if she hadn't outplayed the captain."

"More specifically, given birth to him." I turned a fierce glare on my brother, Asher Galloway, who was too busy bossing the rest of his team around to notice. "But still, he freely chose Dad, Iris, Sutton, Weston, Teri Mason and Hazel Bingham before me. He even chose Edna Evans over me, and he hates her."

"He doesn't hate Edna. He's just scared of her." Jilly's arm pat turned into a gentle poke. "And that's not what's really bothering you, is it?"

"You know what's bothering me. He chose a dog over me." I looked down at my handsome border collie, who warmed me with his brown eye as his mouth dropped open with a pant-laugh at my expense. "The dog is a certified genius, but can he play softball?"

Keats' mouth snapped shut and he mumbled what sounded like an indignant retort. Of course he could play softball. Like everything else, it would be by his own rules.

"If Hazel can have a runner, Keats can have a batter," Jilly said, earning a tail wag for her support. She hugged the orange fluffy cat in her arms tighter. "Percy will have to watch from his cat carrier so that he doesn't get hit by a stray ball."

My fingers reached for my beloved dog's ears. I was proud he was a hot pick but bringing up the rear rankled. As the last of six Galloway siblings, maybe that was inevitable. No matter what I accomplished, I still felt like an afterthought sometimes.

Keats' mumble turned into a reproof. He never endorsed angst when there were so many legitimate problems to worry about. Or, in his case, welcome. This wasn't a dog for leisure, although he did enjoy family get-togethers. I enjoyed them, too, if they involved one of Jilly's superb meals. That's how normal families bonded in adulthood—over a table, rather than standing around a field. "This game is barbaric."

Jilly stopped trying to hide her amusement over my ire. "I wouldn't put pickup softball in the same league as gladiator sports. Or mixed martial arts. Now, those are barbaric."

Our current arena had seen plenty of combat. The diamond was located behind the Clover Grove elementary school, where my sports trauma began. Dodgeball? Picked last. Volleyball? Also last. Football? Last, too. "Everyone here knows I've helped take down violent criminals. I even used a baseball bat to rescue Keats. I'm not the nerd I used to be, Jilly."

"I had a ringside seat for the transformation, my friend, but you're still not exactly athletic." Her prodding progressed to a gentle shove. "You scorn all sports. Proudly."

"Only because they're barbaric. And boring." I moved away from her. "Remember what happened at Flordale? Not only was I picked last, I was also fired from the corporate team for being a liability."

"Oh, the inhumanity of human resources. Didn't we put all that behind us, though? Now we run a beautiful inn on Runaway Farm, where you're picked first often. Who does Mayor Martingale come to when she needs crime-solving help on the sly? Chief of Police Kellan Harper, or his hobby farmer fiancée, Ivy Galloway?"

My lips slid into first base as a smile got away on me. The mayor called on me more often than Kellan liked. Technically, she called on Keats and Percy but we came as a package deal. "Still, I got picked last dozens of times in this very diamond by the same perpetrator—your husband." Asher directed people around with flourishes perfected during stints as a traffic cop. Keats trotted over and added his expert herding skills to the cause. "Ash tried to nab Gertie Rhodes, too. Can she bat with a rifle under that poncho?"

"Probably." Jilly wasn't about to diss our best friends, no matter how quirky. In our circle, senior citizens like Gertie, Edna, Hazel and Buckley Brackens were contenders on and off the field. "Anyway, if Kellan had been able to join us, you'd have been chosen first."

My fiancé had pulled out of the game at the last minute due to an emergency only the highest-ranking officer could handle. It was a convenient excuse to escape the awkwardness of my family at play. If I wanted to make it to the altar, however, I'd need to pretend to buy his story. He bought enough of mine.

With Kellan out of the running, someone else eagerly stepped up as captain of the opposing team: my nemesis, Travis Wigg. The bearded woodsman with the mysterious past never missed an opportunity to undermine me with Kellan and mock my affection for animals. Today, as usual, he wore his trademark lumberjacket. It was too warm for that. My sister Poppy was hanging off his arm like a schoolgirl in a tank top and short-shorts. "What's he hiding under that jacket?" I asked. "A bulletproof vest? And what's with Poppy's outfit? She left her inner rebel at home."

"Don't think I didn't warn her about those shorts," my mother said, joining us. "She's going to slide into home and wear the proof forever. We Galloway Girls are so pale and scar easily."

Mom had taken appropriate precautions. Usually dressed from head to toe in fashion-forward scarlet, she was barely recognizable in jeans, a long-sleeved T-shirt and fresh-from-the-box white sneakers.

"Is that my T-shirt?" I asked.

"Possibly. I don't put nametags in your clothes anymore." She brushed dandelion fluff off her chest. "Remember how you girls used to squabble over the laundry basket?"

"Mom, that shirt was in my bottom drawer and you taught us to ask before borrowing. Same rule applies to you."

My mother spent most of her time in borrowed rooms at the inn while her apartment in town sat empty. After years of living alone in the city, I was glad to have family around but she crowded Jilly more than I liked. Mom also got on Asher's nerves, which I liked just about right.

"Dahlia's above rules," Jilly said. "That's why she crossed sides and assigned herself to Travis' team."

Mom offered a tinkling laugh. "He couldn't say no to his future mother-in-law, could he?"

I turned to stare at the happy couple. "They're not engaged."

"Yet," Mom said. "If she'd stop clinging to him like a life raft, he might have a chance to propose."

"Unless something's changed, you're not Travis' biggest fan, Mom."

"That man has more secrets than your father, and I don't want any of my girls to suffer the fate I did." She went back to work on the dandelion fluff. "However, I learned long ago that showing the slightest resistance would push Poppy in the wrong direction. So, now I'm on Team Travis, as far as optics go."

"I don't know what she sees in him, aside from good hair and teeth," I said. "And a nice build."

Jilly laughed at my faint praise. "Travis is a hottie if you like the rugged type. And I doubt he'll leave Poppy with six children to raise alone, like Calvin did you, Dahlia."

Mom's eyes landed on my dad, who was standing with Travis and Asher. When the captains were done with their flourishes, Dad would weigh in quietly and the younger men would listen. "I *don't* like the rugged type. Not anymore. On the bright side, Poppy is too old to have six children."

"Dahlia!" Jilly signaled for Mom to keep her voice down. "Don't be mean."

"It's not mean, it's math, Jillian. You girls didn't start early enough to replicate my triumph." Mom gestured to her trim figure. "Can you believe I delivered an entire softball team?"

"Only if you're counting grandkids," I said. "And speaking of the twins, Poppy could still match you if she had three sets in quick succession. Daisy had two sets, so it probably runs in the family."

Mom's face paled, making her scarlet lipstick look garish. "Don't joke about that, Ivy. What happened to Daisy was—"

"Inhumane?" Jilly supplied. "If I had *one* set of twins, I'd be so done."

"And yet Daisy let it happen again." Mom's hazel eyes searched out the four boys. "So tragic."

I shoved her hard enough to raise dust around her white sneakers. "Mom, don't say that. You love those boys."

She sighed. "I suppose, although the younger pair are—"

"Hooligans?" Edna Evans, my octogenarian prepper neighbor, filled in the last word. "I don't agree with you often, Dahlia, but you're right about that. The boys are all skilled at martial arts though. You could learn a thing or two from them, Ivy."

"I have. Daisy's basement is fully lined with mats, and the shoulder rolls didn't hurt as much as I expected."

Edna eyed me skeptically. "You can do a shoulder roll?"

"And land on my feet, at least most of the time. Can you say the same?"

She stuck out one leg, swathed in summer-weight camouflage. "All of the time, and in army boots. As can the talented Gertie Rhodes." Plucking off her baseball cap, Edna gave an elaborate bow. "Ivy, I salute you. If Asher and Travis knew about the shoulder rolls, maybe you wouldn't have been the last one chosen today."

"Dahlia jumped the line," Jilly pointed out. "And as much as I hate to disparage my husband—"

"I love disparaging your husband," Edna interrupted.

"I think he deliberately dissed Ivy," Jilly finished. "And he'll hear about it later."

Edna nodded. "Wanted to take her down a peg. Same with Travis."

"Jealous," Mom added. "It's a shame, but men hate being shown up by a clever woman and you do it so often, Ivy. Wait till they hear you can somersault right over them."

"Let's keep that on the downlow, Mom. I think it would upset Kellan."

"Darling, I'm sure he'd be relieved that you're learning to defend yourself from deadbeats and livestock. Kellan's a busy man and can't always be around to protect you."

"He'll worry it'll make me even more—" I turned to Jilly. "What's that word he throws around all the time?"

"Reckless." Jilly grinned. "I'd go with the livestock angle. Nice one, Dahlia."

Pulling a tube of lipstick out of her back pocket, Mom

reapplied expertly without a mirror. "Glad I'm good for something, Jillian. I daresay it isn't catching a softball."

"Me, either," Jilly said. "That's why I declined the opportunity. I'll come to the Galloway family meetings and cook every holiday meal, but I draw the line at sports."

Edna rubbed her hands together. "I'm good with a mitt and even better with a bat. But I accepted Sutton's offer to be my runner."

That surprised me. "The survivalist who crowdsurfed at a rock concert just weeks ago outsources running bases?"

"I'll save my energy for more important things than the Galloway softball team. Why are we doing this, anyway?"

"Daisy's idea," I said. "She always set up a game when we bickered as kids. It was supposed to bring out the team in us."

Mom pulled a visor out of her purse and fanned herself. "It thrilled me to bits when Daisy said, 'let's go and hit a few balls.'"

"You never came," I pointed out. "Not once."

"Exactly. It thrilled me to have two hours of blissful solitude. Since the older twins were accused of murder last month, I expect this game is about solidarity."

Jilly and I winced. Mom wasn't wrong about what happened and it had worked out okay in the end, but it was too soon to joke about it.

"Dahlia! You're up." Travis' shout failed to generate a response and he tried a different tone. "Dahlia?"

Mom applied more lipstick. "I never gave him permission to use my first name."

Travis tried again. "Dahlia?" And then, more tentatively, "Mrs. Galloway?"

She slid the lipstick away. "I sometimes think about going back to my maiden name. But Miss Swingle sounds like a spinster." Directing a gaudy smirk at Edna, she added, "No offense."

Edna beckoned for me to join her in the outfield. "None taken.

I'm a tough old maid with no complaints about my status. Batter up, Dahlia."

Mom's strut on the way to the plate told all assembled that in her own mind, she was wearing heels and red satin. Travis tried to adjust her posture and she said, "Unhand me, you oaf. I know how to hit a ball."

Dad threw out the first pitch and there was a loud crack.

Mom *did* know how to hit a ball. Would she never cease to amaze me?

Running was beneath her pay grade, however, so she flicked ruby-tipped fingers at Beaton, one of the younger twin hooligans. He raced to first base, and then second while Violet and I repeatedly fumbled the ball in the field. It was like Mom put a hex on it.

"Hurry, Beaton," she called merrily. "I'll take a home run, darling."

Finally, I managed to scoop up the ball, run in from the field and fire it toward Sutton behind the plate.

Beaton slid right under the ball and touched home with his sneaker.

Mom tossed the bat to Travis with panache. "That's how *we* play ball, Mr. Wigg."

"*Master* Wigg," he corrected with a smug grin at Poppy, as she walked to the plate.

Poppy hushed him quickly and then scanned the field. When she saw me, she called, "Get back to the outfield, Ivy. Wanna knock your socks off."

Keats left his position to move closer to mine. He was well able to cover both and run the ball in with more efficiency.

"Master?" Mom asked. "Travis, no man will ever master *this* lady again."

Travis wasn't fazed. "Dahlia. Mrs. Galloway—"

"Ms. Swingle. Try that on for size."

"Mom." The complaint came from Poppy as she took a couple of warm up swings. "Just pick one."

"I can never pick just one of anything, darling. As the mother of six and grandmother of four—"

"Soon to be five." All heads swiveled to first base, where Iris gave an innocent shrug. "Or so I heard from everyone's favorite psychic when I called for a reading."

"Iris Gladiola Galloway." Mom's voice had a harsh edge. "Are you saying what I think you're saying?"

Iris grinned. "Probably not."

My phone rang and I hit silence without looking. "Iris, Mom wants to know if there are seeds in the pod. Do irises even have seeds?"

"Got me, but I've pretty much gone to seed, so I'm not delivering grandchild number five."

Now everyone turned to the line of lawn chairs, where Jilly sat chatting with Daisy. The cat carrier jiggled in her lap as Percy got impatient with confinement. "What?" My best friend's eyebrows rose. "Why's everyone staring at me?"

Asher dashed in from center field. "What's going on? You okay, hon?"

Edna's mouth opened to take the lead but Jilly was saved by the bell. Or, more specifically, the phone buzzing in her hand. Glancing at the screen, she said, "Ivy, it's Meryl Martingale. She wants you to pick up."

"I'm busy," I said. "This is a critical family matter."

Not the softball game but the potential new Galloway. Jilly's cousin Janelle Brighton didn't toss her predictions around lightly and I'd seen enough come true to take her seriously.

Jilly tapped on her phone, watched the screen and then shook her head. "No dice, Ivy. Meryl says it's urgent. And that you need to take this one for the team."

I may have held out longer if Keats hadn't assertively poked the side pocket of my overalls while shooting me a look with his eerie blue eye. Whatever Mayor Martingale had to say was more interesting to my intrepid dog than softball. Most things were.

"Time out, please. I need to take this." Grabbing my phone, I greeted the mayor politely, listened for a moment and then blurted, "I'm doing *what*?"

CHAPTER TWO

I shook my head as I drove to the outskirts of town that evening. "I thought better of Meryl. She's become such a disappointment this year."

"She's a good friend," Jilly said, running one hand over Percy and the other over Keats. The double pat always signified nerves, although the mayor had sucked us into worse situations, one as recently as last month. "When she's not being a politician, that is."

"Good friends don't use friends and she's been doing a lot of that. Now she wants us to headline her self-defense class and attract participants. We're busy people."

"She caught the entire clan playing baseball on a sunny afternoon. That's a crowd with time on its hands."

Keats added a mumbled commentary, possibly about idle hands—and paws—serving no good.

"She'll get a big turnout without us," I said. "It's exploitation at its worst."

Jilly's hands paused, the left buried in black fur and the right in orange fluff. "Like it or not, you've become a leader in this town, my friend. You're living proof of why self-defense skills are a good idea. Despite being untrained, you keep on surviving attacks."

"I don't want to be a role model. It's too much responsibility. What if people like Heddy and Kaye Langman start doing spinning sidekicks while parting people from their treasured antiques? Those skills could be used for ill. Even if people were trying to do the right thing, they could get hurt." I reached over to touch Keats. "The only reason I survive deadbeats is heroic pets and there aren't enough of those to go around."

Jilly's fingers started moving again. "Good point. Besides, fewer eyes on you means more freedom to slip around under the radar."

"It's already harder than it used to be, thanks to Justine Schalow." The reporter for the Clover Grove Tattler had made covering my every move her "beat" and she was annoyingly good at it. I hadn't valued anonymity till I lost it.

"Haven't seen Justine around much, lately. Asher implied they've been leaking a few false leads out of town to decoy her."

Keats gave a pant-laugh and I joined in. "Awesome. Although it's a shame our scarce police resources need to be funneled into handling Justine."

"I wonder if she'll be here tonight. Martial arts skills will only make her bolder." Jilly checked her phone. "We're not far, now."

Knowing time was short, I decided to ask Jilly the question that had hung unanswered between us since the family softball game ended with a fizzle. We'd pushed through a couple of innings but the only people who could focus were Keats and me. Having been a first pick for the team, the dog counted as people. Did he hit a home run, though? No, that was me. And, unlike Mom, I'd run the bases on my own with Keats racing alongside for moral support. A round of applause would have been nice but by that time, the teams were packing up. "Speaking of news... Did you hear what Iris said earlier?"

"About the prophesied fifth grandchild?" My friend's fingers wrapped the mystical word with air quotes. "I heard. I'm not the only one of childbearing years."

"I know. But you'd tell me, right?"

"Of course I'd tell you. Maybe even before Asher, depending which shift he was working."

I was both relieved and a little disappointed. "Okay. I just wouldn't want to put my niece or nephew at risk."

"You will, eventually. Twenty years from now you'll still be getting into trouble. I'd put good money on it."

"There are better ways to spend your money. And you're changing the subject." I shot her a glance. "Janelle is your cousin. You're the one she's most likely to make predictions about."

An impatient wave dismissed what Jilly called "psychic mumbo-jumbo." Then she patted her stomach, which was undeniably flat under her yoga pants. "Does it look like I'm packing the next Galloway? Think hard about your answer."

I laughed. "It does not. But you've said you're open to it."

"In a theoretical sense, absolutely. In the practical sense, not quite." Now she glanced at me. "Maybe I'm riding the brakes till you're ready. We could deliver on the same day and have our own version of twins."

"Great idea! But Kellan and I haven't even picked a wedding venue. Twice we've put a day aside to make decisions. Twice crime canceled our appointments."

"It has been busy. I wish you'd let me plan it."

I took the exit that led to a small strip mall on the outskirts of town. "You know I'd love that. The roadblock is Kellan. He's the romantic one who thinks we should plan the big day ourselves." Backing into a parking spot, I sighed. "All I want to do is show up and hit my mark at the appointed time."

"You'll make a beautiful bride, Ivy." Opening the door, she let the pets out. "Just don't get your nose broken today. What if the teacher pairs you with some big bruiser just because you've nailed a few perps?"

I scanned the row of parked vehicles in the lot. "Mostly sedans, which means mostly women." Pointing to a white van squeezed into a tight spot, I added, "With the exception of the bruisers who came in that."

"Why are Edna and Gertie here?" Jilly asked, as we met in front of my truck. "They don't need a self-defense class. They could teach it."

"They'll probably try to do just that unless the instructor is top notch."

Jilly eyed the empty stores on either side of what Meryl had called "the studio." "This mini-mall is a dump."

It always had been. In my memory, Midway Mall had housed a florist, a bookstore, a health food store, a laundromat, a dry cleaner, an electronics store and a pawn shop, among others. The site was unlucky in retail love, possibly due to being nearly surrounded by the forest that always seemed eager to swallow Clover Grove whole. Justine had reported in the Tattler that it was slated for demolition but that didn't mean it was true.

The fluorescent track lighting in the pop-up studio couldn't dispel what felt like vague menace to me. Perhaps Jilly felt it too, because she linked her free arm through mine. Percy dangled over the other, tail swishing irritably against my jacket. Keats' white tuft was aloft and swaying as he led us to the wide glass storefront. Someone more exciting than Edna and Gertie must be here. Or, judging by the movement inside, several someones.

The dog brought us to a stop so that we could case the place before entering. Meryl had obviously spread the word quickly because the turnout was impressive. Most of the crowd was female, with the notable exception of two men in karate whites tied with black belts who were standing with their backs to a mirrored wall. Two other walls were covered in padding that looked brand new. One of the teachers was tall and fair, the other short, dark and bearded.

A third man came out of the back room with the mayor. He

was wearing a familiar lumberjacket, white teeth gleaming out. Sweeping off his toque, he rubbed abundant hair.

I groaned. "Seriously? Travis is the teacher?"

"Master, I'm guessing," Jilly said. "Remember how he corrected your mom earlier? And then looked—"

"Smug? Yeah. He was dying to spring this on us. It was Poppy who wanted to wait."

My lack of enthusiasm for Travis and the romance had done exactly what Mom predicted and pushed the couple closer. Hopefully Poppy knew more about him than I did because the grapevine had been stingy with information. Normally, a few questions could unearth stories dating back to someone's infancy but Travis had hidden his tracks well. My senior friends with their long memories of the area came up empty, as did a trip to the library. If that weren't mysterious enough, Kellan, Asher and the curmudgeonly Pefferlaw brothers were friendly with Travis. The younger Pefferlaw had said Travis was his brother-in-law and a talented woodworker. But no one wanted to say more. Not even the mayor, who'd hired him off the books to provide security recently. I was frustrated with the results of my research but far from done. The only thing the woodsman had going for him, as far as I was concerned, was that Keats didn't hate him. The dog had gone so far as to save Travis from a hat-snatching by Drama Llama. So, he couldn't be all bad. But if he were all good, information wouldn't be hard to find. Despite Poppy's rebellious ways, she was sensitive and a bit gullible. I wanted to protect her.

Jilly's nose was close to the glass. "Where's Justine when you need some reporting done? I don't see her. But the Galloway women are out in force. As you feared, the Langman sisters are here. And Beverly Roxton."

Seeing us, Travis waved, walked to the door and opened it. "Ladies! Come on in. We've been waiting. The party couldn't start without you."

The mayor joined him, somehow managing to look impressive while wearing a high-end track suit. My eyes dropped, expecting to see her usual stilettos, but her feet were bare on the mats that covered the floor. Were we going to toss each other around like crash test dummies?

"Aunt Ivy!" The excited voice belonged to Sutton, my favorite nephew. Weston was right behind him and their eagerness forced my scowl into retreat. Since the twins helped save me from a vicious attack, we'd become even closer. My early martial arts training with them involved more laughter than learning, however, and I'd asked them to keep it between us. They weren't accredited, and I didn't want to get them in trouble.

"Hey, guys." I slung an arm across Sutton's shoulders and peered behind him at the Galloway ladies deep in conversation in the corner. "Where's your mom?"

"Wimped out. Said she had work at the inn." Weston shrugged. "Her loss."

"I've been texting her to let her know Liam is here," Sutton added, gesturing to one of the men in white. The guy was in his mid-thirties and had the same powerful build and confident posture as Travis. That's where the resemblance ended, however. Liam was clean shaven and only had a few tufts of strawberry blond hair left. "We've mentioned him, right?"

"Only a hundred times." I let them tow me to their sensei, who taught out of a studio in Dorset Hills. After shaking hands, I thanked Liam Turco. "Your work saved my bacon last month."

Liam's blue eyes crinkled as he returned my smile. "I heard all about it, trust me. Few of us get to use our training in real life scenarios like the twins did. I'm proud of them. And I hope they never need to do it again."

"Exactly," Travis said, shouldering in beside Liam. "The whole point of self-defense is to avoid conflict altogether."

The third man stared down at Keats, whose tail had dropped. "No dogs in the dojo, ma'am. I mean, it's just common sense."

I waited till his dark eyes came back up. "You obviously don't know me, sir. I'm Ivy Galloway and this is Keats. Where I go, he goes." I gestured behind me to Jilly. "The cat, too. Common sense doesn't always join us."

Travis snorted. "She's right about common sense. Brydon Ting, meet Ivy, Poppy's sister. I can vouch for both dog and cat, if not the farmer."

Brydon's dark brows gathered over a nose that looked like it had been broken a few times. Though the youngest of the three, he was also balding. It was like Travis had deliberately chosen assistants to showcase his abundant mane. "At least take off your boots, ma'am. As a show of respect."

I thought about it and shook my head. "Can't do it, Brydon. I never want to meet an emergency in bare feet. If you have an issue, please take it up with Mayor Martingale. She's the one who conscripted me."

That was enough to make Brydon subside into a muttered complaint to Travis that made Keats' ears flatten.

Travis' shoulders rose and fell under red-checked flannel. "It's a community self-defense class in a makeshift dojo, Brydon. If Ivy wants to wear boots, it means she needs to practice with me." His sly smile suggested that had been the plan all along. "How does that sound, Ivy? We can't have you leaving tread marks on the mayor."

I wanted to back down but a poke in the shins told me to hold my ground. "Perfect. I look forward to kicking you, Travis."

Liam laughed out loud. "That enthusiasm will carry you far, Ivy."

"Not far enough," Travis said. "But let's get started." He clapped his hands and moved with his sidekicks to the front of the room. The mirrored wall behind them seemed like a bad choice for sparring but in one of this unit's many lives, it had been a dance studio. "Eyes front, everyone. Ears open. Mouths closed." His own mouth dipped into a frown as a hand rose. "Yes, Miss Evans?"

"You didn't mention necks, young man, and I'm concerned about the noose around yours. Seems like an accident waiting to happen." Edna crossed her camouflage arms, boots spread wide on the mats. "I should think you'd want to set us a good example."

Travis grabbed the long strip of black fabric looped around his neck and pretended to strangle himself. Most people laughed, none harder than my nephews. The twins had fallen for Travis' supposed charms.

"You raise a good point, Miss Evans." The brilliance of his grin confirmed he'd come out of the woods to see a dentist occasionally. "I'm not one for flashing my credentials but I took my black belt out of mothballs for this." He pulled the belt off, balled it up, and threw it into the corner. "My humor got the better of me. It happens."

"That will make you an easy mark for whatever survives the end times," Edna said. "Consider yourself warned."

The expression on the other men's faces made me laugh, earning me a glare from Poppy and an elbow pinch from Jilly, who'd come up beside me.

To give him credit, Travis laughed, too. "Point taken. And you're right that self-defense begins with being prepared. My best advice is to avoid risky situations in the first place. No matter what we teach you in the coming weeks, most of it will fly out of your head at the first sign of danger. We're going to keep things simple today. When you have no choice but to defend yourselves, you're going to want to know how to jab the eyes, the neck and of course, the uh—"

"The manhood," Edna finished for him. "We all know most attackers are men and most victims, women."

Sutton and Weston looked uncomfortable. "Can you do a

proper demo first, Travis?" Weston said. "Show everyone what you've got."

They weren't calling him "uncle" yet, but Travis was slinking into the family like the boys' wily ferrets.

The woodsman raised his eyebrows at the mayor and she nodded. "If you insist, boys," he said. "Volunteers?"

The twins' arms hung loose at their sides, apparently well aware they were outmatched.

No one else volunteered, either. Gertie flicked back her long gray braid and then crossed her arms under her ratty brown poncho. Edna mirrored the move over her camo jumpsuit. Was Travis intimidating enough to deter my warrior friends?

Keats nudged my hand with a mumble. "What?" I whispered, as his blue eye pinned me. "Are you nuts?"

He nudged my hand again and I lifted it out of reach.

"Ah, I see we have an offer." Travis was delighted. "Ivy, step forward."

Jilly pushed my hand down, and then worked in opposition to the muzzle beneath it. "Nope. You're not trying any flashy moves on Ivy, Travis. She hasn't fully recovered from a concussion."

"We've got helmets in the car," Sutton said. "Mom makes us wear them in class."

"Too small," Weston replied. "Aunt Ivy has a big head. Amazing she doesn't tip over more often."

A snicker passed through the room and anger flamed up in Jilly's cheeks. She stopped fighting Keats and pointed at the twins. "Your aunt's head is exactly the right size to hold an extraordinary brain. If someone needs to volunteer for this showcase, it'll be me."

"Jilly, no!"

My voice was loud but Edna's was louder. "Absolutely not, Jillian. If this overhyped hayseed hurts you or the unborn baby Galloways, Asher would be forced into a duel. Let me do the honors."

Travis bowed gallantly. "I cannot fight a senior citizen, madam. I'm an honorable man."

Edna's sallow cheeks flushed. "You're not the only one with a black belt, Mr. Wigg. Some of us are confident enough to leave it at home."

The flush was contagious. Travis didn't have much real estate over his beard, but his nose and forehead ripened nicely. "Brydon? Thanks for stepping up."

Brydon brought his palms together and lowered his head. "As you wish, sensei."

The crowd backed away to give the men space. Jilly and I took our cue from the dog and eased closer to the large windows. Despite the late day sun that flooded the room, I felt claustrophobic. There were plenty of people I liked here but I preferred the company of animals in wide open meadows.

A strange energy percolated through the studio and I wasn't the only one who thought so. Keats' ruff came up and then settled, and then repeated the cycle. Maybe someone was going to get hurt in this demonstration. I could at least try to intervene. "Travis," I called over the murmur of voices. "How about we stick to your original plan and just go over the basics? Why show us advanced moves we'll never remember under pressure?"

Voices rose in protest, Heddy Langman's loudest of all. Edna shouted them all down. "Ivy's right. I'm skilled in martial arts but when push comes to shove, the basics will keep you safe. Fancy scissor sweeps are best left to the movie stunt people."

"I do love a good chop-socky," Gertie said. "From the comfort of my living room sofa."

Even Poppy shook her head, but Travis had decided. He shrugged off his lumberjacket and tossed it on top of his black belt. Then the two men moved into position, circling a few times. At first it was slow and sedate. It seemed like neither man wanted to throw the first punch. Finally, Travis made a sudden aggressive jab and the game was on. The rest of us moved away as the mock fight got bigger and more flamboyant. Hands and feet flashed in silence broken only by grunts from the men and gasps from the audience of women. I tried to drag my eyes away and find the mayor, but the sparring was riveting. Travis danced back, spun and kicked Brydon so hard he rolled into a reverse somersault. Landing on his feet, Brydon dodged an incoming punch and jabbed Travis in the neck. The next flurry of moves seemed designed to showcase what we'd need to learn: heel of hand to the chin, pokes at eyes and elbows in ribcages. The only thing they *didn't* do was go for the groin. That's how I knew this was still for show, despite huffing, puffing and red sweaty faces. Still, it felt real to me and Keats' hackles stayed in the "on" position. The emotion was too high even without hitting below the black belt, figuratively speaking. Eventually, Brydon went down and pulled Travis after him. The sparring turned into a rolling grapple.

"Would you two like to get a room?" Edna called out. "Because this is uncomfortable to watch."

The men broke apart and bounced to their feet. Travis came at Brydon with a flying kick. I envied his height but knew I'd never achieve it. Brydon leapt aside and struck at Travis, only to have the momentum used against him as Travis pivoted and threw him over his shoulder. Brydon slapped the mat as he went down, but then he caught Travis' feet between his legs and rolled. This time Travis smacked the mat as he connected.

"Stop!" I expected Meryl to call it, but Poppy was the one who broke away from the crowd and stepped into the ever-widening space that constituted the "ring."

The men didn't stop. I responded to Keats' nudge and turned away to face the windows. I'd had too many real-life altercations to take pleasure from watching others fight.

I sensed that neither man was willing to back down. Doing so would probably feel like weakness in front of a senior official. They didn't realize that continuing with tempers flaring was the true sign of weakness. The entire point of the class was to show us how to stay cool in a confrontation.

"Maybe we should intervene before someone gets hurt, buddy," I said. "Each dude deserves a nip. Your choice of body part."

Keats propelled me away from the action, instead. He was mumbling but with Poppy's voice getting loud and shrill, I couldn't pick up on the dog's tone.

When I didn't move fast enough, Keats applied teeth to the back of my leg, making me jump. And then again. And again.

My hopping inside was nothing compared to what was happening in the parking lot.

A large animal with reddish-brown fur bounded across the pavement in front of the windows and vanished from sight so fast it seemed like a dream. Or a hallucination, since sharp teeth continued to prove I was very much awake.

Only a vision so outrageous could pull me outside when tension was building to the boiling point inside. But there was no way I'd let two ridiculous men keep me from my calling.

And my calling was hopping into the sunset.

CHAPTER THREE

"Keats, go!" He raced ahead of me, kicking into low stance and high gear. "Was that what I think it was?"

"Only if you think it was a kangaroo," Edna said, clomping after me in heavy boots. "I saw plenty on my trip down under. Awful creatures."

"Adorable creatures! Those ears. Those big feet. That tail. Edna, it's my dream come true. I've always wanted one on the farm."

She was ahead of me now, camouflage legs pumping. If an octogenarian could pass me so easily, I needed to up my cardio game. "They're ridiculous and fighty." Her voice drifted back. "You don't want a roo."

"Oh, I do want a roo." I picked up speed and we rounded the corner of the strip mall together. "Where'd it go?"

"You said you wanted a wallaby and there's a world of difference between them." Her boots slowed. "Moot point anyway. That roo is gone."

"It can't be. It was just here."

"They can clock 40 miles an hour in a sprint, Ivy. Would your dog be turning back if there was any chance of herding it into your pasture?"

I squinted into the blinding sun hanging above the trees where the kangaroo had disappeared. "I'll need taller fences."

"You'll need a magic bullet, because that thing isn't coming in without a fight."

Pulling out my phone, I texted the co-leaders of a group of animal rescuers from neighboring Dorset Hills, AKA Dog Town. "Then we'll bring the fight. If anyone can capture a kangaroo, it's Cori Hogan."

"I'm guessing it had a hundred pounds on Cori," Edna said. "She'd better bring the magic gun for your magic bullet. Better yet, a unicorn lasso." She watched Keats trot back. He looked dejected. "Even your dog knows it's futile."

"What's going on?" Jilly asked, joining us. "Your sudden exit broke up the sparring, thank goodness. I was embarrassed for them."

"It was a battle between testosterone and smarts and we all know how that plays out." Edna snickered. "In the end, they were saved by the kangaroo."

Little shocked my best friend these days, but her green eyes widened. "Kangaroo? For real?"

"Very much so." I gestured with my phone toward the woods. "Keats kept pushing me to face the window and I turned just in time to see it shoot past."

"There was nothing in pursuit," Edna said. "I guess it was just enjoying freedom."

Keats' ruff was still high and his ears back. He undercut Edna's opinion with a growl.

We all exchanged glances, and then Jilly and I shivered. "Maybe something was chasing that runaway roo," I said, "because Keats isn't thrilled about the situation."

Jilly glanced back at the crowd spilling out into the parking lot.

"We need to tell Mayor Martingale. She'll want to call Animal Services."

"I've called the Rescue Mafia. They'll find a good home for it."

She turned to me, eyes narrowing. "On Runaway Farm, you mean. Everyone knows you want a kangaroo."

"A wallaby, Jilly. Similar but different in all the right ways. Even I know a kangaroo is more than I can handle."

Keats mumbled agreement with that. He was game to take on most livestock but Australian wildlife posed unique challenges. Elaine, our resident emu, refused to submit to my sheepdog and the kangaroo would be even more stubborn.

Jilly smoothed her blonde curls and started walking. "Then maybe we should let Animal Services bring in the runaway."

I followed, keeping pace. "What if it's fleeing abuse or neglect, Jilly? The Rescue Mafia's the best option for placing it properly."

My best friend always moved quickly but on the rare day she wore sneakers she really covered ground. "Fine, I'll try to convince Meryl to let the Mafia give it a try. We'll need to disperse the crowd without alarming anyone."

"I'll manage traffic," Edna said. "Good thing I stocked your truck, Ivy. We're reasonably well prepared, although a dart gun would be nice."

"Let's spread the word about escaped livestock," I said. "It's nearly true and boring enough to send people home without a lot of gossip and gawking."

I was right. Cars left the parking lot as quickly as Edna permitted. She controlled the exit while Gertie and I patrolled the area beyond the pavement with Keats and Percy, now free from the truck. If it weren't for a couple of large, unfamiliar prints in the dry soil, I'd almost have thought Edna and I imagined the large marsupial.

Cori, Bridget Linsmore and Remi Malone arrived in a lime green VW van after nearly everyone else had left.

"You'd better not be pulling my leg, Ivy Galloway," Cori said, jumping out of the passenger seat. The tiny trainer was wearing jeans and a light jacket that looked like they came off the children's rack. Fashion wasn't a priority for her and any spare dollar went into the rescue coffers. She chose to live humbly to serve animal kind. Or so she said. I'd never been invited to her home to confirm it. "Always wanted to meet a kangaroo but wasn't aware of any in the region."

The mayor joined us in time to hear the last comment. "Nor was I, although Animal Services has been monitoring a couple of private roadside zoos."

It was a mild evening, but Cori still wore her trademark black gloves with orange middle fingers. She shaped both hands into pistols and directed them at Meryl. "Roadside zoos should be illegal in hill country. In Dorset Hills, our mayor is cracking down on them."

"Your mayor has a far bigger budget than I do." Meryl cut her eyes at me. "Most of mine goes into policing."

She was implying her crime issues were at least partly my fault, which was nervy when she sometimes deployed me to resolve tricky cases where police red tape slowed the process.

Jilly wouldn't have it. "Don't give Ivy a hard time about the growing crime rate, Mayor. She's always willing to help when you ask for it."

Meryl faked a cough. "Overstatement. Last time, Ivy drove a hard bargain. Her prices have gone way up."

I couldn't help laughing. "Mayor, I accepted your bribe, even though it got me in hot water with Kellan. Much more of that and I'll be jilted at the altar."

That made Jilly stand a little taller. "You owe this to Ivy, Meryl."

The mayor stood a little taller, too. They had a few inches on

Cori, but Bridget and I towered over the rest of the women. "I owe her a kangaroo?"

"I don't want the kangaroo," I said.

Cori snorted. "Liar. You crave that roo like the Langman sisters crave collectibles."

"Fine, I do, but my boss says they're too hard to handle." I looked down at Keats. "Tell her, buddy. Otherwise, the little lady with the rude gloves will stick the big hopper in your pasture."

Keats' mouth opened in a pant-laugh. He adored and respected Cori and her border collie, Clem. But then his mouth snapped shut and his ears flattened to show his true feelings about the problem at hand. A disgruntled mumble sealed the deal.

Cori nodded. "Understood. There's a big learning curve and you've got your paws full already. Let's worry about where the roo goes after detaining it. We'll use typical search formation." She stared over the mayor's shoulders. "Where's the rest of our crew?"

"I sent everyone home, including the men," Meryl said. "Ivy wanted to handle this discreetly and I agreed because Edna said kangaroos are vicious. You've got till ten p.m. to apprehend the marsupial. After that, I'll hand the case to Animal Services and the police."

Our group was small but mighty, and Cori called in more of the extensive Rescue Mafia to help. The pets were an integral part of the search party. In addition to Keats and Percy, we had Clem, Bridget's big black setter Beau, and Remi's beagle Leo. The latter mostly rode on Remi's arm but he'd lend his hound-dog nose to a cause on occasion. I wondered what his olfactory senses would make of this curious target.

Within minutes, we'd gathered all available equipment from our various vehicles and assembled at the edge of the woods. Keats was mumbling a monologue that sounded dubious about the venture. I concurred. Nocturnal excursions into the vast stretches of forested land that covered hill country were never fun for me. It was barely dusk in the parking lot, yet quite dark in the bush. Thank goodness we had plenty of flashlights.

"I'm always worried something will jump out at us," Jilly said, walking right behind me. We were supposed to fan out but silently agreed on single file unless Cori came back to bully us into proper formation. "Today more than ever."

I pushed a branch back to let her pass. "I'm sure that roo was just trying to escape. It looked terrified."

"Sounded like it was moving too fast for you to read its mood. If you even knew how to read kangaroos. Have you met one before?"

"No, and not for lack of trying. I didn't realize we had any in this region. Travel has never been high on my agenda, as you know."

She knew. "When we were execs and could afford it, we were so boring."

"Guess I knew if I took enough time off to visit Australia, I'd never come back to my job." I stepped lightly across rocks through a swampy area. "Didn't realize I was only a prisoner in my own mind." Keats mumbled something and I added, "Then I found the border collie key to get out."

Jilly clutched Percy closer, although the cat was quite willing to walk while on a mission. She met her cat-baby months after leaving corporate America and he was her comfort and joy now. Even on our worst days, which included walks just like this, neither of us had the slightest inclination to go back to our old lives.

We walked on in silence for a bit. The others couldn't be far ahead but the thick bush served as a muffler. Branches crackled underfoot and eventually Percy mewed to get down. I was happy Jilly obliged because it was better to have both hands free out here. The trail twisted and turned as it wound through a gully and back up. I let the light's beam bounce back and forth between the pets and the path. Their tails were at low mast. No one was enjoying this outing.

"What was going on with Travis and Brydon?" she asked, after what seemed like an hour. "It started friendly and seemed to turn real."

"Probably just ego and theater, but Poppy was so upset she left Travis behind. Mom texted to say they're at the farm drowning Poppy's sorrows with peppermint schnapps."

"I'd be upset, too, if Asher risked serious injury just to show off."

"Maybe Pops will think differently of Travis now. At least ask some pointed questions. I wonder how well she really knows him."

Keats mumbled again and the sound made me wonder how well we really knew anyone. I used to consider myself an expert student of human nature but I'd been duped by killers time and again. Luckily, my sheepdog detective was always a few steps ahead of me. It was just a matter of following his lead and getting people to expose their true selves.

"Poppy's pretty far gone," Jilly said, grabbing my shoulder to slow me down. The terrain was rougher now and it would be so easy to trip. "If he's not one of the good guys, her heart will shatter."

"That's what worries me. I wish she'd get a pet. More than any of my siblings, Pops needs an animal shield."

Jilly slowed even more. "Remember, our fur-boys don't hate Travis. Keats tolerates him and Percy likes riding around on his shoulder at the farm. I can't easily write off a man who loves pets."

"Same." I led the way up a small hill. "Maybe his antics today changed the boys' minds."

"Ivy." Jilly turned at the top to shine her light in a full circle. "Where is everyone?"

I stopped to listen. "That's strange. Normally you can hear Cori and Edna barking orders from a mile away. Even when they're quiet, you can feel Cori's gloves gesticulating." I peered around. "There's only one plausible explanation. I think Keats deliberately let us fall behind."

"Keats," Jilly called out. "Explain yourself. Because I never enjoy walks in the woods and this time there's a dangerous animal on the loose."

The defiance in his next mumble said it all. He had his reasons.

I shone my light around, too. "Hey, I think we're nearly back where we started. There's a glow ahead and the sign in front of the strip mall is florescent."

Jilly's chin came up and she smiled. "Well, that's different. If Keats decided we should be safe, I'm all for that. A kangaroo can't kick in a truck door." She turned to me. "Can it?"

The dog continued along the trail and we followed. "Doubtful, although it could probably do some damage." I stopped again on the next rise. "Keats is bringing us out behind the mini-mall where it's much darker. Maybe the roo circled back, too."

"Maybe rethink that, Keats," Jilly said. "What if the runaway is picking through the garbage? Ivy has dumpster trauma."

"You got that right." I'd had some foul encounters with garbage in the line of sleuthing duty, including one that made me faint. "Kangaroos are herbivores, though. Trash won't hold much appeal." I flashed my light at the dog. "There's something Keats wants us to see here."

We came out at the end of the long, slim rear lane and lined up behind a rectangular industrial trash bin. A few yards beyond that sat a black pickup truck.

And beyond *that*, two men argued.

Their voices were low, but one of them sounded angry.

They were about midway down Midway Mall. It seemed like the backside of the martial arts studio. Had Travis and Brydon come back to finish their match?

"Sounds like Travis," I whispered, peeking around the

dumpster. "Should we go out and tell him to stand down? At the rate they're going, they'll scare the kangaroo away."

Keats growled and pushed me back into the shadows. His blue eye glinted briefly as he checked to make sure I got the message.

I got the message. Stay, Ivy. Stay.

"That sounded like a no," Jilly said, picking the cat up again. "Maybe the kangaroo will scare them away instead. I don't like the tone of their discussion."

I squeezed her arm to silence her, feeling the puff of Percy's hackles. The men's voices were rising and the pets weren't happy about it. I could only pick up fragments of the conversation.

"You said you'd never come back," one man said.

"Said a lot of things back then. Meant them, too. But I had no choice."

My own voice was barely a whisper. "Travis. That's him, I'm sure of it."

The first man spoke again, his voice quieter but no less threatening. "You knew what would happen. Now *I* have no choice."

There was a scuffling sound. Were Brydon and Travis grappling on gravel this time? Why didn't they just go inside and roll it out on the mats?

"Idiots," I said. "I'm going out there to tell them that." Keats continued to push me back. "Buddy, they don't know about the kangaroo. Someone could get hurt."

Jilly pulled out her phone with her free hand. "Should I call the police? Just to be safe?"

There was a metallic creak as a door opened and then clanked shut.

"Yeah, text Ash or Kellan. Something feels very off. Maybe they're inside now. Having this discussion with the lights on."

Still, there were noises I couldn't quite place.

As Jilly tapped with one thumb, goosebumps rose on my arms

and a shiver ran from head to foot. The night air seemed suddenly charged with electricity.

Keats felt it too, because he pressed us even further behind the dumpster.

"What's happening?" Jilly whispered, slipping her phone away.

There was a rhythmic vibration underfoot. Someone was running our way.

The thrumming slowed and more scuffling followed with a huffing sound that could be coughing. Or growling.

The metal door clanged again and a whoosh of air seemed to push us back even more.

It wasn't Travis or Brydon rushing past, unless they were so powerful they could cover several yards in a single bound.

"The kangaroo," I muttered, turning to watch the shadowy form enter the trail we just left.

Keats did nothing to stop it. Probably *couldn't* do anything to stop it. He also kept me from trying to follow. It was disappointing but if we somehow managed to corner it now, it wouldn't end well. But our rescue team was down that trail.

"On it." Jilly pulled out her phone again and muttered as she texted, "Incoming roo."

The kangaroo's passing seemed to cause a shift in the atmosphere. A whirl of air blew up a candy bar wrapper almost to eye level and a couple of soda tins rattled on loose gravel and cracked asphalt.

Keats mumbled and poked my shin to let me know it was time to move. Meanwhile, Percy struggled out of Jilly's grip and she nearly dropped the phone. Both pets raced ahead of us toward the spot where the men had argued. Their spat was over now and it was eerily silent.

"Maybe the roo attacked him." There were puffs between the

words as Jilly hurried behind me. "Good thing the police are coming."

Tires screeched somewhere close by and I wondered if they were here already.

"Call Edna and tell her to come quickly. She can deal with medical emergencies."

We walked around the pickup truck and I peeked inside. It was the same model, make and color as mine but this truck had a pink fluffy headband hanging from the rearview mirror. Poppy's.

Keats shot a look back at me with his eerie blue eye that picked up a bit of a glow from the weak light over the mall's middle door. It was propped open now and I knew it was the studio from the smell of off-gassing mats.

But that was the least of our concerns now, because Keats had come to a stop beside a tall man in a denim jacket. At his feet lay the other man.

A burly man who wasn't moving.

"Hello," I called. "Is someone hurt?"

"The police are on their way," Jilly said.

"Too late." The man's voice was low. Somber. Almost sorrowful.

"Too late for what?" I slowed to a stop beside him and turned on my phone light. "Oh."

"What?" Jilly held the phone away from her ear. "What should I tell Edna? She wants to know the man's status."

"Too late." The man with his back to us said again. There was no mistaking the desolation in his tone now.

Jilly was still behind me. "Tell me what to tell Edna."

"Tell her it's a litter box situation. Percy is... well, you know."

The orange cat was pronouncing a death with flourishes of his fluffy orange paws. He was working hard to scrape loose gravel over the man's face.

Travis' face.

CHAPTER FOUR

Percy's paw stuck briefly in Travis' beard. Shaking it free, the cat began scraping again. The ritual was always extravagant but it seemed more so tonight. Perhaps he put extra oomph into mock burials for aspiring family.

"Leave it. Get your claws off right now."

The low voice sounded like Travis. Was he alive after all? Percy had never been wrong before. And he didn't think he was wrong now, because the fluff kept flicking in my flashlight's beam. I aimed the light right at the fallen man's face. His eyes were open, staring at the sky over Midway Mall. If he were alive, he'd blink from the glare.

He didn't blink.

Keats herded me closer and I noticed those eyes were a pale blue.

That was strange, because Travis' eyes were a muddy hazel green. I'd had the opportunity to see the color up close every time he stopped my truck to chastise me over driving with livestock. Had he been wearing contacts all this time? I wouldn't put it past him to fake up a disguise. The lumberjacket looked identical to the one he'd worn in the studio earlier and even at the softball game.

Same white T-shirt under the jacket. Same jeans. Same work boots.

Something else was different. The man on the ground had a crooked nose, and Travis' features were quite classic. A kangaroo was very capable of breaking someone's nose, but surely there would be blood.

"Travis?" I said, just to make doubly sure he was, well... gone.

"What?"

The faint voice came not from the body on the ground but the man standing. He turned and I shone the light in his face till he squinted. When he was able to open his eyes, I saw they were indeed muddy hazel.

"Travis!" My voice squeaked in relief. "This guy looks just like you. A doppelganger."

The hand passing over his beard had a visible tremor. "Or just my brother."

Jilly came up beside me, careful not to step on either Percy or the deceased. "Travis, I'm so sorry for your loss. What happened to...?"

"Knox," Travis said. "Keith, really, but he renamed himself Knox when he was about ten. Because we'd had some hard knocks." His next breath had a hitch in it. "Guess he had the hardest knock of all tonight."

"Was it the—?" Jilly started to speak but I cut her off with a slash of my index finger. Normally she was the discreet one at scenes such as this, admonishing me like a schoolmarm to leave the questioning to the police.

"I don't know what happened," Travis said. "I was nearly home when I realized I forgot my lumberjacket and gym bag, so I turned around. Got an anonymous text to meet back here and found Knox waiting. We argued. I went inside to get money. When I came back, he was... like this."

"It must have been—" Jilly stopped herself this time. "You know."

"Must have been what?" Travis asked. "Knox had enemies. I assume one staked him out. If I'd come out a second sooner, maybe Percy would be scraping gravel into my beard, too. Can you stop him, Ivy? Knox and I haven't always seen eye-to-eye but this is too much."

Before I could ask, Percy amped up his paw work. The police must be close and the window for death litter theater closing. Quelling mild hysteria building inside, I touched the cat with my boot. "Percy, paws down. We got the message."

Boots clomped on pavement from the direction of the dumpster. The wide beam of a high-power flashlight caught us in a bright cone.

"Dagnabit, Travis, did you kill your chop-socky buddy?" Edna joined us with Gertie, while the rest of the Mafia stayed back. "I've seen Percy call it more times than I care to recall. "That man is never getting up. Wait. Is that—?"

"Not again." The voice was so lacking in juice it was hard to recognize as Cori Hogan's. Her grating tone was as much a signature as her gloves. "What is wrong with you people? Always with the bodies lying around."

Jilly signaled Gertie. "Could you take them around the front to wait? The police are on their way."

"Not until Travis coughs up the facts." Gertie crossed her arms over her rifle and her knee-length braid. "His buddies with badges will go soft on him."

Travis seemed to have shrunk to half his normal size and his denim jacket flapped in the breeze. "I didn't kill him. The deer did."

"The deer?" Edna came closer. "Is he high?"

"He's not high," Jilly said. "Delirious, perhaps. This was a major shock."

He turned to face us and tears glistened on his cheeks. "Delirium isn't in my repertoire. And I know a deer when I see it. The thing charged away just as I came outside. A doe or young buck."

Edna's laugh was more of a harsh bark. "Any chance that deer was upright, with big feet and a long tail?"

He shook his head. "Just a regular deer, moving fast. Super fast. Galloping, kind of. I guess it trampled Knox."

"Or kicked in your friend's ribs. That was a kangaroo, Travis." My friend swept off her camo cap in a sign of respect as she bent over the fallen man. "Wait, it isn't Brydon Ting. This fellow looks just like you. He even dresses the same."

"Always copied me," Travis muttered. "Except when it mattered most."

I touched Edna's arm. "It's Travis' brother, Knox. Apparently he came to shake Travis down for cash. The kangaroo was a case of bad timing."

"Shake you down?" Edna straightened and shone her light right in Travis' eyes, which gave him an excuse to wipe his face with his sleeve. "Sounds like your family is no better than mine." She glanced from Jilly to me and back to Travis. "My twin came from Australia to shake me down."

"Yeah?" His eyes filled again as soon as he moved his sleeve. "Where is she now?"

"Same place as Knox, I imagine. Wherever the users and losers end up. I try not to think about it."

"Let's leave the discussion for the police, shall we?" Jilly's inner crime scene schoolmarm surfaced, and she tugged Edna back a few steps. "We don't know much about Knox, other than that he had a rough childhood. You can empathize with that, Edna. Most of us can, I expect."

The murmur of agreement among the crowd startled me. Is that how we all ended up as rescuers and renegades? There wasn't a person here who hadn't broken the law at some point. Our merry band of rebels never let fences or locked doors prevent the liberation of animals in need. I was the worst offender. So much so that it was a wonder an officer of the law proposed. Sometimes, I worried that's why we still hadn't gotten the knot properly tied.

Keats nudged my fingers in what felt like a combination of comfort and tough love. He wanted me to focus. In a situation like this, there was usually just a slim window of time to investigate before being told we could not. It didn't stop us, but it usually slowed us down.

Gertie came up to stand beside her best friend, and Edna crossed her arms, too. "So, you're saying the roo killed your brother, Travis?"

Confusion looked out of place on confident Travis. "Like I said, I *thought* it was a deer. Are you saying a kangaroo's on the loose?"

Edna nodded. "You'd know that if you hadn't been overcome by testosterone earlier. It hopped right past the studio windows."

"Huh. Guess the roo could have done it."

Unfolding her arms, Edna poked him. "Guess again. Because I met a few kangaroos when I was down under paying off my sister's debts. None of them had the smarts or dexterity to strangle a man."

"Strangle? That's not how it happened." Travis stared down at Knox and his broad shoulders spasmed. "Oh."

Keats had gone into a point right beside Knox's head and his white paw dangled over the man's neck.

A black band circled tightly below the beard.

"Choked by a black belt," Edna said, bending to confirm. "And the embroidery says it's yours, sensei."

CHAPTER FIVE

"I did not kill my brother." Travis' voice echoed in the alley. "I spent the first half of my life trying to keep him alive. Why would I kill him now?"

"Brother?" The word came from Poppy, as she rounded the dumpster with Asher. She was wearing pink plaid flannel pajama bottoms and a fluffy faux fur jacket. Her long multicolor hair was in a topknot that made her look far younger. As she walked up beside me, I got a strong whiff of peppermint schnapps. Asher had been at the farm when Jilly texted about Travis and he brought her along. The high-speed commute couldn't have been easy on her digestion.

My brother raced to embrace Jilly and pat her in as many places as she publicly permitted to make sure she was all in one piece. "I'm fine, honey," she said. "Unfortunately, Travis' brother passed away suddenly."

"By roo or kung foo," Edna supplied, cheerfully. She was starting to enjoy herself. "Turns out the surviving Wigg and I have more in common than anyone might have thought."

Poppy turned slowly to face Travis. "What brother?" she asked.

The question said it all. This tragedy had exposed a truth that made Poppy question everything she knew—and didn't know—about her relationship. Her hand rose and then dropped. She wasn't sure whether to comfort Travis for his loss or chastise him for keeping secrets.

"This is—*was*—my little brother, Knox," Travis said. "And I didn't kill him."

Asher twisted an imaginary key in front of his mouth. "Travis, shut it. Wait till Harper gets here before you start talking."

"You won't want to waste a moment when you hear what happened," Edna told Asher. "Knox Wigg died with Travis' black belt around his neck. Apparently, the only witness is a kangaroo."

My brother's hand moved up to rub his forehead. The gesture of befuddlement had become all too familiar to me in the past year. "Kangaroo?"

"Kangaroo," Jilly confirmed. She was probably the only one he'd believe in that moment. "A runaway."

He stopped rubbing his forehead to stare at her. "There's no police report about an escaped kangaroo. Believe me, I'd have heard about it."

"I know, and I'm sorry," she said. "We had the mayor's permission to try to rescue it. Ivy and Cori Hogan were deemed most likely to bring him in safely."

"Ivy?" Cori snorted so loudly I jumped. When I turned, her orange flipping fingers flashed. "If ever a rescue goes spectacularly wrong, it's when Ivy's involved."

I shrugged. "I've had some spectacular wins, too. Granted, I'm less graceful than you are."

Jilly came to bend over the body. She plucked Percy up mid-ritual and his paws kept sweeping as she cradled him in her arm. Then she tapped my forearm. "How about you and Cori debate rescue techniques later? Travis is standing vigil over his long-lost brother. Someone Poppy never knew about."

Poppy released her hair, as if the time for youthful topknots had passed. "I'm sorry about your brother, Travis. But you told me you didn't have family. Many times."

"Binty Pefferlaw is his sister, isn't she?" I asked. "That's what her husband told me."

"We're *like* family," Travis said. "The kind you make, not the kind you're born into, you know?"

I knew all about that. Right now, I was surrounded by a mix of both and it took the edge off a rough situation better than schnapps ever could.

Travis scuffed one boot in the gravel, connected lightly with his brother's shoulder and then backed away. "I'm sorry, Poppy. Knox has been gone for about twenty years and I lived in the bush so long I considered myself an orphan."

Multicolor hair swished over faux fur. She wasn't ready to wave this aside. "Parents?"

His head drooped so low that his beard brushed his denim jacket and his toque nearly fell off and landed on the deceased. "They're around, but we went no contact even before Knox left."

"I don't know what to say." Poppy's hand pinched her throat and I wondered if the peppermint liqueur was threatening a bold return. That stuff had a sneaky kick.

"Here, Poppy," Jilly said. "This will help."

"This" was Percy and judging by his loud purr, he was happy to be deployed as emotional support cat. After finishing his official police deputy duties, being cradled in someone's arm was a nice reward. Even if a small mew suggested Poppy squeezed too tight.

"Poppy, it's not what you think," Travis said. "I never lied to you."

"Withholding the truth is a lie." She glanced over at me. "Isn't it Ivy?"

I wasn't sure what she was inferring, but Jilly's arm clinch kept me from asking for detail.

"Leave that discussion till later," Jilly said. "Come back to the inn and I'll make some hot cocoa."

"Cocoa?" Edna asked. "It's practically summer."

"If it's cool enough for camo, it's cool enough for cocoa," Cori said. "Let's regroup at the farm and then redeploy. We need to bring in the renegade, ASAP."

"You'll do no such thing, Ms. Hogan." My tall, dark and handsome police chief fiancé had finally arrived and his voice was crisp. He wasn't a fan of Cori's at the best of times, and it was far from that. "Officer Galloway informed me about a suspicious death. We don't need your help to investigate or apprehend anyone."

"It's the kangaroo I'm worried about," Cori said, flipping her fingers into pistol formation and aiming at him. "You can handle the murder, Chief."

Asher gave Kellan a quizzical look. "It's not a murder if a roo did it. Is it?"

Kellan turned to me. "You're sure it was a kangaroo?"

"That killed Knox Wigg? On the contrary. A roo wouldn't need a black belt to do that." Gesturing to the dead man, I added, "Someone with prehensile thumbs is to blame."

His sigh was no doubt the first of many gusting my way. "Ivy. I'm only asking if you saw this kangaroo with your own eyes."

"She saw it with mine, too," Edna said. "And you'll see some interesting tracks with yours if you look. That is, if they're not trampled. Did you need to bring an army?"

I shook my head at her. For the moment, our crew still outnumbered the police and we were definitely encroaching on the crime scene.

Kellan looked slightly chastened. Crowds at a crime scene were so commonplace now that he hadn't immediately dispersed us. "Deputy Keats and Special Deputy Clem, could you please escort civilians around the front and corral them into a small area?"

Clem didn't speak cop but he happily followed Keats' lead and herded us up.

"You can't boss my dog around, Harper." Cori skipped a few paces as my dog nipped at her pant cuffs. "We don't even live in your jurisdiction."

"You're currently in my jurisdiction at a potential crime scene. That means you call me Chief." Kellan signaled to a young officer I didn't recognize. "Accompany them around the front and don't let them try any funny business. Ms. Hogan's a dog whisperer and might go rogue."

"I'm a rescue chief in all jurisdictions." Cori's words became staccato as Keats applied more little nips. But then Clem nipped Keats for disrespecting his leader and the two skirmished briefly. "It's my job, and this particular renegade moves fast. Every minute you keep us here is another..." She trailed off and looked at Edna. "Do the mathing for me."

"There's no telling how far that roo's gone," Edna said. "Might lead us full circle again. Seems to like this strip mall. Can't imagine why, when no business ever lasts here."

I couldn't see the attraction either, as we circled the building. It was dreary out front and worse out back. I was happy enough to be told to stand down tonight, since the sky was overcast and it had become chilly enough for cocoa.

Cori didn't resist the young officer's orders to march and the dogs fell back to enforce. The only noncompliant one was Poppy. She tried to step around Keats without success and then repeated the effort with Clem and failed again. That's when Percy gave a yowl of frustration and jumped from her arms to my shoulder. It wasn't comfortable for Poppy or me.

"Just leave it for now, Pops," Jilly said. "Travis will tell you everything soon, I'm sure. This is a very old story."

"So old his jaws rusted shut," Edna muttered. "Never trust a faux woodsman."

I gave her a little shove. "Edna, let's figure out the roo problem and leave the Knox problem to the police."

"Since when do you leave a murder to the police?" Poppy asked.

The young officer turned. "Since the chief said so?"

Everyone laughed except Poppy and me.

"Young man, you're obviously new around here." Edna gave him a smile that was rather ghoulish under the lone light halfway up a pole. "We do things differently in Clover Grove."

His face had that stiff, expressionless mask assigned in cop school. "I read your file, Miss Evans. It's part of the onboarding package."

"You don't say." Edna sounded delighted. Pulling off her hat, she fluffed her perm. "I'll have to thank the chief and request a copy for my autobiography."

"You're writing your life story?" Cori asked.

"No one else could do it justice." Edna carefully settled her hat back on her head. "Besides, if I hope to see it on library shelves, it's a race against the end times."

"You think zombies don't read, old friend?" Gertie asked.

The junior officer waved us into a vacant spot between the two vans with sweeps of his flashlight. "Someone died back there. Do you really think you should be joking around?"

"They shouldn't. You're right." Poppy's voice was sullen. "It's disrespectful."

"It's our way of dealing with stress and you know that, Pops." I tried to catch my sister's eye and failed. "I'm sorry about what happened."

"I didn't even get to meet Knox. He looked just like Travis."

"Very much, yeah. Other than eye color, they could have been twins. I'm sure there was a good reason they were estranged."

She turned toward me and our strong family resemblance struck me again. When Poppy's hair was its natural color, we were mistaken for each other often. "You moved to the city and avoided us for ten years," she said. "Did *you* have a good reason?"

"Actually, no. I never expected it to be that long, and maybe the Wigg brothers didn't either. I didn't consider us to be estranged, though. Just living different lives. You took off for ages, too. Did you keep in touch with everyone?"

"Iris and I wrote letters sometimes." She was defensive *and* sullen now.

"I called Mom once a month. Jilly can back me. It was the only day I drank."

Jilly fought a grin and then surrendered to it. "That's true. I called my mom the same day and we'd toast to daughterly duty done. It was a shared ritual."

The young officer cleared his throat. "Ladies? Can you save the true confessions for later? Chief Harper needs me around the back for a minute. Do not move. Do not cause trouble. Got it?"

"Got it," I said. "And don't worry, Officer. We're all too rattled to do anything but hug it out."

"And maybe sing a little," Remi said, offering Leo to the young man. "Join us in Kumbaya before you go?"

His boots were light and fast as he fled a fate worse than a crime scene.

When he was gone, Cori's gloves got lively. "Rescue 911 meeting at our secret location. Stat."

CHAPTER SIX

The next morning was deceptively bright and cheery. After a murder, I always half-expected thunderclouds and bolts of lightning. The only rumbles I heard came from the passenger seat beside me as I left the farm's lane and turned onto the main road. It sounded like Keats was urging me to drive faster. Perhaps he sensed police coming and our window of opportunity closing.

Asher hadn't made it home and Kellan was too busy for more than a terse text making sure we were all right after our hasty departure from Midway Mall. He'd followed that up with a direct order, in formal cop language, to delay the kangaroo search till he gave the go-ahead. Cori had thrown a tantrum but I felt obligated to back my fiancé and made a case to the Mafia. The first and best way to save the roo was to prove it wasn't guilty of killing Knox Wigg. That meant the police needed to comb the area thoroughly before a big rescue crew trampled over every square inch. The weather was on our side. There was no rain in the forecast to wash away evidence. Further, our mild summer temperatures would suit the kangaroo well. The abundance of vegetation would likely keep it in the area till we could intervene.

"Remind me to do a deeper dive into the care and feeding of

captive roos," I told the pets, as we rolled down the highway. "Hopefully it can stay a little while."

The dog's mumbled response was indifferent. His interest in marsupials hadn't grown. If he couldn't herd an animal effectively, it didn't belong on his farm. Keats was an adventurer and a fine sleuth, but his first job was livestock manager and he took it seriously.

Since we didn't fully agree, I changed the subject. "How do you feel about Travis now? Turns out I was right about his secrets."

The next mumble was equally indifferent. Perhaps Travis' deep dark past—and darker present—didn't concern the dog much. They concerned me. My sister was head over heels for a very slippery guy.

"We found Travis standing over his brother, who'd been choked by a black martial arts belt. Obviously, he's the number one suspect."

Keats mumbled again in an insolent tone. It sounded like "tell me something I don't know." Then he scraped his claws across the glass to get me to roll down the window. He sniffed for about a mile without enthusiasm. Nothing smelled sinister on this fine morning, apparently. That was good, although it suggested our job wouldn't be easy.

A happy pant left a trail of slobber on the vinyl. Easy was for amateurs. Or at least rank amateurs. With so many cases under our belts we'd become *professional* amateurs. Professionals who didn't wear belts. I felt constricted by waistbands and much preferred overalls. A decade of business suits and tight cubicles made me prize ease over presentation.

"Don't let me stay too long, boys," I said, as I parked the truck outside Mandy's Country Store. "We promised to delay a foot search for the runaway roo but there's nothing stopping us from verbally beating the bushes. Someone will have seen something,

I'm sure. You can't hide an animal that big and that unusual for long."

Mandy waved from the window, where she was setting an oversized mug of coffee on the long counter. The glass steamed an invitation that I hastened to accept. Percy and Keats rushed ahead of me up the stairs, tails aloft. Until recently, the cat was confined to his carrier in the store in case he decided to parade around the food counter. Mandy had never asked but it was the polite thing to do. During a recent reconnaissance visit, however, she released Percy herself and I took that as permission to let him loose unless there were other customers.

The cat vanished into the grocery aisles as I greeted Mandy and introduced myself to the bucket of coffee. By the time Mandy had set a platter of sweets in front of me, Percy was back and ready to be adored. He pawed Mandy's jeans until she lifted him and let him settle in the crook of her arm.

"You'll probably want to change that apron after we go," I said, fork hovering over the triple threat of chocolate mousse, lemon-blueberry coffee cake and a slice of rhubarb pie. Rhubarb wasn't my favorite but it was popular among the locals at this time of year. She'd doubled the serving of mousse to compensate. "I figure some pet hair is good for the pipes but others may disagree."

"There's no shortage of aprons. I go through half a dozen a day." She hugged the cat closer. "It's worth it for a dose of Percy."

The store wasn't officially open yet, but the apron was liberally splattered with pink and blue.

"What have you been making?" I asked. "Cake for a baby shower?"

She rocked the cat like an infant and cooed. "Something like that."

"Seems like there's a lot of talk about babies all of a sudden. Who's the lucky mom?"

"I never bake and tell. My business depends on confidentiality."

My fork stopped midair and I tried to catch her eye. "I thought I was an exception to the rule. You're always my first stop when something happens and I bet you heard about last night."

Her pale blue eyes rose and she smiled. "Crime's different. It's just the sweet treats I zip my lip over."

I savored a bite of lemon cake, hoping the zing would fire up my neurons. "Do you know anything about Travis' brother, Knox Wigg? His given name was Keith."

Mandy shook her head. "I can't believe I never heard of the Wigg family. Almost everyone in hill country came through here at some point and"—there was the usual hitch in her breath before she mentioned her grandmother—"Myrtle had a great memory for detail, as you know."

That I did know. Myrtle was a repository of secrets for the community. Maybe the weight of that responsibility had tipped the old woman into sociopathy. Too bad I'd ended up being the one to uncover *her* secret. I'd nearly died for it.

The mouthful I was chewing went down hard. It was strange how the memory of Myrtle attacking me held more weight than the others. Maybe that was because I'd known and liked her all my life. Before Myrtle, I took great pride in my HR skills and ability to read people. After Myrtle, my confidence took a big hit. I still relied on my intuition more than I probably should but I always looked to my animals to back it up.

"It's hard to believe an entire family slipped under Myrtle's radar." I queued up some mousse on my fork. "You're sure the name Wigg doesn't ring any bells?"

Mandy thought for a moment. "Maybe a vague tinkle but not enough to go on." Clutching Percy closer, she added, "We could visit Myrtle if you want."

It was unfortunate the mousse was in my mouth when she said

it. A throat spasm sent a trickle of chocolate down my chin. "That won't be necessary. It's something I'd only repeat for a critical situation. Right now, my main concern is getting that kangaroo home."

"You captured it?"

I grabbed a napkin. "Nope, and Kellan has ordered me to stand down on the macropod rescue till he completes his investigation."

"Macropod? That's what they're called?"

"For the big feet. There are a few others in the family, like the wallaby and quokka. I've done some homework to be ready for the rescue."

The smile Myrtle's memory had banished returned to Mandy's face. "I suppose that macropod is coming in for a landing at the farm?"

I finished polishing chocolate off my own smile. "You know I've been dreaming of owning a hopper. My boss isn't on board, though."

"Charlie? I thought he could handle any livestock."

"The big boss." I tipped my head toward the dog at my feet. "The guy who runs the whole operation, humans included."

"Ah, gotcha. I've heard roos can be aggressive."

"Mainly if they're cornered or courting. Mostly, they flee." I got back to work on my breakfast desserts. "Cori is figuring out how to bring this one in. By that time, I'm hoping to have convinced my canine overlord to allow me to keep it."

"Imagine what Travis would say if you took your hopper for a ride in the truck."

I started in on the rhubarb pie and realized anew I didn't give it enough credit. Mandy's pastry could make any filling divine. "Maybe he'll be in jail by then. He is the prime suspect, you know."

Mandy gasped. "Ivy! Don't say that. He's the love of Poppy's life. I've seen more of her boyfriends come and go than you, and Travis is a definite upgrade."

My mouth puckered, either from the tartness of the pie or the thought of Travis becoming my brother-in-law. "She's not alone in liking him. Somehow, he's won over the guys and the mayor. Everyone is fond of Travis except me."

Her fingers moved briskly over Percy. "I'm not his biggest fan. Most people respect that I'm an introvert, but he's made it a personal mission to draw me out."

"Arrogant," I said, moving back to the lemon cake. "But I doubt he's guilty of killing his brother. Keats would know, wouldn't you buddy?"

He stared up at me with his eerie blue eye, pressed on my boot with one forepaw and mumbled.

"What does he want?" Mandy asked.

I stared at the dog, pondering. "I'd say he thinks you know more than *you* think you do."

She adjusted Percy and reached down to touch Keats' ears. "Really? What do I not know that I know?"

"Maybe it's not about the Wigg family directly. Every mystery is like a ball of twine with twisty knots to untie."

Putting Percy down, she went back to the counter to get the coffee pot and top up my cup. When she was done, she paused, lost in thought. "It's the kangaroo. That's what I didn't know I knew."

My heart gave a little kick. "Really? You know someone who keeps roos?"

"Maybe. Or at least someone who did years ago. The man came up from Waterfield to collect his delivery. One day the packaging was ripped, so I could see inside without getting into trouble from Myrtle for being nosey. It was macropod pellets."

Keats' mouth dropped open in a happy pant. Things getting more interesting.

"Why would the guy come all this way to pick up a parcel?

Waterfield might be too small for a post office, but there are many closer than your store. It's nearly a half-hour drive."

"Kangaroos must have been illegal to keep back then. Myrtle never pried."

I set my fork down. "They're illegal to keep now. I just hoped the mayor would make an exception for me, like she did with the Valais Blacknose sheep. My ledger says Meryl's still down a few favors."

Mandy set the coffee pot on the counter and squinted out the window. "What was that guy's name...?" Her face lit up. "Gilroy Leek. And now that I'm unearthing old memories, I'm pretty sure macropods weren't the only things he was feeding."

Picking up a spoon, I scooped the mousse in a hurry. I could leave the last of the pie but not the chocolate. "An exotic animal collector, I guess. Do you remember his address?"

"Let me check on the system." She hurried back to the counter. "Myrtle kept meticulous records."

Since I had a few minutes to kill, I cleared the rest of my plate. It was likely to be a long day and Waterfield probably had little in the way of amenities.

"Do you want to know a fun fact?" I called over to Mandy.

She glanced up from the computer. "Judging by your smirk, no."

"It's supercool, though. Kangaroos and wallabies have two uteri."

"Like twins in separate apartments? Is there room in the pouch for two?"

I got up and walked over. "See, here's where it gets fascinating. She has a baby the size of a jellybean just thirty-three days after conception. A second baby in the unit next door goes into a sort of hibernation until there's pouch availability. In short, there's a bun in the backup oven."

She handed me a slip of paper. "I don't know how I feel about your fun fact. Or bun fact."

I laughed, as Keats rounded me up. "Feel inspired, master baker. Macropod moms can be perpetually pregnant and handle three joeys at the same time. Put a kangaroo on your baby cake."

"Interesting, but I'll probably go with a classic vibe."

"Suit yourself." I walked through the door when she opened it for me. "But I'm sure your expectant mom client would be fascinated to hear all about roo reproduction."

"Ivy." Mandy rarely sounded stern. In fact, I didn't know her pale eyebrows could gather that way. "Do *not* talk about the baby cake. My reputation rides on this."

Fluttering the slip of paper, I nodded. "Understood. I owe you too much to get your apron in a knot."

"One day the baby cake will be yours," she called after me. "I'll have a roo at the ready."

That idea added a spring to my step and Keats' teeth in my leg did the rest to get me hopping.

CHAPTER SEVEN

J illy and Edna were waiting for me outside the grocery store. They'd arrived separately to avoid questions about our plans. Mom was at loose ends since Poppy hadn't come back to the farm after last night's incident at the mall.

"Bad news, Ivy," Jilly said, climbing into the truck and settling bags of produce at her feet. Investigations inevitably led to more mouths for this chef to feed. "Asher delivered Travis to the inn. He's staying with us until they clear him. Your mom will report on his every move, no doubt, but an officer's on point, too. Not the young one we eluded so easily."

I slumped behind the wheel. More eyes meant less freedom. "Why couldn't Travis stay with Poppy? She has a perfectly good apartment and she actually likes him."

"Didn't sound like it last night," Edna said with her trademark cackle. "After finding out he lied about having a family, maybe she changed the locks."

Jilly adjusted the pets on her lap. It was the beginning of an ongoing process of shifting claws to more comfortable positions. Her jacket was too warm for the day but it looked nice and afforded some measure of protection. "The police are worried that the killer will come after Travis, too."

"Unless the killer *is* Travis," Edna chipped in. "It was his belt, after all."

I pulled out before catching her eye in the rearview mirror. "As much as I'd like to see less of Travis, the chief has spoken. He isn't guilty of fratricide."

"Kellan's certain?" Jilly asked.

"Not that chief." I pointed to her lap. "The other one. He's promoted himself from deputy based on a stellar record."

My friends laughed. "I don't understand what that dog sees in Travis, but he's always liked him," Jilly said. "But then, who did kill Travis' brother? And why did Knox come back after all these years anyway?"

"That's what Kellan, the shadow chief, will be trying to find out while we go about our business." I grinned at her. "You'll think he got the better end of the bargain."

"Our business is roo business, I suppose. You must have gotten a tip from Mandy."

I turned off the main highway and headed south. "Turns out someone used to have macropod feed shipped to the store when Myrtle was around."

"I thought it was illegal to keep kangaroos," Jilly said.

"It is, but when has that ever stopped a collector?" I caught Edna's eye again. "Do you know a man named Gilroy Leek down in Waterfield?"

"Gill? Sure. He came in to see Doc Grainer now and then. Not often enough to gain any sense. Heavy drinker and heavier smoker. Should be six feet under by now."

"Might be. He stopped shipping there after Myrtle left."

Edna wrapped a kerchief around her perm before rolling down the window. The silky fabric was in a camouflage pattern and matched her jumpsuit. "Always figured Myrtle was taking a cut on private packages. I bet a lot of mail was diverted when Mandy took over."

After tapping on her phone, Jilly turned the screen to face me. "Gilroy is still alive and smoking in Waterfield. He's on the town council. Place is too small to have a mayor."

"If he's collecting exotics, that's how he gets away with it." I pressed harder on the gas. "Let's pay a visit and find out if he lost a kangaroo."

She put her phone away. "I made the right choice with the coat. Wasn't sure if we were heading into the woods or the boardroom."

I loved that she was ready and willing to do either one on the basis of one simple text. My best friend was bolder than her husband liked to believe. More so when we were short on guests. I wasn't the only one in this truck who bored easily. All of us did.

The drive went quickly as I shared what I'd learned from Mandy and more information on kangaroos than either woman cared to know. Keats was the one to silence me with a rumble as we came to the turnoff.

"Blink and you'll miss it," Edna said, leaning forward to bark directions. "The Leek manor is set well back from the road and Gilroy has at least a hundred acres, to my recollection. He bragged a lot."

"Plenty of room for an illegal zoo, then," I said. "Still, you'd think it would be hard to hide."

"You can hide anything in hill country. Speaking from experience." Edna cackled again as she signaled for me to turn into an overgrown lane that probably didn't see a lot of traffic. "Still, roadside zoos aren't illegal in many towns. There are restrictions on the animals, though."

Jilly straightened. "What else might he have in this zoo?"

A camo glove came through the seats and patted her shoulder.

"Never fear, Jillian. I equipped the truck properly while you slept last night. We could take down a rhino, if necessary."

"A rhino!" Jilly's voice was sharp. "Don't even joke about that."

"A hippo then. Although the soil is too rocky in these parts for an inground pool."

"Stop it, Edna," I said. "I'm sure kangaroos were as adventurous as Gilroy Leek got. Otherwise, Mandy would have seen the feed come in."

"Gotta give the girl credit for snooping," Edna said. "Didn't think she had it in her."

"She shares some of Myrtle's genes." I steered the truck around the last bend and into an open area. "Don't think that doesn't terrify her."

The Leek manor was similar to other grand homes I'd seen in hill country, most of which had gone to seed. This one was likely well past the century mark and staggering toward ruin. In fact, it looked barely habitable.

Our feet were still on the stairs when the front door opened and an old man appeared in the doorway. His hair was down to a few long white strands combed over a pink scalp and his baggy dark suit had seen better days. Make that better decades.

"Well, well, well, if it isn't Edna Evans," he said, walking across the porch. He probably didn't notice the dog and cat behind him, standing on either side of the door. "Finally came to take me up on my offer, did you?"

My prepper friend didn't blush easily or often but her sallow cheeks reddened now. "Don't flatter yourself, Gilroy Leek. I turned you down fifty years ago and I'd do it again in a heartbeat." She swept off her kerchief. "I'm surprised *you* still have a heartbeat, you old degenerate."

He gave a masculine version of her cackle, showing an array of teeth that were quite likely dentures. "Always liked a woman with spunk. That's why I invited you to dinner every time I came to

Clover Grove. Heard you finally got off your high horse for Buckley Brackens."

Edna's color deepened. "I am and will always remain a free agent, Gilroy. The end is coming, one way or another, and I intend to go down running solo."

He stood at the top of the stairs, blocking us. "Fine. I won't offer again."

Edna backed down huffily. "You shouldn't have offered the first thirty times. Bordered on harassment in my workplace. For some reason Doc Grainer found it amusing."

I finally spoke up. "Edna likes to be the only one harassing people, Mr. Leek. I'm Ivy Galloway and this is my friend Jilly Blackwood."

A frown dropped the curtains over his dentures. "I know who you are. Everyone does. The stories are legend."

It still took me aback when people I'd never met recognized me. My years of corporate anonymity had left me woefully unprepared for notoriety. "Just stories, sir. Probably get more exaggerated the further they roll down the hills."

"Even so, I'd prefer you roll back up the lane and home, young lady. You seem to bring chaos wherever you go."

I nodded, not in agreement but as a signal for my furry spies to fan out. They jumped off either side of the porch and vanished around the house. Gilroy was too riveted by Edna to see the treachery.

"You mean she dispels chaos wherever she goes," Edna said. "What've you got to hide except black lungs and a vexed liver?"

His frown deepened. "That's inappropriate. You're on my property and I'm a respected town councillor."

"He's right, Edna," Jilly said, turning up the wattage on her blazing smile. "We're guests on his land."

"The word 'guest' implies an invitation, which I never issued. In fact, there's a sign at the road that says, 'Keep out.'"

"Couldn't see it in the overgrowth," Edna said. "Would have ignored it anyway."

He groped in the pocket of his baggy jacket. "Then I'll call the police."

"Go right ahead, Gill. It'll take them half an hour to get here from the closest town. I suggest you just relax and this will all be over in minutes. No worse than the tetanus shot I took such pleasure in giving you."

Jilly raised her hand to silence Edna. "We're here to help, Mr. Leek. If you've heard the news—"

"I'm a councillor. Of course I heard the news. Keith Wigg was killed last night. Only surprised it took so long." He gave up on the phone and raked a hand over his strands. "Never thought his own brother would do the deed, but the Wiggs were a bad lot."

"I didn't realize Travis grew up in Waterfield," I said. "He's seeing my sister, you know."

"Send her my sympathies. The stork dropped those two in a dumpster, I'm afraid." His dentures reappeared. "Their old man had a *truly* vexed liver and a worse temper. The family wasn't around too long before I encouraged them to be on their way. Last year, Lenore came back. The boys' mother. She rents a basement apartment across from the town square."

"You mean the gas station," Edna said. "Waterfield doesn't have a square."

His eyes narrowed. "There's a plaque honoring our founder in the vacant lot. We're a humble people, unlike you highfalutin Clover Grovers."

That was the first time I'd heard anyone suggest my town was fancy. The homesteaders who comprised most of the tax base would be affronted.

Jilly intervened again. "Thanks for sharing some of the Wigg history, sir. I'm sure the police will come to ask more. That's not why we're here."

Keats quietly leapt through the railings and sat down behind Gilroy. One white front paw came up in a point, telling me it was time to speak to a man about a kangaroo.

I dug deep for my HR smile. It wasn't as flashy as former headhunter Jilly's, but it usually worked in a pinch. "Mr. Leek, we came to inquire about your kangaroo."

"My *what?*" His shocked expression might have fooled someone without a canine lie detector.

"Your kangaroo, sir. It was at the scene of the crime. As a councillor, I'm sure you heard that, too. Your roo is being framed for killing Knox Wigg."

A brisk wind blew up and his hand anchored the long strands on his head. "Is *your* liver vexed, young lady? Because you sound intoxicated and it's barely nine a.m."

Edna chuckled. "She's not drunk, Gill. If you're having trouble understanding her, I can recommend a good neurologist."

"Let's give Mr. Leek a chance to tell us how his kangaroo got away," I said. "When exactly did it escape, sir?"

He gave up on his hair and rubbed his forehead. "No kangaroo escaped here. I can assure you of that."

It was carefully phrased. Even politicians in tiny towns had guile. "Ah, I see." What I saw was Percy's stealthy arrival on the porch. The cat started scraping invisible litter over the welcome mat. It wasn't the full flourish of last night. Just a light sprinkle to cover a lie, perhaps. "So, you're saying someone *released* your kangaroo. Did that happen yesterday?"

"I'm an old man, as Edna keeps pointing out. Hardly the type to keep an animal of that size, Miss Galloway."

"And yet you did. Chief Harper can send officers to examine your property." I glanced at Jilly, who tapped on her phone. "On their way now. If you care about your macropod at all, you might want to speak up before it's detained."

"Kangaroos rarely go out of their way to kill people. Even a lowlife like Knox." He gave up the pretense and caught my eye in a fierce stare. "Tell me about the roo."

"I didn't get a good look. It was moving fast the first time, and quite dark the second. Hopefully we'll be able to capture it later today."

"You'll need my help. I want to bring my girls home."

Edna, Jilly and I looked at each other, unable to hide our shock. "Girls? Plural?"

"The doe had a joey in her pouch. At least I hope the little girl was still aboard. Sometimes they lose them fleeing in a panic."

I turned to my friends. "There was a baby."

"And that means...?" Edna prompted me. "Surely you remember my health education classes, Ivy. Babies don't arrive by magic, even to illegal kangaroos."

Keats' mouth opened in a pant-laugh, which Gilroy should have heard. "Sir, are you saying there's a buck on the run as well? Presuming it's a red kangaroo, they're huge and unpredictable."

His hand flapped dismissively. "They get a bad rap. Mild as a white-tailed deer most of the time."

"Last night wasn't 'most of the time.' Someone died in an alley with at least one of your roos and they're both still at large. When were they set loose?"

He gave up the game. "Night before last. Someone broke the lock to release the mob. I was out—"

"Vexing your liver," Edna suggested, earning a scowl.

"Didn't think to check on them before turning in and only found out in the morning," he continued.

"At which point you failed to notify the police," Edna said. "Because owning them—a mob, yet—is illegal."

Gilroy ignored that. "I hired a couple of men to search but we figured they'd go south, not north. Surprised they got so far so fast."

I held up my phone. "Research shows twenty-five miles per

hour is a comfortable pace for a roo on the run, with bursts of up to forty-four."

"But they didn't know the turf and I figured they'd take the slow route through the bush. I sent the men the wrong way." He brightened. "Now, we can refocus our efforts."

"You'll need to leave that to the experts, sir," Jilly said. "It's in good hands."

Percy brushed against Mr. Leek's leg and the man let out a small scream.

"Toughen up, Gill," Edna said, laughing. "You wouldn't last a day in the apocalypse."

"Don't be so sure, Edna. I've been kicked more times than you can imagine."

She laughed harder. "Don't underestimate my imagination."

Gilroy turned back to the house and almost tripped over Keats. "Have these pets been running around my property? I'll have them seized."

"Wonderful," Edna said. "Then your roos will have company."

"They hate dogs." He turned back to offer me a flash of dentures. "Been known to kick out their entrails. Or drown them, if they get the chance. How does your fine lad feel about that?"

A shudder passed over Keats from ears to tail, and he ran down to join me. "My fine lad feels like you have more to tell us. You must have some idea who freed your roos?"

He thought about his answer for a long moment. "Figured it must be animal rights weirdos like you. My enclosure is sufficient for macropods but you people are beyond reason." He gestured at Jilly, who was now rocking Percy in her arms. "You treat animals like babies."

I brought my hands together to entreat him. "If you care about *your* baby, sir, please tell us what you know."

His gaze sharpened and I saw a familiar gleam—the one that was in the eye of every collector. "Do you think your chief would send her home? She's priceless. To me, I mean. I'm very fond of her."

Not if I had anything to do with it, and I very much intended to have plenty to do with that baby roo. My HR smile did its best to say the opposite. "Stranger things have happened when politicians are involved, sir. Help us find her." I pointed to the camera on a post. "What did you see on your security feed?"

"It was disabled, along with the others, unfortunately." He turned to the house and called back, "If you want to know more, I suggest you ask the surviving Wigg."

He thought he had the last word, but that was never guaranteed when my dog was around. Shaking off the horror of drowning by roo, Keats raced up the stairs and delivered a nip to Gilroy Leek's calf.

The old man howled and hopped to the door. "He punctured my suit."

"That thing should have been retired forty years ago," Edna said. "With you."

"I liked you more in a skirt, Edna," Gilroy called out, while yanking the door closed. "Brackens is welcome to you."

Jilly giggled as we walked back to the truck together. "Isn't that sweet, Edna? Maybe you and Buckley can ride off into the sunset on matching kangaroos."

"So romantic," I said, jumping out of reach of a backhand shot. "Be sure to wear your kerchief, Edna. The road to happily ever after can get mighty windy."

CHAPTER EIGHT

Jilly groaned when I turned away from the highway at the end of the Leek lane. "Tell me we're not visiting the grieving mother, Ivy." Her hand sank deep into orange fluff. "Or, what if she's *not* grieving because she doesn't know Knox is gone?"

"If Gilroy knew, she'll know," I said, as Keats diligently applied his muzzle to the open passenger window. "Kellan and Asher knew more about Travis than we did. I'm sure they sent someone down to break the news."

"Even so, she won't welcome a visit from strangers. Imagine how she must feel. Her youngest came home after decades and died right away. Lenore's heart must be doubly broken."

"It's an intrusion, no question. But Keats wants us to go, Jilly. Lenore must know something about the kangaroos and we need to find them before Gilroy. His men might get to them first and stash them in even worse conditions." Jilly wasn't convinced, so I kept going. "Think about the other mama out there in the bush. Lost and scared. Do you know what they call female roos in Australia? Jills! Isn't that funny?"

A withering look came my way. "Hilarious. You're just trying to distract me from this horrible breach of etiquette. We don't even have flowers or a card."

"Let's give her the fruit you bought earlier. It's like a fruit basket. Without the basket."

Jilly groaned again. "I'm sure there are easier ways of finding these kangaroos."

I pointed to the dog, whose entire head was now out the window. "If he thought so, we'd be doing it. Keats normally takes the shortest route to the goal. In case you hadn't noticed, this dog likes to win."

Her withering continued. "I noticed. You both do. And you egg each other on."

I touched the dog's backside. "She means that as a compliment, buddy. Jilly admires our chutzpah."

Keats turned his muzzle to eye Jilly and a long trail of spittle hit the glass. Then he mumbled something sassy.

"Contrary to what you and Keats believe," Jilly continued, "this dog is not the chief of police. That job still belongs to Kellan and he wouldn't like this."

Throwing Kellan at me meant she really was uncomfortable about barging in on Travis' mom. "Jilly, come on. My sister is practically engaged to Lenore Wigg's firstborn son. That makes us family."

Edna snorted from the back seat. It was the first sound out of her since we left the Leek estate. Our teasing about Buckley must have really rattled her. I'd probably feel guilty about that later, but for the moment, I was tickled. Getting one-up on Edna was nearly impossible.

Jilly was more compassionate and threw our friend a rope. Nothing made Edna feel better than sharing her knowledge. "Edna, you visited a kangaroo sanctuary when you were down under. Do they really call females 'jills'?"

"Jills and flyers are both common names for does," Edna said.

"Males are called jacks, bucks or boomers. I learned so much when I visited that I'm worried about that joey. Gill was right that a baby can bounce out of the pouch as a jill flees. The sire is useless, as with most species. More likely to be off boxing the competition than protecting his kin."

"Poor baby," Jilly said. "If that happens, will she come back for it?"

"Depends on the circumstances. Some say jills deliberately jettison the joey to make an easier getaway. In just a month, she can have another in its place."

"I don't believe she tosses the joey on purpose," I said. "Kangaroos have strong kinship ties, especially among jills in a mob. But if Gilroy's jill lost her baby near Midway Mall last night, she may be afraid to come back with all the police around."

"Can we go with 'flyer'?" Jilly asked.

"'Jill' is more common." Edna's voice regained strength. Jilly had been the first to tease her about Buckley and the balance of power needed to be restored.

I parked near the vacant lot that comprised the town square. There were dozens upon dozens of quaint small towns in hill country. Waterfield wasn't one of them. Aside from the gas station, there was a scattering of stores that looked like they didn't want to be seen together. The community had little appeal and that was probably exactly what Councillor Gilroy Leek wanted. Some towns welcomed growth and others repelled it.

The repellers were the places the police really needed to worry about, yet often lacked a presence. Crime flourished in towns like this. No one in Clover Grove or Dog Town could get away with an illegal zoo for decades.

We collected the fruit from the back of the truck and let our pet posse lead the way. There were only a dozen houses to choose from, and one had a row of potted pink begonias leading down the side of the house. Keats paused at the end of the driveway and lifted his paw.

"Gilroy said Lenore lived in a basement apartment," I said. "That's probably the entrance."

Jilly rearranged the fruit in the bag to be more appealing and then straightened. Her shoulders went back and her chin lifted. "I'm only doing this for the baby roo. Let's keep it short, though."

The Wigg family connection was immediately obvious when Lenore came to the door, wearing a navy blue dress. Her dark, wavy hair was threaded with gray, but it was nearly as abundant as that of her two sons. She had hazel eyes like Travis but hers were puffy from crying.

The bad news had definitely reached Lenore.

Thrusting the fruit toward her, Jilly blurted, "We're so sorry for your loss, Mrs. Wigg. I'm Jilly Blackwood and this is—"

"Ivy Galloway. I know." Her bloodshot gaze landed on me. "I hear my son is engaged to your sister." She swallowed hard. "My surviving son, that is. Hoyle Junior. He goes by Travis now."

I plucked the easiest thing from the thorny greeting. "Engaged? I didn't know it was official."

"Nothing official, I suppose. He just said she's the girl he wants to marry." Lenore backed up to let us into the small entrance and led us downstairs. The apartment was small but very neat. Large patio doors to the yard let in streams of sunlight. "That's not something I ever expected to hear from Travis. He was staunchly against marriage and kids." She gestured to a worn couch and the three of us sat down. "Can't blame him, given his own childhood."

Edna leaned forward and offered her hand. "Edna Evans. Survivor of the worst childhood imaginable."

After releasing Edna's hand, Lenore sat down opposite us in a rocking chair. "I doubt that, Edna. You seem robust and lively. My boys were broken. And it was my fault."

"Not broken," Edna said. "At least, not Travis. Despite what happened early on, your son is well regarded by the police and even the mayor. He's a cockroach, like me."

"A cockroach?" Lenore's thin hand rose to her cheek. "That's awful."

Edna leaned back and crossed her legs primly, as if she were wearing a skirt instead of an army jumpsuit. "Coming from me, it's a compliment. Ivy's a roach, too. Jillian's aspiring."

My best friend and I glanced at each other and let it go. We'd be paying all day for our comments about Buckley. It was worth it.

I sent Keats to offer his soft ears to the grieving mother and he obliged with an impatient mumble. "Mrs. Wigg," I began, "we came about—"

"Knox's death. You want to know if Travis killed his brother."

Keats mumbled again, more encouragingly this time, and she rested her hand on his head. "Actually, no," I continued. "I don't believe Travis killed his brother. We're curious to hear about Knox's homecoming."

Her fingers slid from Keats' ears to his back and Percy left Jilly to join the effort. The cat strutted across the coffee table and invited himself onto Lenore's lap. With both hands busy, her tongue seemed freer. "Knox was only here for a moment, two nights ago. He said he was on his way to see Travis about something important. I'm his mother and I haven't seen him in twenty years, but he wouldn't even sit down. Seemed like he only came to Waterfield for what he called 'unfinished business.'" Keats nudged her hand to urge her on. "It was all about Travis. They were inseparable, those boys. My Irish twins."

"Irish twins?" Jilly asked.

"Born less than a year apart," I explained. "My mom has two sets of Irish twins, too, Mrs. Wigg."

Her gaze cleared and she nearly smiled. "Really? Poor woman. I couldn't keep up with mine. They were always in trouble. And their father… Well, in today's lingo, they'd call him a deadbeat. Wasn't around much and when he was, he was intoxicated. I only wish I'd left sooner. The boys never forgave me for putting up with Hoyle."

Percy rolled onto his back to offer his apricot belly. In terms of feline emotional support, he was pulling out all the stops. The roar of his purr filled the room.

Jilly backed him up with words. "What a difficult time you had. How did the boys cope?"

"They escaped to the woods. My husband worked construction all over the region and was gone for weeks at a time. When he came home, he showed his frustration with his fists. Eventually, the boys started staying away until Hoyle left again. A week, sometimes two in the bush when they were no more than nine and ten."

"Impressive," Edna said. "I did the same for similar reasons. You don't see kids these days doing things like that. It builds independence."

Jilly stared at Edna. Tart words about child protective services might have followed if not for the grieving mother.

"Do you know where your boys went when they ran away?" I asked.

She shook her head. "Couldn't have been too far. All they had was a salvaged dirt bike. I overheard them talking about backup camps, as well."

"Savvy." Edna's voice revealed increasing respect for Travis. "How did they feed themselves?"

"No idea. I didn't ask because I didn't want to hear they were robbing the grocery store. My best pot and some cutlery went missing, and I know they checked out garage sales and picked through trash. Very resourceful, my boys."

"Did their father ever find them?" Jilly asked.

Lenore's fingers ran over Percy's belly. "Didn't try, as far as I know. Hoyle isn't a woodsman. Only cared about the bottle. Wish I'd known that before we married."

"Isn't?" Edna uncrossed her legs and leaned slightly forward. "Is Hoyle still alive?"

Lenore nodded. "Not for much longer. He's in palliative care in a nursing home near Fleetborough. Surprised he's made it this long, to be honest."

"In my nursing experience, the stubborn ones always outstayed their welcome." Edna chuckled. "I'm sure it'll be a relief to you when he sheds this mortal coil."

Lenore's eyes closed and she rocked the chair gently. "It won't change what happened. Hoyle connected with the wrong people and brought enemies to our very door. Once Travis joined the army, I'm afraid Knox followed his father down the wrong path. Then, like his mother, he fell in love with the wrong person. Travis came home and convinced Knox to leave for his own safety. Found him a job on an Australian oil rig and delivered him personally."

"Poor Knox," Jilly said. "He really did have some hard knocks. That's what Travis said last night."

Opening her eyes, Lenore glanced at a photo on a shelf of two young boys. They had a lot of hair even then. "Knox was a sweet boy. An animal lover like me." She still had one hand on my dog and cat, so I knew it was true. "His father got rid of every pet Knox brought home. Said he was weak in the head."

"Strong in the heart," I said. "Mrs. Wigg, I'm an animal lover too, as you probably know."

Finally she smiled and I saw where Travis had gotten his sparkling choppers. This woman had been very attractive before abuse and worry stole her youthful joy. "Travis says you drive around with livestock in the cab."

"Only when necessary." A blush tickled my neck but I willed it back with deep breaths. It was time to press for the information we needed. "When Knox was here, did he mention anything about kangaroos?"

Her smiled faded and she shook her head. "He only wanted to talk about finding Travis. I walked him out and realized someone was waiting for him in the van."

"What made you think so? Did you see a passenger?"

"Too dark, but there was a thump from inside, like someone was telling him to get a move on it. I got the sense they were in trouble and they must have gone to Travis for help."

"Probably," I agreed. "Can you tell me about Knox's interest in kangaroos?"

"We couldn't speak often when he was overseas but he told me about volunteering at a kangaroo sanctuary. Nothing made him happier than rehabilitating an animal and setting it free again." Her sigh blew Percy's fluff around. "He was doing so well there. If only he hadn't come home."

"Do you think he had old enemies waiting?"

Her expression soured. "Ivy, I don't need to tell you that grudges never die in hill country. You've seen the results time after time."

"Even in my own family, Mrs. Wigg. How did Knox feel about Gilroy Leek?"

"Hated him." The two words shot out. "Gilroy basically drove us out of town after finding Knox trespassing on his land. It was so hard on the boys. We had a nice house on the corner of Elm Street, and they felt safer here than they ever had, thanks to their camp."

Edna nodded. "That's the beauty of bunkers, in a nutshell. They're an escape clause."

"So, Gilroy wouldn't have been thrilled to see Knox back. Anyone else?"

Lenore stopped rocking. "Ivy, if I knew more about Knox's

enemies—or Hoyle's, for that matter—I would have told your brother when he visited last night. My boys didn't share information like that with me. For my own safety, they said."

I took the opening. "What about Travis? Is he into shady dealings, too?"

Her eyes sharpened. "On the contrary. He works hard to support you folks up in Clover Grove. I believe he only came out of hiding to help your fiancé and brother."

That gave me pause, so it was Edna who prompted. "Go on."

"After the issue with police corruption, there were more problems in your area than your men could handle." She pointed from Jilly to me. "My Travis agreed to lend a hand, and now look what happened."

"How long had it been since your boys were together?" I asked.

"Oh, decades. Knox never came back after Travis shipped him out. I think that was the agreement."

"To keep Knox safe?"

Her gaze traveled out to the yard. "Probably to keep Travis safe, as well. When Knox was gone, Travis quit the army and moved into the backwoods. For many years we had no contact at all. Once they made those burner phones, we could chat now and then. I was happy when Travis came out into the open again. Worried, but happy he could have a life. Until now, nothing happened except losing his heart to your sister. I hope this business gets sorted out soon so that they can marry and start a family. I'm sure he'll make a wonderful father."

My stomach shot a little acid up into my mouth. This was not the life I wanted for Poppy. Backwoods, burner phones and bad guys. The only good part of this story so far was Knox freeing the kangaroos from conditions he likely found inhumane.

"I'm sure he will," Jilly said. "Although Poppy and Travis haven't been seeing each other long."

Edna smirked. "You and Officer Bumble weren't seeing each

other long before he ripped his heart from his chest and offered it on a platter."

"Edna, Officer Bumble is my brother and I'd appreciate it if you didn't disparage him during a criminal investigation. One that affects Mrs. Wigg deeply."

"Touchy." Edna smoothed her camouflage. "Asher's a decent man, when all's said and done. But he wouldn't last a week in the backwoods."

Jilly glared at her. "Of course he would."

"As long as you were there to feed him, I suppose. He's used to the perks of a luxury inn."

I thought my friend might snap back, but Percy flipped and sauntered over to her. Keats returned to my side, as well, suggesting the information pipeline had dried up. I wondered if Lenore had shared all of this with Asher, too. My brother was a smart cop who was getting smarter all the time with Kellan's support, but Ash also had a kind heart and may not have pressed.

Jilly made the first move to go, and Lenore trudged up the stairs ahead of us. Her youngest had bounced out of her metaphorical pouch permanently today yet it seemed like she carried the weight of the world.

Outside, beside the row of cheery begonias, she let the tears fall. "I failed my boys. Both of them."

"Don't say that." Jilly's arms opened and she went in for a hug. "You did the best you could with what you had. That's all any of us can do."

Even Edna murmured agreement with that. "Older means wiser, Lenore. You still have one son and he's making quite a mark in Clover Grove."

Pulling away from Jilly, Lenore wiped her face with her sleeve. "Thank you for that. I only wish I could have given you more help."

Keats trotted away to the truck with Percy. Two tails lifted more with every step. "You gave us plenty of help, Lenore, and thank you," I said, following the pets. "I know just what to do next."

"You do?" Jilly asked, coming after me.

"I do, my friend, and it's going to be so much fun."

CHAPTER NINE

I t wasn't fun.

It was downright terrifying.

It was worthy of the screams I let out at irregular intervals.

And it was going to hurt like the dickens tomorrow.

"Slow down!" My shout turned the helmet into an echo chamber. "Slow down right now or I'll heave."

"Go ahead," the shout came back to me. "That'll teach you."

Teach me what? Not to barf in a helmet? Or not to joke about my second-best friend riding into any sunset with any suitor on any variety of animal.

Edna did not do romantic sunsets.

She most certainly did do dirt bikes. And she probably took a sadistic glee in hitting every root, every rock and every stretch of muck that splattered my overalls.

I flipped up the visor and raised my voice. "Stop, Edna. You've hit rewind on two years of concussion recovery. My brain's rattling around like candy in a piñata."

She still didn't slow down. I'd hit rewind plenty of times on my concussion so the guilt trip held no weight.

"I'll report you to the nursing registry," I said.

"I'm not registered to practice nursing anymore. What are they going to do to me?"

"It's about your reputation as a longstanding health-care professional, but if you don't care, I don't care."

She slowed so suddenly that I slid forward and crashed into her back. "There. Happy?"

Easing back, I groaned. "Happy that my chesticles deflated? I don't think so. I wanted to keep those, at least through the wedding and honeymoon."

"Chief Harper isn't the kind of man to worry about that. He has more important things on his mind."

"Newsflash, Edna. Betrothed men have the capacity to focus on saving the world while still appreciating their fiancée's bosom."

"I'll be sure to ask him about it," she said, leaning on the gas again.

"You do that. And I'll do the same with Buckley. Something tells me he still has that gleam in his eye."

She hit the brakes, but this time I was expecting it and braced myself.

"Get off," she said, cutting the engine. "You can walk the rest of the way."

I dismounted, already feeling stiff. When Gertie had joined us with her late husband's dirt bikes in the van, I was game. Saul's snowmobiles had already given me the worst ride of my life, thanks to an oversized helmet that completely blocked my view of snowy woods. How bad could this be?

Worse, as it turned out. Far worse.

Slapping Edna's camouflage back, I said, "Off you go. Good luck finding the place, because the dog stays with me."

The dog rumbled a protest I could hear just fine through my helmet. He would stay with me, I had no doubt, but the mission was his and it would hurt not to be first on the scene.

Gertie came up behind us and cut her engine, too. "What's going on?"

"We're bickering, that's what's going on. Edna's driving like a maniac. Meanwhile, Jilly's getting a sedate Sunday drive."

"It was no Sunday drive," Jilly said, dismounting, too. "Gertie's only going easy on me because I have a baby on board."

"A baby!" Was Jilly the one in Janelle's prediction after all?

Percy meowed from his backpack carrier and my friend shifted slightly to remind me the cat was there. We'd debated leaving him behind in the truck while we searched for the Wigg brothers' old camp but it seemed too risky when we didn't know how long we'd be gone.

I turned to Keats. "How much further?"

His excited spin was all I needed to know we were close enough to walk.

"Do you really think this is worth the pain and suffering?" Jilly said, following me as I skirted around Edna and started walking. "There are a dozen other things we could be doing today."

"I defer to the tails, as always." I pointed at the jaunty white tip waving ahead of us. "You know Keats isn't a wagger. He's onto something."

The trail was old, slim and nearly blocked with overgrowth in places, but even my untrained eye suggested it was worth a look. The entrance was only two blocks from the Wiggs' original home on Elm Street. Broken branches at the trail head suggested someone had passed through recently. There was barely enough room for the dirt bikes, however, so it was clear Knox hadn't come in with a van.

"What makes you think Knox actually stole the kangaroos?" Jilly asked, stopping to release Percy. The cat was wailing in righteous indignation over Keats getting the lead alone.

"Lenore thought someone was waiting in the van because of

the banging sound. There are other things that go thump in the night."

"Why wouldn't he just set them loose and run?"

I stood on tiptoe to catch sight of Keats, now well ahead of us. "If Knox cared about animals as much as his mom said, he wouldn't want them loose and at risk of Gilroy recapturing them. So, I bet Knox was trying to take them somewhere safe and wanted Travis to help."

We came to a swampy patch and I turned to offer Jilly my hand. Edna was a few yards behind, pushing her dirt bike and complaining to Gertie about young people today not respecting their elders.

Jilly grinned at me. We rarely got called "young people" anymore. "I can't imagine how Knox would get two adult roos into the back of a van," she said. "They don't sound that cooperative."

"Netting? Sedation? Wish I knew because we might need to do the same." Pushing branches aside, I pondered. "Knox probably learned roo management at the sanctuary."

"Or his mom could have been right, and there's another ne'er-do-well lurking here now."

I waited for her to catch up. "Possibly. Either way it's a good lead. Any pal of Knox is likely to know the backstory on the kangaroos."

Keats circled back, mouth hanging open in the pant of success. His posture and prance suggested he'd found the camp and it was worth the trip.

Jilly must have gleaned the same from his message because she caught my arm to slow me down. "What if the kangaroos are here? I don't like the sound of those big boomers. We know they—uh —*pick on* dogs."

For Keats' sake, she left out the word drowning. He didn't deserve to have his jubilance undermined by fear of being doused.

"Packs of wild dingos are their main predators, aside from

humans," I explained. "But I doubt Keats would look so perky if they were here. It would have to be a pretty fancy camp to be worth the hop back from Clover Grove."

Edna got over her snit in time to charge ahead of us into the clearing. I hadn't expected much from the two Wigg boys, but they'd created an impressive "safe house." Quite literally. There was a small cabin built out of reclaimed barn board. A few bits were missing but when I poked my head inside, the place was still relatively dry.

"Good job, good job," Edna said, stooping to go in for a look. "Can you imagine how much work it was for two boys to haul everything back here and build this alone? What a grand adventure!"

I thought about the clubhouse my brother and his friends built in Huckleberry Swamp, near Edna's house. This one surpassed their efforts by far, probably because the need for escape was greater. Asher's youth wasn't without challenges, but no one was waiting at home to beat him in a drunken rage. It reminded me to have more compassion for my mother. Like Lenore, she'd done her best with what she had.

Keats came over and nudged my hand. Memories like that could swallow me whole if I didn't step lightly aside.

"Over here," I said, following the dog. "There's a pen and I see fresh hay."

The small pen was considerably more dilapidated than the cabin and if someone figured it would hold two adult roos, he was mistaken. Several boards had been bashed out, perhaps by big feet. Signs of digging confirmed the roos had been determined to make a break for freedom.

"A good plan gone wrong," Gertie said, flipping her rifle over her back to kneel. "There are tracks. What do you make of this, old friend?"

Edna knelt, too. "Macropod. And look at that." She pulled out her phone and snapped a photo. Then she tapped and waited a second. "Aha, kangaroo scat! Confirmed by my app."

"There's a scat app?" Jilly asked.

"Of course. There's an app for everything. Birdsong. Flowers. Scat." Edna grinned over her shoulder. "It's one reason I keep that smartphone, despite my fear of overreliance on modern conveniences. "Years ago, I'd have made an educated guess. Can't deny it's nice to have confidence we're on the right path."

I stared around the clearing. "There must be a road, because no matter how good Knox was with animals, he didn't lead a boomer in here on a leash."

Gertie straightened and pulled her rifle around. "I'll look for another way out."

The rest of us joined Percy beside a fire pit that still smelled of smoke. His paw reached out and raked over the ash, touching lightly to leave faint claw marks.

"Looks like Knox stayed the night," I said.

Edna poked around in the ashes with a stick. "*They* stayed the night. And I don't mean just the kangaroos."

By the time she'd finished excavating, there was a heap of evidence that Knox had human company. Two mugs. Two plates. Two forks. Two spoons. Six empty tins that had likely held baked beans and canned meat. Prepper cuisine.

"Mrs. Wigg was probably right about Knox having backup," I said. "He must have connected with an old pal."

Gertie was back before long. "I found a road in, and the earth was damp. Two sets of boot prints. Both men likely over six feet and around two hundred pounds."

"Don't tell me... there's an app for that, too," Jilly said.

Gertie grinned. "There is, and it's almost as good as police forensics. But there's no substitute for the naked eye and experience. When treasure hunters were trespassing on my land I got quite good at identifying people. It was one of my more useful hobbies."

Edna clapped her best friend's shoulder. "Gertie's got me beat by a mile. Sometimes we skip Sunday target practice to go tracking the old-fashioned way. The apps are just a bonus."

"You guys are awesome," I said, and Jilly echoed the praise.

"Oh, we know," Edna said. "That fiancé of yours would be wise to get us on retainer."

Gertie headed back in the direction of the dirt bikes. "He might if you could legally drive, old friend."

Edna followed, cackling. "Good thing I can illegally drive, because there's nothing I enjoy more than the wind in my perm."

Looping her arm through mine, Jilly sighed. "I doubt I'll enjoy dirt bikes in my eighties any more than I did today. Pretty sure I forfeited the capacity to have children."

"Me, too." I laughed as I shot her a glance. Jilly had been my prime suspect in Janelle's baby prediction but her willingness to get on a dirt bike suggested otherwise.

Unless she didn't know herself.

And we still had to get back.

Keats supervised Edna and Gertie to bring over the bikes. They were small and light. Small and vicious. Small and deceptively powerful. Even with a small motor they could reach 50 miles per hour.

Our prepper friends went past us to the road Gertie had found on the other side of the clearing.

Meanwhile, the dog herded Jilly and me around, sniffing for no apparent reason. Only there was always a reason.

"What's going on, buddy?" Jilly asked.

I jumped ahead of his nip and failed. "Ow. Leave it, Keats."

"He's agitated," Jilly said. "Do you think the roos are in danger?"

"Maybe. Probably." Even after two years of studying this dog, I couldn't always read him. "But there's more. I guess we'll find out in due course."

Jilly twisted her curls into a ponytail. "It's not even noon, but I feel like we've had a week's worth of adventure already."

The dirt bikes roared and Edna bellowed, "Your chariots await, ladies. Hop on if you dare."

"Slow and steady," I said, slinging my leg over the back of Edna's steed. "Jilly and I have plans to reproduce, you know."

Edna scoffed. "If the human race were that fragile, we wouldn't be heading into the apocalypse. Your babies will be cockroaches."

"I heard that and register my objection," Jilly said, from the back of Gertie's bike. "And furthermore..."

The howl of Edna's engine drowned out her complaints, and my subsequent screech did the rest.

CHAPTER TEN

Jilly shifted uncomfortably in the passenger seat when I turned onto a side road. "You said we were going back to the farm, Ivy. My butt is on strike."

"Your butt's been overruled," Edna said, from the back seat. I'd expected her to ride with Gertie but she elected to oversee us instead. "Ivy's making the right choice."

I gestured to the white paws on the dashboard. "In all fairness, I barely have a thought to call my own. My canine overlord suggested a diversion."

"Wait a second." Jilly became suspicious. "Are we going to Fleetborough?"

A happy pant from her lap confirmed the good news and I added, "Figured Uncle Sterling might feed us lunch."

"Oh, please. When has he ever fed us a meal? Last time I had to scrounge up stale crackers and moldy cheese."

I grinned at her. "The olives were an elegant touch, though."

"When you get to our age, meal preparation is exhausting," Edna said, with a chuckle.

The fierce prepper who had boundless energy for apocalyptic

activities, took quite a few of her meals at the inn. Only my mother's frequent presence at the dinner table kept Edna from scoring more. I could hardly complain when Edna regularly worked around the farm and refused to accept a penny. She said she didn't want to be "chained to the man," in this case me.

"If the cupboard is bare, we'll pick something up in town on the way out," I said. "I'm still riding a sugar high from my stop at Mandy's."

"Sterling will crash that high," Edna said. "Never met a crankier man."

Jilly and I glanced at each other. We knew plenty of cranky men, and Edna outdid them all.

Uncle Sterling was standing outside at the top of the stairs, as if he knew we were coming. In fact, I'd wager a bet that he did know, because he was wearing baggy khakis and a tan jacket. Normally, he didn't bother changing out of his bathrobe before noon.

Gertie pulled up beside my truck, jumped out and saluted Sterling with Minnie. "Where's your rifle, old man?" she called. "With your rep, you can't afford to be standing outside without it."

"Check under your poncho," he called back. "I'm a magician."

They both laughed. Like all my senior friends, they loved busting each other's chops. The digs were so outrageous that no one's feelings ever got hurt.

The gun was leaning against one of the posts, along with the cane Sterling rarely used. When we first met he had a limp, but it was mostly gone. Perhaps it had always been an excuse to carry another weapon.

"Hi, Uncle Sterling," I said, as the pets raced up to greet him. My great-uncle was at the top of a fairly short list of their favorite humans. Jilly and I followed more slowly. "You were expecting us. Does that mean lunch is ready?"

"Sure," he said. "Toots knows her way to the kitchen."

"Toots" shook out her blonde curls before kissing the old man's cheek. "We already ate the olives. What else do you have on hand?"

He flicked his fingers. "Don't ruin the surprise."

Jilly went inside with Gertie and Edna, while I lagged behind. "How'd you know we were coming?"

"I'm a smart man, in case you hadn't noticed. The grapevine interrupted my favorite crime show last night and I've been standing here waiting for you ever since."

"Lies," I said. "Asher called, didn't he?"

Sterling laughed. "Dropped by after visiting Lenore Wigg, like you probably did. Predicted you'd slide down here under cover of a kangaroo. What's that word he likes to use?"

"Sneakery?" I suggested.

"That's the one." Sterling held the door for me like a gentleman. "Said you were his twistiest sister."

"Possibly, but all of the Galloway Girls are capable of a few twirls."

"That's your mother coming out." He walked over to his recliner and dropped into it. "Never met a sneak like Dolly. My nephew fell under her spell and never got out."

I perched on the chair opposite, while Gertie and Edna took the couch. Jilly made a show of banging around the kitchen, although she was probably happy to be on her feet after our dirt bike adventure. "Dad got out for decades, as I recall," I said.

Sterling crooked a silver eyebrow. "And now he's back, sleeping in the barn and waiting for her to relent."

This silenced me quite efficiently. My father had become a quiet, constant presence on the farm but he avoided my mother as much as possible. If he still held a torch for her he hid it well.

"I've advised against it," Edna said. "Dahlia could do so much better. She was the belle of the county until Calvin came back and stole her mojo. Now, she's frozen in time, like one of those bugs stuck in amber."

"A comparison Dolly would love," Sterling said. "It's almost worth a text but I don't like to encourage her. Always turns into a rant or a string of drivel. She hasn't realized I only reach out if I want something."

"Hence the rant or drivel," I said. "Mom's a master of evasion. You ask a simple question and flee in a hail of sewing trivia." Keats directed a blue eye and a mumble my way. It felt like a wake-up call. "Aha! Sterling is doing exactly the same thing only without buttons and bobbins."

"She's right," Edna said. "We can spend our visit talking about sewing if you like, Sterling. Last time we were here you were worried about losing testosterone, as I recall. We could drain off the rest of it with light conversation about needlework."

He shoved the recliner back with enough force to add another chip in the paint. "I'll pass. My favorite niece so rarely visits."

"I don't need to visit because you're at the inn for dinner quite often. That senior meal service you mentioned must have let you down."

"It's fine if you like your food soft and flavorless," he said. "I don't."

Jilly came in with a platter of fruit, sweet baked pecans, and a large chocolate bar in pieces. "Someone won a basket at bingo."

He smiled. "I was targeting the whiskey but someone beat me to it. There's also a full selection of herbal teas for you, ladies."

I was happy enough to get fruit and delicious nuts. On days like these, meals could be hard to find. Fast food joints were few and far between in hill country. "Eat fast, Uncle Sterling. We've got to get moving."

Chewing the handful of nuts he'd poured into his mouth, he crooked the other silver eyebrow. "We going somewhere?"

"That's why you put your pants on, isn't it? You don't usually make an effort just for us. I guess Hoyle Wigg is worth suiting up for."

He swallowed before answering. "Hoyle Wigg isn't worth the lint on Gertie's poncho. A man who abuses his wife and kids isn't worth my khakis, let alone a suit."

"Then put your bathrobe back on," Edna said. "They might mistake you for a patient at the nursing home, but why not live on the edge?"

Percy got into Sterling's lap and flexed his claws. "Ow. Would you mind? I'm eating lunch."

Gertie pointed to the bird feeder beyond the sliding back door. "They get more hospitality than your human guests."

"Well, they sing for their supper and more or less leave me in peace. You want me to go with you to interrogate a dying man."

"We don't feel comfortable going alone," I said.

"Or at all," Jilly muttered.

Sterling eyed me shrewdly. "Meaning, you don't think you can get into the nursing home without me. An old and reluctant acquaintance of Hoyle's."

I nodded, ashamed but still determined. "All we want is a quick visit to see if Knox stopped by to see him."

"The guys with the badges will ask all the hard questions," Sterling said. "If they haven't already."

"Yeah, but we're interested in completely different crimes, Uncle Sterling."

He helped himself to more nuts when Jilly offered. "You don't say. So, you have your own personal crime to solve? Something to do with the kangaroo, I suppose."

"Plural," I said. "Knox broke into Gilroy Leek's private zoo two nights ago and stole a pair of adult kangaroos and a joey. We figure he drove up to Clover Grove with them to see if Travis could help and they got away. I need to get them to safety before Gilroy finds them and hides them better. Percy declared their living conditions objectionable."

"Well, I doubt Hoyle Wigg was Knox's first stop for rescue tips," Sterling said. "Unless he wanted to get his old man discharged and let the roos drown him." He smirked at Keats. "They do that to dogs, you know."

I snapped my fingers to stop Keats from punishing Sterling's ankles for the insult. As spry as he was, my uncle's skin was paper thin and he already had a couple of Band-Aids on his wrist. "Don't taunt my dog. He's doing his best to recover these animals before they get hurt. You can do the same by getting out of that recliner and working your famous charm on Hoyle."

Edna smoothed her jumpsuit. "Famous? I've seen nothing of this so-called charm."

"I don't waste it on soldiers, Evans." Sterling pressed a lever and the recliner snapped up. "Besides, I never mow another man's lawn."

"Excuse me?" Edna jumped to her feet. "What is that supposed to mean?"

Sterling got up and dumped the cat to the floor. "It means Brackens has filled your dance card." He hustled past her with the gait of a young man. "Guess I should have moved a little faster. Gertie, you still available?"

Gertie swatted him hard enough to bruise. "Take that for insulting my friend."

"Schoolyard shenanigans," Jilly said. "Sterling, you're worse than the twins."

"Only the first set," he said. "When is your set arriving, Toots?"

I circled through the kitchen and met him at the front door. "Don't bait the dog. Don't bait the preppers. And don't bait my bestie."

"What does that leave?" he grumbled, walking through the door I opened.

"The cat and me." I passed him on the stairs and went to the truck. "We're clawed and waiting."

Jilly picked up a potted plant from the porch and followed. It was a bouquet for Hoyle. Minus the vase. Minus the flowers.

Sterling elbowed me out of the way and went to the driver's door. "Ready for a thrill park ride? Because I'm driving."

CHAPTER ELEVEN

S terling did exactly as I feared and took the back country trails to the nursing home. It wasn't far and it probably would have been faster to take the main roads, but my uncle enjoyed shaking things up. More specifically, shaking people up. He had that in common with Edna.

Since I already felt bad for putting Jilly through the dirt bike ride, I gave her the passenger seat and sat squished between Edna and Gertie in the rear, holding the potted plant in my lap. Both women were slim but they took up plenty of space, what with the poncho, the rifle and various other mysterious objects stuffed into pockets. Neither seemed aware that I was compressed like the filling in a lunchbox sandwich. They were too busy directing Sterling, who knew the local route better than they possibly could, rating his stick-handling on the curves and cackling gleefully when the earth seemed to fall away in the valleys.

Jilly lifted her hands off the pets in a plea. "Slow down, Sterling. I'm feeling sick."

"Are you with child, Jillian?" Edna demanded. "I knew it! The Kangaroo Prophecy is about you."

"Ooh, I like it," I said. "The Kangaroo Prophecy."

Jilly turned to send a glare between the seats that was hot enough to toast the entire prepper sandwich. "If I left home in the family way this morning, the dirt bike ride took care of this jill's joey."

"Dirt bike ride?" Sterling asked.

Edna did the honors. "We headed into the bush to check out the Wigg brothers' first campsite. The route was rough enough to rattle some ovaries." She turned to look at me, her face a little too close for comfort. "How are yours doing, Ivy? Still humming a merry tune?"

Sterling shook his head. "I don't want to know about my niece's ovaries. She's still a child herself."

We all laughed, including Jilly. "Our days of ovarian opera are passing all too fast, Sterling," she said.

I leaned forward to pat her shoulder. "If only we could make like kangaroos and have a backup bun in the backup oven. They're a model of efficiency."

"I don't particularly want to know about kangaroo reproduction, either," Sterling said, navigating the rest of the trail like a Sunday driver. "What I want to know is how you intend to get an inveterate crook like Hoyle Wigg to tell you anything useful."

I shrugged. "No idea. But Keats wants us to go so he must know something."

My uncle caught my eye in the rearview mirror. "That dog just likes a joyride. He's yanking your chain."

A muzzle crossed the space between the seats and I saw a gleam of teeth. "Don't, Keats. A bite might send us into a gully never to be seen again. What would your livestock do without you?"

His ears flattened but his muzzle withdrew and he resumed coxswain position. A grumble told Sterling in no uncertain terms that he was crossing too many lines.

"The dog's not wrong, Sterling," Jilly said. "You're jacked up on bingo nuts."

I leaned forward again. "Could you tell us more about Hoyle? Lenore was reluctant to talk about him even now."

Sterling's shoulders shifted uneasily. "That's how abuse works. Even after he dies she'll hear his voice in her head." He circled a hill and came down the other side slowly. "I didn't know Hoyle well and I liked it that way. As you know, I've kept my nose clean since I moved to the Fleetborough area. But I saw how he carried himself and how his family cowered. I also heard from people who didn't keep their noses clean that Hoyle was the one you went to when no one else would do the job. If my intel is correct, and it usually is, he was on his way to jail when cancer issued its own life sentence. He's not so much a patient here, but an inmate."

Leaving the trail, he turned onto a side road with a long, two-story building. There was nothing quaint about its gray cement exterior. I couldn't imagine what it had been before. The main floor had no windows at all.

"Used to be a slaughterhouse," Edna said. "Someone got the idea to slap another floor on top and call it a nursing home." Turning to me again, she added, "Remember, you and Jillian are my executors. Not to be mistaken for executioners. If you put me in a place like this, I'll find a way to cross back and exact vengeance."

"Relax," Jilly said. "That's not in our plans."

After a pause, Edna took the bait. "What plans are those?"

Jilly pretended to pass me a baton and I picked up the story. "Sometimes, when we're bored, we plan your send-off. Do you go down in swordplay? Bunker dive gone wrong? Skydiving accident? However it happens, we'll have a themed party."

"Punt her off Garnet Point," Sterling said. "I'll go with her." He smirked over his shoulder. "If Brackens lets me."

"Forget it," Gertie said. "Edna and I are like a prepper version of Thelma and Louise. We go together."

The two old friends bumped fists across me, sending warmth into my heart. I hoped it would be many years before they put their pact to the test.

We had no trouble finding parking and I wondered if anyone came to visit the patients here. Were they all former deadbeats?

Sterling had a word with the security guard at the front desk and we walked to the end of the corridor. Hoyle Wigg had his own small, dour room. He was propped up in bed watching re-runs of an old sitcom on TV and laughing out loud. Maybe the police had decided to spare him the bad news about Knox. Could I pump the ailing man for information without revealing what we saw? It wasn't my place or my goal to make his last days harder.

He glanced away from the TV when we came in and then turned up the volume. "No visitors. This is my favorite show and I'm busy."

"You've probably seen that episode a hundred times, Hoyle," Sterling said. "I have."

"Yeah, and it never gets old." He stared at my uncle, eyes still bright in a gaunt face. "Unlike us, Sterling."

My uncle nodded. "I got at least ten years on you, pal, and my day will come. We won't keep you from your show for long. Just a couple of questions for another old-timer. First, let me introduce—"

The remote control in Hoyle's frail hand pointed at each of us in turn. "Nosy do-good animal freak. Scary poncho nutjob. Sadistic nurse zombie slayer. Cop bunny toxic chef."

"Nice," I said. "We've been called worse."

Jilly bent over to set Percy down. "We have? Cop bunny toxic chef is a contender for worst."

The cat immediately jumped on the hospital bed. Hoyle tried to swat him with the remote control but an orange paw was already flying over the man's blanketed legs with grand sweeping gestures. "Get that thing off me. What is he doing?"

I set the potted plant on Hoyle's side table and collected

Percy. "Sorry, sir. I think he was trying to rearrange your blanket for you. He's an emotional support animal, just like my dog, here."

The dog in question was staring up at Hoyle, one paw raised to suggest there was something here worthy of our visit.

Clutching the blanket to his chest, Hoyle leaned away from the dog. "Ugliest farm cur I've ever seen. Get him out of here or I'll call—"

Edna plucked the buzzer off the tray beside him. "Fear not, this sadistic former nurse won't let you die on her watch."

"You might want to, though," Gertie told Hoyle. "Even this poncho nutjob finds the zombie slayer hard to handle."

I decided to press forward before things went completely off the rails. "Mr. Wigg, I'm so sorry for this intrusion. I just want to speak to you briefly about your son."

He turned up the volume again and stared at the screen. "I know about what happened. Chief Do-Good called last night."

"I'm so sorry for your loss," I said. "I hope you had a chance to see Knox before he passed."

"I didn't and that's fine with me." One more notch on the TV. "He was a disappointment. They both were, but Keith especially. He had a free pass and wasted it."

"Free pass to what?" I had to raise my voice over the sitcom and worried it would bother other patients close by.

His face scrunched in an obvious "duh." "A ticket into the good life. But Keith was weak, like his mother. Hoyle Junior was stronger. Learned a few tricks in the army that could have brought honor to his family. A sniper in hill country? That's a prize. But Hoyle wouldn't play the game. Haven't seen him in over twenty years. Left me for dead long before there was an ax hanging over my head." He gestured to a photo tacked to the wall of an actual ax. "Get it?"

I couldn't help smiling, but Jilly took over. "Family can be so difficult," she said, catching Percy as he tried to repeat his maneuver. "I'm sure we all know how that feels."

Hoyle directed the remote at her and pretended to press a button repeatedly. "Off. Off. Bye-bye, cop bunny. You're easy on the eyes but you married a dope."

Jilly pressed her lips together before trying again. "We'll be glad to leave if you'll just tell us about Knox's homecoming."

He flung himself back and closed his eyes. "Didn't see him. Didn't hear from him. Don't know what he did or didn't do to get himself clipped. All that boy cared about was animals. Always said he was weak in the head."

"But strong in the heart," I said. "It's a wonderful quality I share."

"Knox wanted to work in a veterinary clinic, if you can believe it? People like us don't do jobs like that. It's stamped on your forehead when you come out of the womb."

"What is?" I wondered if he was feeling remorse or just self-pity.

His eyes opened and pinned me. They were blue, like Knox's, and as sharp as icicles. "You came into the world with a golden spoon in your mouth. All smooth sailing and good luck. Just like your brother. It isn't like that for the Wiggs."

"Wasn't like that for me, either," Edna said. "My spoon was made of— Wait, I didn't get a spoon at all. They missed my order."

He ignored her. "I did my best. Should I have been tougher on the boys? Sure. I let them run off for days at a time when I could have been educating them on the hard facts of Wigg life. Maybe then, Knox would have had the sense to latch onto the gig I found him. Instead, he fell in love with a girl and got even softer."

Keats' ears came forward and he turned his blue eye on me. "Which girl is that? I didn't know he was married."

The remote came up again. "Travis intervened before that could happen. Too much personality by half, that girl. Guess what they say about redheads is true. For the long haul, you want someone you can mold, like Lenore." He traced the remote buttons in silence. "Good lady, my wife. Until she started getting big ideas." Hitting mute, he dropped the remote and sat up a little. "Happened when Knox left the country. Said she refused to lose another child to"—he shaped frail fingers into air quotes— "'intergenerational trauma.' Had to look that one up."

"So, you let Lenore go," I said.

"Seemed like the right thing to do." His fingers dropped to the blanket and picked at the fabric. Finally, he poked the remote and brought the sitcom laugh track booming back. "Especially with the court order."

I glanced down at Keats but the dog wasn't satisfied. There was more to learn here. "Mr. Wigg, can you tell me about Knox's former sweetheart? The redhead?"

Another poke at the volume nearly drowned out my own thoughts. "I'm done. Let Nurse Sadist take the final jab if she wants."

Edna's chuckle had a dark note. "Maybe I want to, but I won't. I only have a couple of decades left on this earth and I intend to do good with them."

Hoyle snorted. "Couple of decades? You're nearly a hundred now."

"Time works differently for people like me." She looked my way. "Ask Ivy. I'm ten years younger than when we met."

"More," I said. "Every time you save a life you lose five years. Pretty soon you'll be younger than me."

Gertie gave her best friend a little shove. "Maybe the Kangaroo Prophesy is about you."

A caustic glance from Edna only made Gertie grin harder. "Watch your mouth, Poncho Nutjob. I have enough people depending on me as it is."

"Kangaroo?" Hoyle said. "I heard Knox spent a lot of time and all his money on a sanctuary for them. What an idiot. People raise them for chow now. Does anyone have a cow sanctuary? A pig sanctuary?"

"Actually, yeah, Mr. Wigg. My farm is a sanctuary for all kinds of animals. I admire that about Knox."

He grunted. "Probably why he didn't come back earlier. Couldn't leave his beloved hoppers." His eyes drifted from the TV and found mine. "They're illegal here, right?"

I nodded and checked in with Keats again. He slipped in front of me to ease me away. It seemed like our work here was done.

Percy had other ideas and jumped back onto the bed. This time Hoyle ignored him.

The others said goodbye and Keats herded them out, leaving me alone with Hoyle and the deafening laugh track.

"Thanks for seeing us, Mr. Wigg," I said, backing toward the door.

"Like I had a choice." If I thought the television's volume was at its highest, I was wrong. "Tell Travis to visit his old man."

"I'll tell him," I called back from the door. "Seems like you've had time to reflect here."

"Forced sobriety. But it's not one of those deathbed makeovers." Hoyle had to shout over the TV, too. "Wiggs don't get showy like that. But I wouldn't mind seeing him once more."

I held onto the doorframe to resist Keats' effort to evict me. "I'll definitely let him know, sir."

Finally, he hit mute again. "Travis didn't kill his brother, Nosy Do-Good. Why would he spend his life protecting Knox from me, only to off him?"

"Doesn't make sense, does it?" Keats was going for my shins now. "The police will prove he's innocent."

"Never trusted the police." His eyes fell to the border collie menacing my cuffs. "Or dogs. But I hope that cur can help my boy. Travis deserves better than I gave him."

I let go of the doorframe and nudged Keats away gently with one boot. "Sounds like it, sir."

The volume came up again. "And he deserves your sister, Nosy Do-Good. In case you had any doubts about that."

"You think? Poppy isn't easy to mold, Mr. Wigg. Far from it."

"New generation. My way ends here. In this room." He looked down at Percy, busily scraping at the blanket. "After your cat finishes burying me. How many days do I have left, fluffer?"

Not many, I guessed. The paws were flying.

"Enough to see that episode come around again, I bet," Sterling said, poking his head back in. "The show's running on five other channels, Hoyle."

"I know. Sometimes the remote's too heavy to bother looking." Hoyle caught Sterling's eye. "You know the girl?"

"The redhead? Brandi Brownhill, yeah. Crossed paths a few times."

Sterling disappeared again and Hoyle gestured to the potted plant. "Take it. I was never good at looking after things."

Percy jumped down and slipped past me before Keats took one last lunge at my legs. "Travis learned how to look after himself and we'll help, Mr. Wigg. Don't worry."

"Life's too short to worry, Nosy Do-Good." I could barely hear him over the laugh track. "Take my word for it."

CHAPTER TWELVE

K eats blocked me in the hall of the nursing home, letting the others go ahead to the truck. Apparently, we had more business.

I peeked into the room two doors down and saw another man a little older and only slightly healthier than Hoyle. He sat propped upright in bed with a magazine in his lap.

"Spurned your plant, did he?" the man asked. "Hoyle Wigg wasn't much good at looking after things."

"He said so himself, Mr.—?"

"Call me Pops. Everyone does." Looking down, he smiled. "Handsome pets."

Grumpy pets. Two lashing tails told me the boys weren't particularly thrilled about our diversion, although Keats had planted the seed. Percy wasn't in the mood for more paw flourishes, although this man probably warranted them, too.

"I call my sister Pops," I said. "Short for Poppy." Proffering the potted plant, I added, "Would you like what Hoyle spurned?"

He tilted his head to the windowsill, which held about a dozen plants and three vases of blooms. "Add it to the others. It's like a funeral before I'm even gone."

I walked around the foot of the bed and made room for the new addition on the sill. There were several photos of family, some from long ago. "Are these your parents, sir?"

He nodded. "Good people who taught me the value of hard work and loyalty. I've passed that down the line. There's nothing more important than family and we all look out for each other."

I couldn't help but notice the contrast between the two men and the two rooms. This man was revered by his clan. Picking up another photo, I stared at it. Two boys with reddish blonde hair looked back at me from their father's knee.

"My grandsons," he said, flicking the pages of his magazine absently. "I leave our legacy in good hands."

Keats came over and looked up at me with his blue eye. His ears flicked, too. He was done with this nursing home. I let him herd me back to the door. "Sounds like you have every right to be proud, sir."

"Pops," he said. "I am, and I'll be helping my family until I can't."

I smiled. "Pops, then. What more could you want at the end?"

He shrugged. "A better neighbor? Hoyle has the TV roaring all day long. A man can't hear his own thoughts."

That was very likely Hoyle's intention. To drown out rumination and sorrow when alcohol couldn't do it for him.

"I imagine you'll have visitors before long. With more flowers."

He smiled and there was something vaguely familiar about it. "Always liked gardening. Had the best roses in hill country."

Once again, I held onto the doorway as Keats tried to evict me. "I love roses. What's your secret?"

"Fertilizer. The quality really matters."

He was speaking my language. "I spend a lot of time cultivating good fertilizer," I said. "Care to share your recipe?"

"Wish I could, but it's unique and stays in the family." He cocked his head to the hall. "What's going on?"

Voices rose as my senior friends skirmished in the distance. A loud "dagnabit" convinced me to let the gardening conversation go before other patients complained. "I'd try to twist your arm about that recipe but my adult kids are fighting."

He fluttered the magazine to flush me out the door. "Thanks for the plant. You take care, now."

When I reached the entrance, I found Edna, Gertie and Sterling bickering over who would drive back on the trails. I held up the key and cast the deciding vote. "That would be me. And we're taking the main roads."

"Who were you talking to?" Jilly asked, climbing into the back seat between Edna and Gertie.

"Some nice old man. I gave him the plant and we talked about fertilizer."

That was enough to quell everyone's interest, and we pretty much fell silent for most of the ride to Sterling's. A visit to palliative care was bound to leave people with feelings to process. Percy circulated from one lap to the next, confirming everyone needed some kitty care. Keats eventually parked himself on Jilly's lap in the back seat and caught a short nap. It was good to see him relax. Learning to take breaks when they came was an important lesson for me. Sprinting might get me to the marathon's finish line, but at what cost? If my restless dog could pace himself, I could, too.

"I'm going to skip the visit to Brandi Brownhill," Sterling said. "After a ride fueled by estrogen I can't handle relationship talk."

I suspected he was right to take a pass. Knox's former girlfriend was more likely to spill to Jilly and me alone. Nurse Sadist and Poncho Nutjob would probably dissuade girl-talk, too. That took a certain kind of fertilizer, normally best distributed by Jilly's velvet glove. "Is there anything we need to know about Brandi?" I asked.

"Used to run with the wrong crowd but she's settled down some," Sterling said. "If you have questions, swing back when you're done. But don't come hungry. You ate me out of house and home."

Jilly laughed. "I'll freeze some meals for you, Sterling. I don't like the idea of you gumming down gruel."

"I'll happily accept everything but your toxic stew. Remember how you nearly killed a logging crew?"

"As if I could forget. That pot of stew nearly ruined my reputation as a chef. Haven't been able to make a batch since. Or chili, the loggers' other favorite."

I caught her eye in the rearview mirror and smirked. "Is that why you haven't taken Travis up on his challenge to a backwoods cookoff?"

"Toots is afraid of losing," Sterling said. "As she should be, because I've had Travis' chili. But that's all he's got. He's a one-dish wonder."

I nearly swerved onto the shoulder as I turned to look at my uncle. "You've had Travis' backwoods chili?"

"Sure." Sterling gestured for me to keep my eyes on the road. "Ate it in the backwoods, too."

"You mean you knew Travis before he was a thorn in my side? You never told me that."

"You never asked. And to my recollection, you basically invited that thorn out of the backwoods."

The truck drifted across the middle line and his hand came up to grab the wheel. I swatted it away and got back on track. "Hardly. Explain, please."

"Not if you're going to veer into the ditch. I have no desire to beat Hoyle into the grave."

Edna's hand rose. "Let me dumb it down for you, Ivy. When Kellan was away, and you and Asher exposed corruption on the police force, Meryl Martingale saw the benefit of having a trained sniper underfoot. Under *your* feet in particular. Makes sense, doesn't it?"

It made sense. I didn't like it, but it made sense.

"There isn't enough coin in the hill country police budget to keep a lid on what's going on now," Sterling said. "Ever since you came home you've been kicking a hornet's nest."

"Me? It's not my fault."

"Of course it's not Ivy's fault," Jilly said. She probably would have squeezed my shoulder if she could avoid disrupting Keats. I suspected the dog wasn't even asleep. He was opting out of a conversation he didn't care to join.

Sterling's hand kept trying to reach for the wheel and I blocked him with my elbow. "All I'm doing is helping animals in need."

He laughed. "That's it? No kicking of hornet's nests?"

"If that happens, it's accidental." I put my right hand back on the wheel. "Mostly."

I was happy to end the conversation by the time we pulled into Sterling's driveway. "Be careful, Ivy," he said. "I'm going to check my traplines, but I've heard a little buzzing. Maybe somebody powerful wanted Knox to leave and didn't expect him back. Ever."

"Now, there's an idea." An idea that made me even more worried about the kangaroos. Being stuck in the middle of a hill country vendetta was precarious. "Keep me posted about what you learn."

Sterling slid out of the passenger seat. "I'll keep the folks with the badges posted. You focus on the mob in your purview. Specifically, kangaroos."

Jilly joined me in the front, while Gertie and Edna climbed into the van to follow us discreetly, in case we needed backup. It was a short drive through Fleetborough to the address Sterling gave us. Jilly and I walked up the front stairs behind the pets, while our friends parked just out of sight. There was no point overwhelming Knox's first love with the entirety of our eccentric posse.

Brandi Brownhill's hair flamed through the screen door she cracked open a few inches. It wasn't naturally red anymore, but a fiery orange that came out of a bottle. A black tank top and shorts revealed plenty of freckles. She was likely around Travis' age, although she looked older.

Brandi had been crying. Her eyes weren't as puffy as Lenore's but with her fair complexion, it showed more. She pulled a tissue out of her pocket and honked before saying, "If you're selling makeup or collecting for some worthy cause, forget about it."

We'd found the rare person who didn't recognize us—or was too upset to make the connection between us and the media coverage right away. She held the door open just enough to allow Percy to slip past her into the house. Meanwhile, Keats sat down beside me to take Brandi's measure with a keen blue eye.

My best friend moved a half step forward to let me know she would dive in first. Brandi was emotional and potentially volatile, thus requiring the Jilly Blackwood touch. "We're not collecting or selling, Ms. Brownhill," she said. "We got your name from a friend of ours, Sterling Fable."

Her frown eased slightly. "How do you know Sterling?"

"He's my great-uncle," I said. "I'm Ivy and this is Jilly."

It seemed wise to skip the last names and coast on anonymity as long as we could.

"Can you make this fast? I'm having a bad day." She chafed at her nose with the tissue. "An awful day. Something terrible happened to someone I know." After another honk, she corrected herself. "Knew."

"That's really why we're here," Jilly said. "We learned from Sterling that you and Knox Wigg were friends at one time. Ivy and I never met Knox but we do know his brother, Travis."

Brandi's bloodshot eyes narrowed. "Whatever you want, no comment. Knox and I were over a long time ago."

"We guessed that, because he's been overseas for so long. But people do manage to keep long-distance relationships going sometimes." Jilly smiled a little. "Not me. Guess I'm too high maintenance."

"Not me, either," Brandi said. "Although I initially bought Knox's promises. He was full of them, but he only called a few times before ghosting me for good." Her eyes watered up. "We'd talked about marrying. Having kids."

"It was harder to stay in touch then, wasn't it?" Jilly said. "Nowadays, technology means you can be in constant contact."

"True. He had to find a pay phone that couldn't be traced." She pressed her lips together, probably fearing she'd said too much. "But where there's a will there's a way."

"If what we heard was true, Knox spent a lot of time on an oil rig and in the outback. Anonymous calls would have been difficult. I'm sure he wanted to stay in touch. His father said Knox fell hard for you."

There was a flash of white as the hand holding the tissue dropped to her side. "You spoke to Hoyle?"

"Just an hour ago," Jilly said. "He thought Knox might have stopped here on his way to see Travis."

The tissue came up again and patted her eyes. "I wish. But I wasn't his first priority when he got here. Not by a long shot." There was a hiccup in her voice. "It was always about Travis, the heroic big brother who hated me."

"Maybe Travis was threatened," Jilly said. "They'd always been so close and then you stole Knox's heart. That happens."

"Maybe. But he told Knox I was a bad influence." She stuffed the tissue into her pocket and pulled a fresh handful from another. The door opened a little wider, revealing several more on the floor inside. An orange paw swatted a couple away in the hall as Percy did his due diligence.

"Hoyle was pretty open about being the bad influence in Knox's life," Jilly continued. "You're not on the hook for that."

"Thank you for saying so." She clutched the tissues to her

chest, where the freckled skin was covered in red splotches. Grief seemed to be flooding her system. "Knox and I did a little business together but he was a very willing party."

Keats' paw rose. "What kind of business was that?" I asked.

Too soon. Timing was everything and I'd asked too soon. Brandi backed up, taking the door with her. "I'm not up to talking about the old days," she said.

Jilly tried to course correct. "We're really here to invite you to a celebration of life for Knox."

The door opened again and a half smile dawned on Brandi's face. "You are?"

I was surprised too, but it was a great idea. "His life should be acknowledged," I said. "Especially his good work to help rehabilitate wildlife in Australia. Animal causes are very close to our hearts."

This time she deliberately dropped a tissue. It was more of an impatient toss. "Roos, roos, roos. That's all Knox wanted to talk about. After he left, I mean."

"What about when he visited last night?" I asked. Percy's huffy exit, tail lashing, suggested Knox had been there.

"He didn't visit last night." She bent to pick up the tissues, and a pendant escaped from her tank top. It twirled till a sunbeam hit it.

"The night before, then," I suggested, when she straightened. "I assume that's when he gave you the pendant. What a pretty little kangaroo. Is that an emerald chip for the eye?"

"Topaz." Her own eyes withered me. "Knox wouldn't spring for an emerald. Every spare dollar went to the sanctuary."

Now that we'd established he'd been here, I got to the point. "Did he ask you for help to hide the kangaroos, Brandi?"

She clasped her fingers around the pendant. "What kangaroos?"

"The ones in the back of his van. We know he liberated them from Gilroy Leek."

The golden kangaroo bounced on its chain as she released it. "That was stupid. So stupid. Gilroy has connections and he couldn't take the insult lying down. I told Knox he'd better run. I wasn't about to help him and bring criminals to my door. These days all I sell is luxury water filters. There's a lot of money in health and wellness."

"Any idea what happened next?" I prodded gently. "I don't suppose you have a secure shelter big enough for two adult kangaroos?"

"This isn't a farm, Ivy. And yes, I know who you are now. Took a minute to put the pieces together." She glanced around. "Where did your dog go?"

Keats had made a stealthy exit with Percy, and two tails flashed as they rounded the side of the house.

"To check out your yard, I suppose. He has a good nose for livestock so perhaps he smells Macropodidae."

"Macro*what*?"

I pointed to her pendant. "Just like that, only six feet tall. The jack at least. The jills are smaller."

"Can't you call them does?" Jilly asked me. "I really don't care for the association."

The front door slammed in our faces and I texted Edna to join us out back with Gertie. If Brandi was hiding a mob of roos in her yard, we'd need all the help we could get.

A padlock on the gate forced us to wait for our prepper friends. Keats had likely gone under the fence, as there was a freshly widened hole just big enough for a canine genius. Percy likely took the high road over to keep his fluff clean.

"You can't trespass on my property," Brandi shouted from inside the yard. "Get out of here."

"My property is on your property. I have to come in. You'll never get my pets out of there alone."

"I'll hit them with a shovel and throw them over. Call them back, or that's what'll happen."

"I wouldn't take a swing at them, young lady." Edna had arrived to snap the lock with her handy bolt-cutters. "Unless you want your ears pierced. The dog is famous for that and the cat for scarring scalps. Up to you if you want to sacrifice beauty. I never did."

We walked into a large, deep backyard bordered by tall fir trees. Keats and Percy were dancing just out of reach of Brandi's spade. Both pets seemed to be enjoying the game, so I doubted there was an imminent threat.

"Satisfied?" Brandi demanded. "No kangaroos."

Keats darted away to stand by the trees lining the back of the grassy area. His paw rose in a point and he looked back at me with his blue eye. Pricked ears suggested curiosity rather than concern. Whatever he wanted me to see here was unlikely to drown or disembowel dogs.

Keats' mouth snapped shut and his tail dropped, perhaps sensing my traitorous watery thoughts. Then he started moving through the trees.

"Allow me," Gertie said, hauling Minnie around in front. Edna graciously yielded the lead. She didn't like to be encumbered by a longarm and Gertie felt naked without one.

Brandi waved her shovel around. "You can't just break in here and do what you like. I'm calling the police."

"No need." Jilly held up her phone. "I already texted. My husband's a police officer."

"I'd put my money on roos against Asher," Edna said. "He's too nice."

I nodded agreement. "Cori Hogan's a better bet if kick comes to punch. She's so agile. We'll need to be very careful."

"Hello? Are you listening?" Brandi's voice was high. Frantic. "I said there are no kangaroos here."

"There's a shed," Gertie called back through the trees. "A small barn, really. If I had roos to stash, here's where I'd come."

We all pushed through the trees and Brandi turned to confront us as we emerged in the open space. There was indeed a small, weathered barn with double doors.

"Do not open it!" Brandi's voice spiked another notch. "I'm warning you."

Minnie spun around to take a closer look at Brandi. "Or what?" Gertie asked. "Tell my rifle all about your plans."

"Maybe we shouldn't open the door," Jilly said. "The last thing we need is kangaroos bounding away."

Edna shook her head. "Unlikely. I expect the roos are still up in Clover Grove. Stressed animals wouldn't willingly hop all this way to take cover in a shed."

"Unless there were more," Jilly countered. "How do we know Gilroy Leek was telling the whole story?"

"You've got a point, Jillian. Gilroy Leek has never told a whole story in his life."

Pointing to the pets, I weighed in. "It's not a huge threat. Keats and Percy are too relaxed."

Brandi lowered her shovel. "Good. Listen to your pets if you won't listen to me."

I thought about it. "Unless it's the baby roo. We can handle a joey easily enough."

The shovel rose again. "There isn't and never was a kangaroo in my shed."

"But Knox was here and his first priority was to safeguard those roos," I said. "And if there's a clue as to what happened, we owe it to Knox and Travis to find out."

"There's nothing. No clue." Brandi's frantic tone was back.

"Knox came, tried to woo me with his pendant and left when I laughed in his face."

Keats was pant-laughing in her face now, but Brandi didn't notice. "Then there's really no reason you couldn't let us take a peek inside," I said. "Just to put our minds at rest. For Travis' sake."

"Why would I care about Travis' feelings? He never cared about mine. He's the reason Knox left me, and now look what happened."

"Not the only reason, at least according to Knox's parents," I said. "We'll get to the bottom of this story, Brandi. You can take my word for that."

"I'm not taking your word for anything." Her voice was like a jackhammer to the ear. "Leave. Now."

I might have done just that, or at least waited for the police, had the shed door not opened without our help.

It wasn't a kangaroo inside.

It was something even bigger.

CHAPTER THIRTEEN

The young man standing in one half of the barn's double doors had to stoop to get out. He was well over six feet tall and broad-shouldered enough to give a buck kangaroo a good fight.

He looked to be around 17, give or take a year. His hair was thick and dark, his beard a bit sparse and his eyes bright blue. Still, I didn't make the connection till he smiled.

It was the Wigg smile. I'd seen it on Travis often enough, and even, however briefly, on Lenore's face. Was this strapping youth Knox's son by way of Brandi Brownhill? Or did he belong to Travis?

"G'day mates," he said, answering the question with a handy cliche.

"Who are you and what are you doing in my shed?" Brandi demanded. She was either truly shocked or her acting skills had improved markedly in the past half hour.

"I'm Camden. Camden Betts. Sorry for camping here without permission."

His Australian accent was so perfect it sounded put on, but that smile didn't lie. Knox Wigg had clearly brought his son with him to meet the family. Or at least, Travis.

"Camden Betts Wigg?" I suggested.

He shrugged. "I guess. Knox was a stranger to me till a few weeks ago. My mum raised me alone and never talked about him. But then Knox tracked her down and there's a resemblance Mum couldn't deny."

"There is indeed," Edna said. "You look just like your Uncle Travis, too."

Camden nodded. "That's what Knox said. He really wanted me to meet his brother. That's why we came."

Brandi shoved the spade's blade into the soil and leaned on it. "Who is your mother? Knox always said he didn't want kids. Because his own childhood was—"

"Awful," Camden interrupted. "That's why Mum didn't tell him. They worked together at a sanctuary until she broke up with him and moved away. If he hadn't looked for her, I wouldn't be hiding in your shed, ma'am."

Jilly finished tapping on the phone and gave the young man her full attention. "Camden, we're friends of your uncle, Travis."

"Speak for yourself," I muttered, while aiming a grin at Camden. "Travis is seeing my sister. He's smug and overbearing."

"Knox said that too." Camden grinned back. "But he also said he wouldn't be alive today if not for Travis."

My grin faded and my throat clenched. Camden didn't know what had happened to Knox. It didn't feel like our place to tell him the father he'd only just met had been murdered—and that his new uncle was a suspect. Jilly flashed her phone to let me know the police were on their way. Someone with a badge could deliver this terrible news. They had advanced training in shattering dreams and breaking hearts. As a former HR exec with a specialty in terminations, I supposed I did, too. But that wasn't my job anymore and I'd lost my ability to shield my own heart.

Brandi started to speak but Gertie shushed her. When she

persisted, Brandi got a more personal introduction to Minnie, who started to nudge the redhead back through the trees.

"You can't shoot me, lady," Brandi said. "This is my property and Knox Wigg did not have permission to store junk in my shed. Not anymore."

Jilly gave Camden a kind smile. "Don't worry about Brandi, Camden. She used to date your father and seeing him again brought up a lot of grief and anger."

Camden watched her go. "Knox said they parted on bad terms but he hoped she'd be over it by now. I waited in the van while they were talking back here. Couldn't make out the words, but it got pretty heated."

Jilly mouthed a warning at me to wait for the police but I couldn't let the opportunity pass. The stolen kangaroos would be their last priority, whereas they were my first. "Camden, were you waiting in the van with stolen kangaroos?" I asked.

Camden paused too long for Keats' liking and got a nip for incentive. Meanwhile, Percy began scaling the young man from behind, making him squirm.

"Easy, boys," Edna said as the cat crested the summit and took his parrot perch on a broad shoulder. "No need for torture unless he doesn't spill."

Camden's face had flushed up to his thick, wavy hair. The Wiggs were truly gifted in the follicle department. "I wouldn't say stolen. Liberated was the word Knox used. My mum rescued plenty in her time, too. This pair was in a small, rundown pen and deserved better. I wanted to help. Knox didn't make me. In fact, he told me to sit out the rescue but I knew two roos would be a handful. Plus, we had to be extra gentle with the jill and joey. Roos stress easy."

"So, when Brandi refused to help, did you visit Lenore? Your grandmother?"

He nodded. "Well, Knox did. I stayed in the van. He said we'd come back and do it properly after seeing Travis. Lenore knew he was teaching a self-defense class the next night."

"And that's when you went to the old campsite," I prompted.

Camden's face brightened. "It was cool. We had dinner and slept under the stars. Well, I slept for a few hours. Knox had to stand guard because the roos wouldn't settle. The pen wasn't in good enough shape to keep them there, so we had to move on the next morning. Knox tried other barns and even garages to hold the roos, but nothing panned out. Eventually we just drove up to that mall to—"

"Stake Travis out," Edna interrupted.

His nod was sheepish. "Pretty much, yeah. We hid the van in the bush and talked for hours. When people started arriving for the class, Knox left me in charge and went to watch for his chance to—"

"Ambush Travis." Edna's comments were the prepper equivalent to a sheepdog nip and irritating for more than the recipient.

"Basically. He was hoping Travis would be last to leave so they could talk. Travis wouldn't pick up Knox's calls. Didn't recognize the burner, I guess. So, Knox walked over to see if he could intercept him."

Jilly couldn't help herself from asking, "Then what happened?"

Camden began to pace in a tight circle. "It was a long day and the roos were frustrated and restless. They were thumping around and I decided to open the back door to see if they were okay. I was worried about the baby." Now both hands were in the luxurious Wigg mane. "The jack jumped out like a superhero on steroids. Scratched me up and knocked me right over." He pulled up his sleeve to show claw marks and then turned so we could see the pocket hanging loose on his jeans. Percy held his position with admirable grace. "By the time I got up, the jill was gone, too."

"You called Knox?" I asked.

"Yeah, yeah. He didn't answer the first few calls. When he finally did, all he said was 'run.' I told him I'd come back here and wait for him. He still hasn't checked in."

Camden's blue eyes shot a questioning glance around the circle and we all looked down at once to avoid answering.

"Where's the van now?" Edna asked.

"Up the street a bit in the brush. Same place Knox parked when we visited Brandi. Said he was used to hiding there to unload."

"Unload livestock?" I asked.

Camden's hands dropped into his front pockets. "Dunno. I didn't want to ask too many questions at once. After the roo rescue it was kind of a blur. We mostly talked about their childhood. The best parts. Growing up wild in the bush. Knox just kept saying, 'Travis will know what to do. He always knows what to do.'" He met my eyes squarely for the first time. "Is Travis good with animals?"

As much as I enjoyed dissing Travis, this kid deserved to hear something kind about his newfound family. "He is, yes. A few months ago, he helped me rescue a ton of beehives and kept a lot of them. He's a skilled beekeeper. Sometimes he helps my sister around my farm and seems to enjoy it."

Camden leaned against the shed, looking relieved, drained or both. When Percy yowled a complaint, the young man quickly straightened. "Then Travis will handle everything. He'll catch the roos and you can keep them on your farm."

Jilly groaned. "That's exactly what I'm afraid of. I help run an inn on that farm and we don't need our guests getting scratched up like you did."

"It's illegal to keep kangaroos here, Camden," I said. "Gilroy Leek was breaking the law, which was why he had them hidden away in squalor."

"Then maybe they're better off free." He winced as Percy came down his arm and leapt off. "There's plenty of land and forage."

I shook my head. "They've been captive all their lives and don't know how to take care of themselves. Some farmer would end up shooting them."

"Besides," Jilly added, "the police already know."

Sirens screaming close by indicated our time had run out. "Don't worry, we'll find the roos and get them somewhere safe. We have an amazing group of rescuer friends."

Car doors slammed out front. Lots of them. This yard was going to get busy.

Camden huddled against the shed, seeming to lose inches, pounds and even years. He was a gangly kid without parental support and my heart went out to him.

Jilly's did, too, because she tried to lighten the mood. "Camden, did you sleep all right?" Poking her head into the shed, she gasped. "Oh, dear. Percy, what are you doing?"

I walked past her with Keats and turned on my phone light to get a better look. The cushion from a chaise lounge was spread on the floor with a tarp draped over it. Good thing it hadn't been too cold because a tarp was far from cozy. "Percy, where are you, my friend?"

"In the corner." Jilly stood behind me in the doorway. "He's doing... you know what."

"His business?" Edna called.

Jilly stuck her head out. "His *other* business."

"Oh dear," Edna said. "Again?"

Percy was indeed scraping invisible litter over something in the corner. I stepped across the cushion and bent to take a closer look.

That's when someone shouted, "Ivy Galloway, *stop*. Whatever you're doing, just stop."

CHAPTER FOURTEEN

Okay, maybe it wasn't a full-on shout, but my nervous system experienced it as one and I froze with my butt in the air. Heat and frost seemed to collide in different parts of my body and sweat beaded on my forehead before chilling. The reaction reminded me of encounters with killers, and Keats poked my hand repeatedly to ground me in the moment.

In all our exploits, with all my foibles, Kellan had never done more than raise his voice in frustration, and even then, only rarely and privately.

Now he was shouting at me in front of a crowd.

Keats' ears went back. Some chief's cuffs were in very deep peril.

Another avenger got to Kellan first. "What's got your uniform in a knot, young man?" Edna said. "As Dahlia always says, no one likes a shrew."

Laughter threatened to bubble up in my throat. Mom did say that often. To my sisters and me. Not the chief of police.

"Miss Evans, desist." Kellan's voice returned to near normal level. "Only you find yourself amusing."

"Not true," Gertie said. "Edna is highly entertaining. Sometimes intentionally."

After a general chuckle subsided, Kellan said, "Ivy, please come out of the shed. At your earliest convenience."

I wasn't sure sarcasm was a big improvement, but Keats decided to round me up and get the herd of one moving.

"It's fine," Jilly whispered as I walked slowly to the doorway. "He's just worked up. The mayor's probably on his back."

The mayor was on Kellan's back frequently and it didn't translate to yelling. I'd cut a few corners today, for sure, but I'd done far worse in my quest for animal justice. What was it about this case that had Kellan so riled? More specifically, *Fiancé* Harper. *Chief* Harper was quietly severe. Intimidating. Ominous. Only the fiancé got emotional. What was worrying my betrothed?

"Someone's in trouble." My brother's voice had a singsong quality. "You better come on out, Twisty."

I hated it when Ash called me that in front of strangers. Camden I wasn't so worried about, but Brandi Brownhill might spread that around.

The redhead's smirk as I finally joined Jilly in the doorway confirmed it.

"What's going on?" I asked, scanning the growing crowd of police officers for Kellan. When I found him, I looked slightly away, as one would with any potentially aggressive animal, including one's betrothed. "I was just fetching Percy." For the benefit of the new faces, I added, "My cat."

Asher flashed his infectious grin at me. I'd always found it insufferably bright until Travis came along with his brilliant choppers. The Wigg genes were also kind in that respect. "Why is your cat contaminating a crime scene before authorities can investigate, Twisty?"

"You've solved plenty of crimes with a few orange hairs in the mix, Asher."

He crossed his arms. "You said he was doing his business. How will forensics get to the bottom of that litter box?"

Jilly walked toward him with her own arms crossed. My brother backed up a few steps until he hit Kellan. He was a brave man, Asher. Daring, even. But he didn't mess with his wife when she was protecting me. It would be a wonder if she let him anywhere near his own kids when they arrived. Jilly was fierce, loyal and loving to the underdog.

Or, in this instance, the under*cat*.

"I was the one who said Percy was doing his business," she said, glaring up at Asher. "And I meant that metaphorically."

The brief pause that followed allowed Edna to slide into the conversation. "Did you miss that day in English class, Officer Galloway?"

Asher probably knew what "metaphorical" meant but his expression was confused. When Jilly got riled, it was like his bones melted from terror. She'd married him happily and had no regrets, but he worried that he was just one small blunder away from losing her. I could empathize because I knew the fear stemmed from our father's baffling departure when we were kids. Maybe that's why my own bones had just melted in the shed. Falling in love wasn't simple for Galloways. It left us constantly vulnerable to abandonment and pain.

Keats pressed his head under my fingertips and mumbled something encouraging. It sounded like he was taking his share of responsibility for pushing Kellan's limits. Percy hit me midback and scaled to his shoulder perch in solidarity. Another quiet chuckle rippled through Kellan's staff but they choked it off quickly.

Jilly was still on the offensive. "Chief Harper, Percy did nothing more than swish around in that shed. Otherwise, all is exactly as we found it when we encountered a stranger." She gestured to the silent young man who was trying unsuccessfully to blend into lilac bushes. "Allow me to introduce Camden Betts Wigg." She let that sink in for a moment and then turned to Camden. "Please meet my husband, Asher Galloway, as well as Chief Kellan Harper. The chief is Ivy's fiancé."

"He was this morning," I muttered. "Before yelling at me."

Edna raised her hand. "Add a no-yelling clause to your vows. As your bridesmaid, I recommend several amendments. For the record, Chief, the word 'obey' isn't even on the table."

Kellan wasn't anywhere ready to be amused. "Our vows aren't on the table right now, Miss Evans. Not when you've apparently discovered a relative of Travis Wigg."

"A nephew," I said. "Camden only recently learned about Knox Wigg being his father."

Jilly gave Kellan a significant look. "He isn't aware of what transpired last night. Perhaps you or Asher would like to take him aside and chat?"

Kellen nodded to Asher and gestured for Camden to join him. My brother led the young man back through the trees to find some privacy. Then Kellan directed someone else to pull Brandi aside and question her. The rest of the staff dispersed to investigate the site.

After that, he turned to me. "Walk with me, Ivy."

Keats beat me to him and delivered a preliminary nip to chiefly cuffs. He didn't like Kellan's tone or the fact he was cutting me away from my herd. In situations such as this, a wise sheepdog knew it was best to keep allies together.

Nonetheless, it was an invitation we couldn't refuse, so we followed Asher back through the trees and walked around the front of the house. Normally, I was quick to jump in with nervous babble but this time I decided to wait Kellan out. There was a chance he didn't know all we'd done today and I might save some of the news to share later. Via phone, perhaps. Or a polite text. Snail mail, even.

The dog circled to press us back from the road, where police vehicles formed a long line. He wanted to stay close to the action. When Kellan didn't move fast enough, his pant cuff got evened out with a nip to the front. And another for good measure.

"Leave it, Keats," I said. "I pay for the dry cleaning and darning, you know. The last repair cost me thirty bucks."

"What's his problem?" Kellan sounded irritable, although this was far from unusual with Keats. The dog doled out nips like candy at Halloween. I could stop him, and sometimes did, but I relied on his instinctual behavior too much to dull his edge. He needed to trust his own judgement and I backed him in that. It was something I'd learned from the master trainer, Cori Hogan. Her border collie had torn my pant cuffs, although Keats hadn't done the same damage to Cori's. He admired and respected her too much. The same did not apply to Kellan. At least, not today.

"You didn't say please," I said. "And you were curt. When you yell at me, you yell at Keats."

Percy, still on my shoulder, reached out and swatted Kellan, leaving light scratch marks on the fabric of his jacket.

"It wasn't yelling," Kellan said, "although I suppose I could have moderated my tone."

"Apology accepted. You're having a tough day."

It wasn't an apology but in due course it would become one. I just leapfrogged to the destination to help my betrothed out of his dark mood. Maybe that's how a good marriage flourished. I wasn't quite sure as I'd never had one modeled to me. My parents split, as did Kellan's and Jilly's. Since I moved back, I'd seen far more examples of poor relationships than otherwise. We would need to carve our own path.

"I only regret my tone," he said. "My anger is justified. You promised to stand down until we were finished examining the crime scene."

I wanted to shrug but Percy's weight suppressed the urge. "I promised not to search for the roos around the mall and I haven't. Their safety is my first priority and I don't like knowing they've been loose up there. A farmer could shoot them. There's a baby involved."

"I know. You mentioned."

"Exactly. I mentioned it in one of my many texts today updating you. Jilly sent others."

His exasperation came out for a showing. "And did you notice I replied asking you to stand down? I believe my exact words were…" He pulled out his phone. "Ah yes, here it is. 'Go back to the farm and stay there.'"

"Huh. Must have missed that one in the flurry. Did you say please? Were you curt?"

"I believe I sounded exactly as any chief of police would in the situation."

"But what about a chief fiancé? You wear two hats, you know."

He ruffled his dark hair. Normally, I wanted to take over that job for him, but not right now. I preferred to keep my fingers.

"Ivy, I spoke as both when I asked you to stay out of harm's way. Didn't think I needed velvet gloves when there's a killer on the loose."

"That's not so unusual in hill country, is it?" I stared at him, trying to figure out what was different about this case. "Is the mayor hassling you?"

He rubbed his eyes now. "Of course she's hassling me. She's come to rely on Travis lately."

"Ah, yes. Her own personal sniper. Who *wouldn't* get attached?"

His hand shifted and he stared at me. "Who said that?"

"Hoyle Senior." I sidestepped the lecture by forging on. "Anyway, it's not like we were creeping in alleys, and I had plenty of company. *Armed* company."

"Armed risk-loving company. Sterling should have known better."

"You know he's a softy about animals. Besides, when it comes to my crew, Jilly's the only voice of reason. The voice we talk over. Or bark over. Or meow over."

A mere hint of a smile formed but Kellan converted it into a pucker of disapproval. "I can't believe you descended with an entourage on a grieving mother and then a dying man."

"It was for the kangaroo cause. Every step we've taken today is for the roos. Mandy told me about Gilroy Leek, the illegal zookeeper Knox busted. Gilroy told us about Lenore Wigg, and I figured Knox had stopped there. She told us about her ex, Hoyle, and he told us about Brandi. We haven't found the roos, but we did find Travis' nephew. Did you know about Camden?"

He shook his head. "We had reports that Knox wasn't alone but figured he'd hooked up with an old friend. They didn't fly together and used burner phones." Glancing back at the house, he sighed. "Brandi denied she'd seen Knox when I sent someone down to speak to her."

"The kangaroo pendant was a giveaway. I really don't think she knew about Camden. He hid in the shed on his father's orders after things got tense at Midway Mall. The animals escaped by accident but it sounded like Camden sensed Knox was in trouble by then." I waited till Kellan's eyes refocused on mine. "Did Travis know about Camden?"

"He hasn't mentioned him but Travis isn't exactly an open book."

Percy was bored of the discussion. He leapt from my shoulder to Kellan's and then onto the roof of a police vehicle. Then he paraded down the hood and onto the next one, leaving prints in the dust. As he continued, it struck me how many cars were here. There was a time—only last year—when you could hardly scare up a uniform beyond Dorset Hills and Dog Town. Meryl wasn't wrong about budgets being allocated to policing. There was more going on behind the scenes than I knew, and that's probably what made Kellan so irritable.

I walked after the cat, and Kellan followed me down the street, hopping a little as Keats assisted from behind. Percy wasn't going to stop till he reached the end of the row. The cat made his own fun and his own statement. Sometimes, the price tag in dirty paws was worth it.

That reminded me of his signaling behavior earlier. "There may be something under the floorboards in Brandi's shed, Kellan. She got very agitated when we got near it, yet didn't know about Camden. Percy suggested you focus on the northwest corner. He was curious, but not corpse curious."

"Thank goodness for that." My fiancé watched Percy leaping from one car to the next and shook his head. "Maybe Camden or Knox stashed luggage."

"Think bigger. I got the sense Brandi and Knox used to do some business together of the illegal kind. Fencing stolen goods or something like that."

"Something like that," he repeated.

It was enough confirmation for me to jump to conclusions like Percy jumped between cars. "Maybe Knox came back to claim money she owed him. To help with his son, or the kangaroo sanctuary. Maybe Brandi was worried he'd expose their past and decided to kill him."

"And maybe you could let me follow due process to investigate." His tone was milder now, and he threw me a bone. "It would be difficult for a woman of Brandi's size to strangle a man of Knox's."

"I guess. Unless she trained in martial arts."

"Even then. He had a black belt, too."

I pushed my luck a little. "What about the guy Travis sparred with? Brydon Ting?"

"Alibis for both instructors. First thing we checked."

We'd reached the last vehicle in the row, which I knew from the plate was Kellan's. Percy started chasing his tail on the roof, making an intricate pattern in the dust. I turned sideways and leaned on the SUV. "Did Knox have a record in Australia?"

Kellan paused, perhaps weighing what he wanted to share against what he wanted to glean about my day. "No criminal record. It seemed like he'd succeeded in turning his life around. Travis had no idea he was coming back."

"It's about Camden," I said. "Knox only found out about his son a few weeks ago and he must have wanted to introduce him to Travis. I'm sure it was hard to be half a world apart when they were once so close."

I filled him in on everything Lenore and Hoyle had told us about their Irish twins.

"A hard life," Kellan said. "What you've said matches what Travis told me. He doesn't know about his father's change of heart."

"Hoyle definitely has regrets. Maybe they can reconnect now, before he passes." I brushed my fingertips along the SUV, leaving a trail in the dirt. "That won't undo what happened, though. The Wigg boys raised themselves in the bush."

Kellan jumped back to avoid Percy's arrival and failed. The first step toward clean paws was scraping off the excess on a uniform. "Has this story changed your mind about Travis?" he asked.

While he was trying to dislodge Percy, I traced my initials in the dirt on his SUV door. "I have more compassion for him, but I still worry about Poppy. Travis was already loaded with baggage and now there's tragedy. It's a lot to put on a relationship."

"Poppy has issues of her own. We all do. The best we can hope for is to find someone who helps us heal those wounds." He half-smiled at me, still holding his teeth in reserve. I wasn't out of the woods yet. "Look at how Asher has changed since he met Jilly. He's become a very good cop under her watch."

"He'll make a great father," I said, continuing my etching in the dust. "I hope the kangaroo prophesy is about them."

Giving up the effort to evict Percy, Kellan allowed himself to take the bait. "Kangaroo prophesy?"

"Janelle Brighton predicted someone in Clover Grove is with child, like the jill kangaroo. It makes sense, doesn't it? But Jilly denies it and willingly took a dirt bike ride this morning."

"Dirt bike?"

"That's how we got to Travis' camp. Terrifying. And it probably would have shaken the next Galloway spawn loose."

His smile was still blooming, despite the persistent cat and dirty pawprints on his shoulders. "She might not know yet. Or it's a secret baby."

"Like Camden. Imagine discovering you have a grown son."

"Luckily, I don't need to worry about that. I expect to be there when my children arrive and shadow them like an overprotective hawk till I'm in Clover Grove Cemetery."

"I hope you're not called away on a case when they arrive," I said. "Crime doesn't stop for incoming babies."

Finally, a mere hint of teeth. "I hope *you're* not called away on a crime or a rescue. My child could get a dirt bike debut." He shut his eyes, perhaps trying to block images of the ways I could disrespect his newborn offspring. "Or on the end of a crane."

I was right about the images. "Deputies Keats and Percy will need to deploy with others when the time comes. Unless..."

I paused strategically.

"Unless what? Are you contemplating a surrogate?"

"I'm contemplating kangaroo modifications. Did you know the baby is born after just a month's gestation and tucks itself into the pouch to mature? And all the while, there's a backup baby in the backup oven. Mother Nature was really cooking by the time she got to macropods."

He pretended to think about it. "You could pull off a pouch. With those overalls, no one would know."

I pulled out the fabric to test the give. "No room for twins. That's a risk with my family."

Percy swished from one shoulder to the other across Kellan's face. "We'll be lucky to raise one without incident."

"You underestimate our social supports. There's an entire network of good people to make up for my maternal deficits."

Keats took his cue to circle us, mumbling an order to get moving.

Pulling me away from his vehicle, Kellan slung an arm around my shoulder and turned us to face Brandi's house. "The people in that yard—and many more—would follow you into battle without question."

"My point exactly. Someone would follow with our baby and keep it safe."

The chiefly head shook. "You're too much, Ivy. Too much."

"I'm just enough." I resisted the urge to look back at my handiwork on the car. "Exactly the right amount."

I hoped he wouldn't look back, either, but he must have sensed my suppressed glee and turned.

On his car door, I'd traced his initials plus mine in a fat, slightly misshapen heart.

Dropping his arm, he went back and bent to smudge out the message with his sleeve before his staff could see it. When he straightened, however, I saw all the teeth a besotted hobby farmer could ask for.

"You're right," he said, leading me back into battle. "You're just enough. No need to add a pouch."

CHAPTER FIFTEEN

J illy and I got up before dawn, packed everything we'd need for
a long search in the forest for the kangaroos, and hit the road
before anyone was up except my father, who merely waved as
he did my chores without being asked.

"He's a good guy," Jilly said. "I didn't expect to like Calvin, but
I do."

"I guess." We rolled under the black iron arch that said
"Runaway Far." My mother repeatedly asked me to replace the
"m" to class up the inn's image but I was all about quirky and
rustic. Besides, it still gave me sparks of satisfaction to defy Mom.
I'd been a model child and teen and had some catching up to do in
the parental rebellion department. Figured I might as well get it
out of my system before becoming a parent myself. "I like Calvin
as a person and I'm grateful for what he does for me on the farm,
but it's hard to erase all the years he was erased from our lives.
Mostly I think of him as a kind, older friend who camps out in the
barn. He doesn't feel like a dad, per se, but I don't really know what
that feels like."

"Same." Jilly let the pets wrestle for position in her lap without
complaint because she was in rugged rescue gear. No need to

worry about dirt, hair or catches in fine fabric. "My dad is only a vague memory and still hasn't surfaced."

Sharing a common loss might have been one of the many things that drew Jilly and me together in our college days. Back then, it wasn't something that I thought about much and she didn't talk about it, either. It was just part of our identity. We chatted more often about it after Calvin came back, probably because we began looking forward to having children of our own. We'd both chosen men who showed all signs of staying the course. Asher would only be pried away from his family by the cold undead hands of zombies. And Kellan... well, I kept putting him to the test with new animals and escapades and he cleared the bar with room to spare. Our children would be lucky to have him.

"Your mother never married again?" I asked. It was dangerous territory. Jilly and her mother had a strained relationship and my friend had actually been relieved when her mom missed the wedding. She'd never once visited Clover Grove and aside from one trip, Jilly hadn't left the farm. Like me, once her boots touched down, she was anchored. Home. I hoped we would grow old together here with our families, though in time I knew she would need her own house, with its own fabulous kitchen. There was plenty of room for several houses on my property or the neighboring land Dad owned, providing we could get zoning approval. It seemed like the ideal future, with children and animals running around all day, safe under the eyes of family and Edna's surveillance gear.

"Mom dated a few guys but she always had one foot out," Jilly said. "Or maybe she's found someone and hasn't said so. She's a very private person." Smirking a little, she added, "The exact opposite of Dahlia. Mousey and dull."

"Mousey? That's hard to believe. All the Brighton women I've met are gorgeous and outgoing."

"She was the odd woman out and wanted it that way." Keats

pawed at the window and Jilly rolled it down for him. "We give each other plenty of space. It's for the best."

Turning, she stared out the passenger window and I took my cue to drop the subject. "I hope we find the mama roo quickly because she must be terrified in the bush on her own. From what I read the males aren't exactly doting dads. He's probably partying in some farmer's field."

Her sigh fogged up the glass. "I'm dreading this, just like every other search, but at least we have a big team."

Edna had gone ahead with Gertie to fight for leadership with Cori Hogan. We had lined up all the usual suspects, with the Thistledown folks on standby.

I looked longingly at Mandy's store as we passed but Jilly had packed sensible food, and thermoses of coffee. "I wonder if Poppy will show up."

Asher had collected Travis from the farm to meet Camden yesterday but they hadn't returned. I wasn't sure where they were staying. I'd offered to host Camden at the inn, too, but Kellan had other ideas and wasn't sharing. The stakes had apparently changed when the young man came into the picture. Happily, the cop assigned to watch the farm was gone, too.

"Probably not," Jilly said. "Can you imagine how rattled Pops must be after learning all this about Travis?"

"I can imagine it, but if you decide to date a man fresh out of the backwoods, you've got to expect a few surprises."

My friend blew out another sigh that made Keats turn and squint at her. He didn't like gusty breaths close to his ears, or the emotions they signified. "That's one reason I love Asher. He's an open book."

That was mostly true. I'd fully believed in his transparency until I found out he'd been keeping in touch with our father for years on the sly. Since I came home, plenty of secrets about my family had been exposed and there were probably plenty more.

That was one reason I preferred the company of my friends. If Edna or Gertie revealed a secret, it was par for the course. I didn't expect to know everything about them, as I did with my family.

Keats grumbled at me and I nodded. There was plenty I didn't tell them, either.

"What was that about?" Jilly asked, as we took the last turnoff to Midway Mall.

"I was just musing about family and secrets and—"

A ping interrupted me. Pings weren't unusual, but when they came from Jilly's phone and mine in stereo, it was occasionally cause for concern.

"Just Cori I bet," Jilly said. "Wondering why we're late."

Our phones pinged again.

And again.

Enough times that we also groaned in stereo over the last one.

"Tell them we can't go," I said. "A roo on the run outranks any family meeting."

Jilly gave me a second to reflect. "Do you really want to say no? It sets a bad precedent."

"They're always bogus. Just an excuse for Asher to remind me to stay out of police business. Kellan probably puts him up to it."

Keats usually enjoyed a family meeting, no matter how fractious, but he wasn't giving his usual happy pant today. The hunt for the roos was a priority matter not to be delayed.

"We've got to go, Ivy. One day it might be *my* emergency and I want to know everyone will show. Those meetings are one of the reasons I married into the Galloways."

"Seriously? Why?" I pulled onto the shoulder of the highway and made a U-turn. "They're excruciating."

"It's community at its very essence. Everyone comes. Everyone communicates. It's like a family dinner with none of the cooking."

"And none of the courtesy."

Keats grumbled along with me as I gunned it back to Daisy's

house. Meanwhile Jilly stick-handled Cori on the phone. "It's okay," she said, when she hung up. "The Mafia called in the Thistledown crew and Keats will help us find them when we get there."

"Maybe it's for the best, because Maud will bring Frost and Annie. More noses for the cause."

Keats mumbled something that sounded vaguely insulting, no doubt directed at his sister from another litter. He adored Annie, their dam, but Frost annoyed him. She had most of his gifts and a few uniquely her own. Maud had been teaching Frost and her pups to "speak" using pre-programmed buttons. I'd offered to do the same with Keats and he refused with a mumble of disgust. Every time one of those buttons squawked "outside," "walk" or "park" he cringed. My dog managed to communicate his needs just fine without buttons.

Asher's police SUV blocked Daisy's driveway and it seemed like a sign of how this was going to go. There was plenty of room on the road but he chose to make us circle his official vehicle. He might as well flash his badge and be done with it.

Jilly pursed her lips as she walked around the SUV and up the driveway. "I wonder if there's a good reason for that. It looks like a statement."

I thought so, too, and family statements were so often unpleasant and directed at me.

With the meeting inevitable, Keats allowed himself to enjoy it. His tail was high as he raced up the stairs beside Percy. The cat was unburdened by inner conflict. This house held ferrets and his passion for finding them never waned.

Asher was in his usual place propped against the refrigerator when we walked into the kitchen. He pushed himself off and dropped a kiss on Jilly's cheek, before she moved on to take a seat at the table with Iris and Violet. Poppy was missing in action, but Mom was very much present, perched on her stool at the counter in a suit that featured mismatched textures and fabrics in shades of red. It was an interesting look. Certainly creative.

When clean freak Daisy turned to spritz the fridge with vinegar spray to erase Asher's smudges, Mom quickly poured her coffee from a colorful mug into one of the empty white china mugs waiting for Jilly and me. Then she planted a red lipstick kiss on the rim before my sister could take her cup privileges away.

I poured coffee into the other white mug for Jilly and took Mom's castoff. There was no reason to serve Daisy a fight on a platter. Since her eldest boys had escaped the slammer with inches to spare, she'd doubled down on her constant cleaning. She'd even added floral print aprons over her jeans, both at home and at the inn. Perhaps they felt like armor against the perils of raising kids in Clover Grove.

"What's so important we had to postpone our search for the kangaroos?" I asked. "Kellan only gave us the green light this morning and I don't want them roaming a minute longer than necessary."

"Finally, something we can agree on," Asher said, sliding back into place when Daisy was done with her polishing. "What if they get in the way of a car or worse, a train? People could be hurt."

I met his blue eyes and shook my head. That sentence summarized our perspectives perfectly. "And the roos more so. One of them had a baby in her pouch, you know."

Daisy turned, spray bottle dangling. "How wonderful. I can't wait to see it at the farm."

"They're not going to the farm," Asher said. "First, they're illegal here. Second, I'd be chasing escapees all the time. Guaranteed."

Mom turned her hazel eyes on me. It looked like she'd gotten eyelash extensions. They were long enough to get stuck in her brows, if not her actual hairline. "I have to agree with your brother, darling. Kangaroos are deadly creatures."

"Lots are deadlier," I said. "But they have a particular disliking for dogs, so the Rescue Mafia will need to find the right home for them."

Asher scowled. "In one of the few states where they're legal."

I swapped my cup for Mom's and got to work on the lipstick mark with a tissue. "If we're here so that you folks can convince me not to keep the roos, everyone should be satisfied. Can we go join the search party?"

"That's only one reason we're here, darling," Mom said, trying to reclaim the white cup. "Have you noticed someone's missing?"

"Where is Poppy?" Jilly asked. "Is she okay?"

Mom flipped manicured hands palms up. "She's not taking anyone's calls. For all we know, she could be dead in a ditch—a victim of the Wigg enemies, Travis himself or a kangaroo. I don't know which is worse."

"That's not funny, Mom," Iris said. "She's not dead in a ditch. Tell them, Ash."

My brother nodded. "She answered my text after I threatened to send officers over to do a wellness check."

The front door banged open and the woman herself walked into the kitchen.

More accurately, she was hoisted inside by the two older twins while Reese and Beaton pushed from behind. Getting Poppy here was a four-teen job.

"Darling! How wonderful to see you." Mom actually slid off her stool and went over to force a hug on her cactus of a daughter. Though no fan of public displays of affection myself, Poppy repelled them like teflon, even at the best of times.

It wasn't the best of times. Her tri-color hair was in wild disarray and she was wearing a fluffy pink bathrobe over mustard plaid pajama pants.

"Well, it isn't wonderful to be here. I was sound asleep when these ruffians broke in and kidnapped me."

Sutton shot me a wink. "It's not breaking in when there's a spare key outside."

He'd obviously heard about how often I used that excuse with Kellan when I was unofficially trespassing.

"And you weren't asleep," Weston said. "You were on the couch crying over some lame reality show and crunching cheese snacks. No excuse to miss a Butter Tart 911. Mom always says they're mandatory."

Poppy checked her orange-stained fingers and then shoved them in her pocket.

"Junk food for breakfast?" Mom clucked in disapproval. "Darling, didn't I teach you better?"

The word "no" came in a chorus of voices. When we were kids we foraged in the mornings and grabbed what we could. Mom's grocery shopping was spontaneous and erratic. Whatever was on sale came home and I started many a school day with stranger things than cheese snacks or Mandy's desserts.

The boys headed into the basement and Poppy took her seat at the table, bleary eyes fixed on me the whole time. "Why aren't you out searching, Ivy?"

I gestured around the kitchen. "Ask them. I was on my way to find the kangaroos when the call came."

Poppy pulled out her right hand and flicked orange fingertips at me. "Forget about the roos. You're supposed to be finding evidence to prove Travis didn't kill anyone."

"Excuse me." Asher shifted into cop mode. "That's my job. The entire department and beyond is working on this case."

"They'll figure it out, Pops," Iris said. "No one believes Travis would kill his brother. Especially with a kid in the picture."

Poppy's mouth dropped open. There was a ring of orange around it. "A kid?"

"Travis didn't tell you?" Violet asked. "Ivy found the kid last night."

"I tried to call you a few times, Pops," I said. "Figured you'd already heard and turned to the comfort of peppermint schnapps. Glad it was only cheese snacks."

Mom looked stunned. "Why don't I know this?"

It was an unusual lapse on the part of the Clover Grove grapevine. News like this was the currency of our community.

"Because you ignore the rumor mill," Iris said. "I opened the salon early and people were beating a path to the door."

Jilly leaned over and squeezed my sister's fluffy shoulder. "I tried calling, too. We didn't want to drop it in a text, Poppy."

"But I didn't hear it from Travis. That he has a... a kid."

"No," Jilly said, giving pink fluff a little shake. "Not Travis. Knox. He brought his teenaged son to visit and sent him into hiding. Keats and Percy found him at an old girlfriend's place."

"Knox's old girlfriend," I added, lest there be any confusion. "We met Travis' mom and then his dad and that led us to Brandi Brownhill's where we found Camden."

She looked confused, and I could hardly blame her. It was a lot to take in. "You met my in-laws before I did?"

"Your in-laws? Did the grapevine miss the proposal, too?" I asked.

Violet leaned forward to join the discussion. "You'd really marry him after he basically lied about his whole life?"

Slumping in her seat, Poppy shrugged. "We're not engaged. But we've talked about it, and I obviously don't know a thing about him." She pulled a tissue from her pocket and chafed at her fingertips. "If he can't be bothered to loop me in, I guess I don't want to know."

"Cool your cheese snacks," Asher said. "Travis is in a safe house with Camden and they don't have phones. Chief's orders." Jilly tossed him a look and he continued, "I thought you knew about the kid. I'm sorry, Pops. I've just been busy chasing after Ivy and cleaning up her messes."

"Messes?" I reached for Keats and his ears were there. "All I'm doing is trying to follow the kangaroo trail and if my pets reveal a few clues along the way, I figure that's a good thing."

He straightened. "My life was a whole lot easier when you were working in HR in Boston."

Jilly intervened. "When Ivy and I were both working in Boston, you mean. Life was easier then?"

He morphed into a lovestruck teen immediately. "That's not what I mean, honey. But if I could have you here while Ivy cooled her corporate heels in Boston, life would be perfect."

"We're living in my best friend's home, Asher. Where I help run her inn. I'm failing to see the perfection in your scenario."

"Darlings, stop," Mom said. "We're all on edge over Poppy's woodsman beau, but it will work out. It always does."

"He's not my beau." Poppy gave up on her fingers. That orange powder was nearly as stubborn as a permanent tattoo. "Not anymore. Couples tell each other everything."

I raised my hand. "Not always. At least, not always right away."

Jilly raised hers, too. "Ditto."

Asher glowered at me from the fridge but stayed out of this one.

Meanwhile, Daisy lowered her cleanser. "They're right. It's all about timing."

She probably had the biggest family secret of us all but I'd certainly never share it.

Walking over to Poppy, I tried touching her shoulder and succeeded only in making her sink even lower to avoid me. "Just hang tight, Pops. There will be an explanation for all of this and Travis will fill in the pieces he skipped. Then you can decide. Right now, the most important thing is to keep him and his nephew safe."

She shrugged me off. "Why do you care? You hate Travis."

"I don't hate anybody." I thought about it. "Not even Myrtle McCain, or the half dozen other people who've tried to kill me."

"Two dozen," Asher muttered. "More. I don't have enough fingers."

His little jump a moment later assured me his uniform cuffs were suitably punished for his insolence. If that weren't enough, Percy hopped onto the counter, then to the top of the fridge and stepped onto Asher's head.

While he struggled to dislodge the cat, Daisy lunged over to scour where orange paws had touched. "No one hates Travis, Poppy. But it wouldn't matter if they did. Yours is the only opinion that counts when it comes to a partner."

"Your sister is right," Mom said. "My parents hated your father and we didn't let it stop us." She pulled out her lipstick and twirled it up. "In retrospect, we probably should have, but that's not how our family works. There's a long tradition of disliking spouses, finally broken by Jillian."

Daisy turned and confiscated Mom's mug. "What about Roger? The father of your grandchildren?"

Mom applied her lipstick carefully and wound the tube back down. "You're right, Daisy darling. There's nothing to dislike about Roger because he's so rarely around. But he does throw twins, and I think everyone would agree that singles are better."

Indignant voices drifted up the stairs from the basement. "Except us?"

Daisy gave a double spray to the counter and succeeded in making Mom sneeze. "Ivy, can you call it? I love you folks, but I want you out of my house."

"Happily. I call the meeting adjourned."

She aimed the spray bottle my way. "That's not what I mean. Poppy needs your assurances that you'll fix this. We all do."

Asher managed to shift Percy onto his shoulder but it was a

fight to keep him there. "What is there for Ivy to fix, other than the kangaroos?"

Daisy raised her shammy as if to swat him and likely thought about the germ influx. "Poppy can't marry a kangaroo, Asher. And as much as we all respect your work and Kellan's, sometimes Ivy's team gets to the truth faster. She saved my boys."

"They saved me," I corrected.

"You got that right." Another shout came from downstairs. I often wondered if they eavesdropped on us and now I knew. "Someone needs more training."

I *did* need more training, but I ignored the boys. "Travis didn't kill his brother, Poppy, and the police will prove that while I find the roos."

"A kangaroo obviously killed Knox," Mom said. "That's why we can't have them on the farm."

"A kangaroo doesn't have the dexterity to choke a large man in the way Knox died," I said. "I emailed an expert in marsupials with a hypothetical question. From a fake account."

Asher tried to glare at me through fluff as Percy crossed shoulders. "Improbable but not impossible." His voice was muffled. "According to *my* marsupial expert."

"Long shot, Ash. Really long," I said. "This is far more likely linked to hill country grudges, don't you think?"

"Speculation. Kellan told me not to indulge you. This time you're not getting into my head with your sneakery."

I let Percy do another pass before responding. "I trust you and your colleagues will comb the criminal archives to find out who might have wanted Knox dead. Or wanted Travis dead and got Knox by mistake."

"*Ivy!*"

There was another chorus and this time Jilly's voice was in there.

"What? I'm just saying Travis isn't guilty. The verdict came by way of Keats. He still likes Travis, which is definitive as far as I'm concerned. I'll wrap up the roos and the police will do the rest. Satisfied, Asher?"

Percy shifted enough for him to assess my expression. At one time, he would have taken me at face value—literally—but he was wiser now. "That's exactly what the chief wants. I suggest you stick to that story for a change."

"Okay, so now we're adjourned. Daisy, can you lend Poppy some old clothes? She needs to lay off the cheese snacks and I've got just the thing to distract her."

"I'm not going into the bush looking for kangaroos, Ivy." Poppy nearly slid under the table and then pushed herself upright in a hurry. "Ouch! You are not the boss of me."

Keats came around the other side and got ready to dive at her bare ankle again.

"Up you get, Pops," I said. "Relief is just a hop, skip and a jump away."

CHAPTER SIXTEEN

"How will we ever find everyone?" Poppy asked as we pulled up among a dozen vehicles outside Midway Mall.

At a glance, I recognized Bridget's lime green van and Gertie's white one. Maud Gentry's car was there, as well as pickup trucks owned by Wendel Barrick and Buckley Brackens. The rest of the vehicles belonged to various Rescue Mafia members. It was an excellent turnout. Once again, I was touched at how far people would go to help animals in our region. Even exotic ones. Here, an animal in need had friends indeed.

"Don't worry," I said, letting the pets out of the truck and following. "Either the crew or their dogs will find us. There are three other border collies, a beagle, a setter and more."

Jilly joined me at the tailgate to collect her backpack. "Aren't they worried about the dogs getting attacked? Aren't you?"

Keats gave a humblebrag that lacked some of his usual swagger. There was water in those woods. Small deep pools with a habit of ambushing us. Ponds like that were a kangaroo's refuge in case of emergency. I was optimistic the female would skip that option while carrying a joey. Surely, she wouldn't risk drowning her baby to drown my dog-baby.

Or me.

"If we get into a bind, someone can take off with the pets," I said, presenting each of them with a leash. "Plan B."

"As if I'd leave you to be taken out by a malicious macropod," Jilly said, sliding her arms into the straps of a backpack.

Poppy smirked, not realizing the impact was lost because of the orange cheese snack stains on her face. "I would. Plan B is all mine."

"It's settled then." I shouldered my pack and handed one to Poppy. Edna always left an extra in my truck for herself. I wondered how many go-kits she had stashed around between Gertie's van and various bunkers. She was always prepared, and because of her, I usually was, too. "From their reconnaissance, only the jill is still in the area."

"Confirmed sightings?" Jilly asked. "Is the grapevine all over it?"

I shook my head and led them around the mall to the trail's main entrance. "Drones. The Mafia has a few and Edna has some, too. I'm surprised Kellan hasn't stopped them from flying over the crime scene and surrounding area, but they've been doing it since the night of the"—I glanced at Poppy and switched words— "incident."

We all stared down the back alley, which looked strangely empty. Even the dumpster was gone.

Jilly jumped in to keep the conversation on track. "So, they've seen the doe recently? Note that I'm taking a stand on 'jill.' To me, this thing is a doe or female."

"Understood. And yes, the doe was seen crossing fields late yesterday and even in someone's garden having a light meal. That prompted the Mafia to set up bait stations with critter cams. Hopefully one will fire while we're out in force."

"What about the joey?" Jilly's voice was tentative. "Still on board?"

"Unconfirmed. I think Cori's examined the images from every possible angle and she seems cautiously optimistic."

"With Cori, that's pretty positive," Jilly said, picking up Percy. He liked to walk on a mission, but she probably needed the comfort. The woods were not our happy place.

We started down the trail single file, with me in front and Jilly in the rear. The larger group had fanned out and combed every inch of the area while we were at the family meeting. At this point, we just needed to catch up to them. I had general coordinates and we were in text contact. That said, we weren't the best navigators in our larger crew and everything looked different in the woods. I counted on them, in particular the pets, to make this reunion happen.

Poppy was silent for the first 10 minutes, enveloped in Daisy's castoff coveralls and a cloud of crankiness. She wanted to be back on the couch watching reality TV with junk food, but this would do her more good. Being part of something bigger than herself. Helping animals. My sister had a tough veneer but she was very gentle with my livestock and had even developed something of a bond with Wilma, the fractious sow, by bribing her with apples.

Eventually, Poppy found her voice. "And if we should happen to run into this protective mother alone, what's our strategy?"

"We won't," I said.

"Denial isn't a strategy." My sister squinted at me. "I told myself Travis would be cleared instantly and all it got me was a secret nephew."

Jilly rested a hand on Poppy's backpack. "The Mafia is nothing if not thorough, Pops. There's no chance of something as big as a kangaroo slipping through their human net. Once we reach them, they have the tools they need to subdue the fugitives."

"And what are those tools?" Poppy wasn't in the mood to indulge ambiguity.

I took over from Jilly. "Rope for lassoing. Strong nets. At worst, sedation."

Poppy finally perked up. "Cori has a tranquillizer gun?"

"I didn't ask for details, because that's the surest way to shut Cori down. This is probably illicit."

"Makes me feel better," Poppy said. "I may be depressed but I don't want to die out here from a flurry of kicks."

"Roos are good with their front paws, too. I read they can grab you by the head, balance on their tail, and kick your guts out with their feet."

Poppy shoved me from behind. "Stop it. If I can manage Wilma, I can manage a roo. You're just trying to scare me."

"Make that prepare you. As far as self-defense goes, the best strategy in a roo attack is to drop to the ground right away, tuck your knees into your chest and protect your head and vital organs. Don't be a hero."

Jilly coughed conspicuously from the rear. "Ivy, that's probably enough information. I'm confident Cori and Edna will handle this with panache."

"Exactly, and once the doe's detained, Edna will bring in an ATV and trailer to transport her back to the van. They'll drive to the farm, where Dad and Charlie have secured the pasture. After the buck joins her, they'll be off to a new home."

"Promise?" I could feel Jilly's green eyes boring into the back of my head.

I turned with a grin. "Why doesn't anyone believe me?"

"Because you're an animal addict," Poppy said. "They'll have to pry you off that joey with a crowbar. Guaranteed."

"I'd keep them if I could, but it turns out roos aren't safe with cats around. And thanks to Dad's weakness for strays, we have a growing colony in the loft."

"Cats?" Jilly was surprised, and judging by his little mew, she'd squeezed Percy too tight. "How can a cat be a threat to such a large animal?"

"Cat feces can transmit a fatal infection to kangaroos. We'd never be able to keep Dad's barn cats out of the pasture, let alone Percy."

"That's terrible," Jilly said, although she actually sounded relieved. She knew full well I'd exploit any loophole, like a true addict. Now I was backed into a real corner. Laws may not necessarily stop me from hoarding furry treasures, but disease sure would.

I expected Keats to show some enthusiasm about the roo news, but his next mumble was more of an alert.

That progressed to a warning. I glanced down, but he had left his lead position. Then Percy let out an eerie yowl.

Uh-oh.

None of us should have let down our guard for even an instant.

I didn't see anything coming but I felt it. The ground seemed to tremble under my boots and when I listened hard, I heard thudding, along with the crunch of sticks. There was no sign of kangaroos, however, or an indication of which direction they were going. Maybe they would run away from us. Kangaroos were flight animals, after all, and humans were their main predator. On the other hand, these were somewhat domesticated and familiar with Gilroy Leek, and probably some zookeepers. Since there was plenty of room for all of us out here, we didn't pose an immediate threat. There was no reason at all for a stampede.

But that was a very human point of view. Kangaroos were prone to stress and this trio had been through a lot in the past two days. Stolen from their home, no matter how squalid. Shoved into a van. Stashed in a shabby pen at a campsite. Back into a van. Released at a strip mall no one had ever liked. And then witness to a tragedy.

Looking at it through roo eyes, I could totally understand how Camden got scratched up. He was lucky it stopped there.

Since then, the roos hadn't had the time and peace to find a new equilibrium. If they were around today, they weren't likely to be reasonable at all.

"Do you feel that?" Jilly asked. "It's a vibration."

"Yeah. Definitely." Spinning, I spotted Keats behind us, looking in the direction we'd come. His ruff and tail were puffy. The roo was following us. We could either go forward or risk a collision on a narrow trail. There was a steep slope on one side and rolling wouldn't be fun.

"What do we do?" Jilly asked.

"Run," I said, pushing them ahead of me. "Put Percy down so you don't fall and then follow Keats."

"I can't leave Percy to—"

"Jilly, he can climb. We can't. Let's go!"

Our boots drummed the path as we charged down the trail, which narrowed quickly. The dense foliage of the forest had never felt so aggressive. Branches smacked me in the face after Poppy pushed through and it was a wonder no one tripped on roots or stones. On one side, a rock face appeared. It was one of the many small cliffs that probably bordered a lake a thousand years ago. Edna loved this type of landform because it held natural caves for satellite bunkers. Today, however, it blocked us on one side, with the downslope on the other.

Then Jilly yelled out one of the words I dreaded most. "Swamp!"

Fabulous.

Soon, we were sandwiched by rock on one side and water on the other. Where there was swamp there were pools, and kangaroos didn't mind a dip nearly as much as I did.

Why hadn't the search party warned us about this treacherous section of the route? Maybe there were so many of them filing through they weren't worried.

Plus, at least three of them had rifles, whereas we were unarmed. Well, our go-kits likely had weapons but I hadn't investigated and now was not the time to take inventory. Edna would be disgusted. The whole point of preparedness was being aware of your surroundings and your tactics for dealing with threats.

"Opening up," Jilly called back. "A clearing."

The rock face declined into rubble and a wide space in the trees appeared. I was surprised to see the sun shining down. In the dense wood it felt like dusk, whereas it wasn't yet noon on a fine day.

"Stop and regroup," I said, puffing hard. "The roo may not have pursued. I couldn't tell once we were running."

"I'll text the others," Jilly panted, groping for her phone.

Poppy said, "I'll just yell."

She did that, bellowing Cori's name and then Edna's. The words echoed and seemed to clash overhead. We were in a valley.

"I don't hear anything," I said. "Keats?"

Flattened ears confirmed he heard something and he mumbled another warning.

Looking back, I saw the female kangaroo emerge from the trail we'd just left. She was more of a grayish-brown than her ruddy partner and considerably smaller than what I remembered seeing fly past the studio window. The joey had remained on board through a very bumpy ride.

"Stay," I said, holding up my palm as if she were a trained dog.

She wasn't and she didn't.

It only took two impossibly long bounds for her to cross the clearing and collide with me in what could best be called a body slam. The impact sent me staggering to one side.

The swamp side.

"No way, lady." I flailed to keep my balance and succeeded, and then moved back. "Not swimming today. Jilly, get Keats out of here."

The doe returned the way she came. Unfortunately, it was only to take a second run at me.

"Is this where we drop and curl?" Poppy yelled.

It was a little late for that. The doe touched down and started swatting me with her front paws.

"Stop that," I said, lunging back. "I can't hit you. You're a mother."

She wouldn't take no for an answer and advanced to rake my neck with her claws. I had no choice but to shove her away.

"Run, Ivy," Jilly called back. "Or curl up. Don't be a hero."

"I can get her," I said. "Just need to calm her down."

"By shoving her?" Poppy asked. "You're giving her room for the kick, Ivy."

I dropped my hands. Maybe if I looked defenseless, she'd relent. "Can we just talk?" I asked the roo.

Waving the white flag did nothing to mollify her. Instead, she came forward fast, head back, front paws out, and gave me a hard shove.

It sent me reeling exactly where I feared. The short flight into the swamp gave me just enough time to wonder if my fears had manifested this very outcome. I'd attracted exactly what I didn't want and landed in the water. The silt gave way and plunged me into what felt like a bottomless, fetid and very cold pit. There was nothing under my thrashing boots and I swished my arms to keep my mouth above the surface. I'd tasted bog water before and the memory lingered.

The roo stood at the edge, watching me. What if she came in and tried to hold me under, as I'd seen them do to dogs in videos? I outweighed her but she had feral on her side. Not to mention a very long tail to prop her up.

In a match between hobby farmer and protective macropod mother, it was sure to end badly for me.

Instead of joining me, however, she just stared, and the joey stared, too.

Treading water, I tried to stay calm. "We're trying to help you, Hildy. You and Rooby can't stay out here. It's not safe. Come back with us."

"Seriously, Ivy?" Poppy was both scared and exasperated. "She doesn't speak your language."

Maybe not, but the mama roo didn't come into the water, and she didn't go after Jilly, Poppy and the pets. So, I kept on talking despite the chill of the water, the slime on my hands and the dank smell in my nostrils. I told her about the farm and all the people who wanted to help her. I made big promises of a good home far away from Gilroy Leek. "We'll catch your fella and then you'll ride off into the sunset together," I concluded. "Sound good?"

"Sounds like you've gone off the deep end," Poppy said.

"Literally, this time." I kept my voice soothing. "I think she's done fighting. Any chance you guys can rope her?"

"Rope her?" Jilly called from the far end of the clearing. "Are you kidding? I can barely tie my own shoelaces."

Poppy sidled toward the roo. "Maybe we can sort of hug her into submission. Jilly, bring the rope. Ivy, you get out and help."

I wanted to laugh but couldn't risk a mouthful of swamp water. "If I could get out, I would. I'll need to be roped, too."

"Okay. Okay." My sister edged toward the kangaroo. "She's settled down. I'm gonna grab her."

"Poppy, don't," Jilly said, fumbling in her backpack. "Are you insane?"

Apparently, my sister was indeed insane. Poppy tried to slip her arms around the kangaroo and with a quick flick Hildy sent her after me. My sister hit me harder than the roo had, and we both shouted unsisterly things at each other.

Now, Jilly was on her own with the pets. Keats remained crouched and ready to spring at the roo on command. I gave him bonus points for being willing to defend his people in the face of not only a terrifying kangaroo but also a bog. Percy's bright fluff moved up a series of rocks as he tried to get a better angle on the jump, if needed.

The kangaroo's big ears flicked and she turned in Jilly's direction. Was she going to pick off the last of us?

"Jilly, watch out," I called.

A voice shouted over me. "Dagnabit, Ivy. How many times do I have to tell you not to play in the swamp?"

Someone else yelled, "Deploy."

There was a whistle overhead and a loop fell over the kangaroo. The doe struggled but her front paws were pinned to her body. Powerful legs pushed off, but in that instant, a net came down.

Edna and Cori charged past Jilly, and together they grabbed the kangaroo's tail through the net.

"Walk her backward," Edna said. "Nice and easy."

It wasn't easy at all. Hildy wasn't going down without a fight and she spun around and around with her captors hanging on for dear life.

"Don't hurt the baby," I called.

"You just enjoy your swim while we do the dirty work," Edna grunted.

Cori, smaller and slight, didn't waste her breath. She just kept steady traction on the roo till they got her into the widest part of the clearing before shouting, "Now."

A dozen other people surged forward to subdue the runaway, and between the net and many hands, Hildy finally gave up the fight.

Her head turned toward the bog and even through the webbing, it seemed like she looked resentful. As if I'd fed her a bunch of empty promises. But she hadn't played nice, either.

"Welcome to the Runaway Farm menagerie, Hildy," I called. "Please enjoy your stay."

CHAPTER SEVENTEEN

K eats had a lot to say as we walked back up the trail. Much of it appeared to be a tale of how he could have handled the whole situation alone if I'd just let him.

"You're all talk, dog," Poppy said. "Because lemme tell you, that thing was strong."

Even soaked and disheveled, she looked a lot happier than she had at the family meeting earlier. As expected, the mission had shaken her out of her lethargy. The swamp water had probably soaked the orange stains off her fingers, too.

"That was brave of you, Pops," I said. "Trying to tame a roo with a hug. I didn't think you were one for public displays of affection."

She laughed. "It was worth a try. Tough love got you nowhere fast, didn't it?"

"I went easy on her because of the baby. But it definitely pointed to the need for self-defense training. The only move I know is the shoulder roll and I didn't think to use it. That's the challenge, I guess. Remembering to use what you know when a crisis arises."

"You were supposed to drop and curl," Jilly said. "You told us so half an hour ago."

"I remember that. *Now*. In the moment, I was sure I could get her. Roos are so cute it's hard to believe they pack such a wallop."

Keats wanted to stop to investigate the cliff but I pressed on. A chill was working its way into my bones and the sunshine beyond the forest would warm me. There were coats and blankets in the truck, too.

His next mumble sounded like "your loss," which was enough to make me look back. Was there really something worth seeing in that rock face? If so, it would still be there later, when I was dry and the other kangaroo had been secured, too.

"Pick it up, Ivy," Poppy said. "A hot shower awaits."

"I feel like we should stay. The crew still needs to get Hildy into the van. And her boyfriend is at large."

Jilly came up behind us. "You heard Edna. We're to go home and be ready to receive the new guest. There are plenty of people to deal with her and the buck, if he appears."

"Nearly half of those people are seniors," I pointed out. "Some quite advanced."

"Oh, yeah? Well, none of us oldies got punched out and tossed into the drink, did we now?"

The question came from Buckley Brackens, who was possibly the most senior of my friends, with Wendel a close second.

"Buckley, why are you following us?" I asked.

He marched briskly up the trail with his rifle propped over his shoulder. "I was voluntold. Someone needs to make sure you get back to the truck. Specifically, someone with a gun."

"You can't shoot a kangaroo."

"I can and I will if Jilly's welfare is at stake. Who else is going to cook holiday dinners?"

Jilly laughed. "That's so gallant, Buckley. You have a standing invitation."

He used that free pass far more often than holidays. All of our close friends gravitated to the inn and it wasn't to see the cute animals.

"I have my orders to watch you actually pull out before I bring back the ATV," he said. "Remember, it's not just kangaroos on the loose. Knox Wigg's killer hasn't been found and she might very well be hiding out here."

"She?" I said. "I highly doubt a woman strangled Knox. He was a big man."

"Just trying to be inclusive." He flushed us ahead with one hand and grinned. "Ladies can be criminals, too. I bet Edna could do it. Choke a man, I mean."

"Probably. Gertie, too. They say it's all about the angle."

Maybe if I hadn't been shivering so hard, I'd have noticed sooner that Poppy had gone silent. Now she turned on me. "I'm glad you think this is funny. Travis lost a brother he practically raised and I'll never get to meet him."

Jilly came up between us and thrust Percy into Poppy's wet arms. "We know, Pops. Ivy always jokes around when she's in shock. You can't take her seriously. I never do."

"I never take Ivy seriously, period," Buckley said. "And you're in shock too, Poppy. You don't get trounced like that by an animal and come out unscathed."

Poppy clutched Percy tighter and despite his distaste for dampness, he didn't protest. The cat was willing to offer therapeutic services for most of my family if the need arose. My sister was one of his favorites and he often kept her company when she did chores. Once, I found them asleep in the empty stall together.

Buckley was revved and ready with the ATV by the time we left. The ride back to town was quiet. Jilly was the only one remotely comfortable and she probably didn't want to give two trapped Galloway Girls anything more to argue about.

I dropped Poppy at her place and she jumped out without saying a word. "Thanks for your help," I said, before the back door slammed. "Enjoy your cheese snacks."

Jilly rolled her window down in time to hear more unsisterly talk drifting back. "Was that really necessary, Ivy?"

"Actually, yeah. Sibling friction has warmed me all my life."

She laughed. "Just give Poppy some space. She really needs to talk this out with Travis."

"I know. But I'm happy he's in a safe house that isn't *my* house right now. I've got enough to worry about with an incoming pugilistic roo. If females are the docile ones, I dread meeting Hildy's paramour."

"Where did that name come from?"

I shrugged. "Dunno. Animals seem to arrive in my life with mental name tags. This one's Hildy Hopper. Gilroy Leek said the joey's a girl, so I'm calling her Rooby Roo."

We drove down the twisting lane into the farm too fast and I was glad no one was coming out. Jilly left me to check out the pasture modifications and started up to the house. "Don't be long," she said. "You'll catch a cold before you catch the buck."

"Maybe I'll catch a break, too," I called after her.

That wasn't to be. Someone in a lumberjacket was standing with his back to me beside the upgraded pasture. When he turned, the Wigg smile switched on. Not to its usual wattage but it was very much a Travis special.

"Did you go for a snorkel?" he asked, bearded chin rising as he sniffed. "And roll in dead fish?"

"Why aren't you at the safe house being safe? So that I can be safe from your wit."

"Aren't you even moderately impressed I have wit left after everything that's happened?"

Keats circled the woodsman, sniffing too. The slight flattening of his ears said he wasn't impressed in the least. It wasn't a canine criminal conviction but Travis had been downgraded in the dog's estimation.

"Impressed isn't the word. Suspicious, maybe. Keats thinks you smell a little off, too."

He looked down at the dog. "I thought you liked me, buddy."

"He tolerated you but you've lost credibility."

Travis' smile vanished. "I didn't kill my brother, Ivy."

"If I thought you had, you wouldn't be here on my farm. The welfare of my animals is always paramount. The chief of police knows that."

"Chiefheart delivered us personally, so that should tell you something." His teeth came back out. "Camden and I aren't suspects. And someone else has been detained."

That got my interest. "Who?"

"An old rival of my father's was released from prison a couple of weeks ago. The police think killing Knox was a last jab at Dad before he passes."

I turned to lean against the fence. The shivering had slowed but my legs felt weak. "Do *you* believe that?"

"It's possible. Also possible that this guy had a grudge against Knox directly. My brother was into some shady stuff when I strongarmed him onto that plane to Australia." He stared over my head and out into the meadows. "Knox was so angry. And maybe a little heartbroken because I abandoned him. Deep down he knew I was trying to save his life. That's all I'd been doing since he came into the world right behind me."

"You kept in touch after he left?"

"Not much and not often. I didn't want anyone locating him through me or Mom. Plus, it was just easier to cut it off." He rubbed a hand through his abundant hair. For once he wasn't wearing a hat. "I don't think he was in contact with our father, but I don't know. When he was gone Knox seemed to forget just how horrible that man was."

"He knows it," I said. "Your father, I mean."

Normally I only got to surprise Travis when he found me driving around with livestock, but hc was shocked today. "You spoke to my dad?"

"Hoyle Senior. Yes. I visited the nursing home with my uncle. After seeing your mom first."

His surprise turned to displeasure. "I don't appreciate your invading my privacy like that."

Keats didn't appreciate Travis' tone and told him so with a nip that the man barely noticed.

"Travis, I found you in a dark alley with a body and a kangaroo. I'm never going to ignore animals in need and I had to source leads to help me find them. Besides, you're dating my sister. At least, you were."

His lips pressed into a thin line and his eyes narrowed nearly as much. "I'm not just dating Poppy. We're practically engaged."

"And yet she thought you were an orphan until two days ago. Suddenly, you're a son, a brother and an uncle. How is she supposed to feel?"

Both hands landed on his head and he started to pace. "I was trying to protect her. The less anyone knows about my family, the better."

Keats sat on his haunches and studied Travis. He wasn't calling fake on this display of emotion. "Look, Travis, I've been known to sidestep the truth a few times with Kellan, but only temporarily. There's no way we'd contemplate marriage without knowing almost everything about each other. The best way to protect someone is to share it all. For better, for worse, right?"

"You guys don't have a history like mine."

I pointed to Calvin riding the tractor behind the barn. When I was distracted, he liked to scale down my manure pile, always leaving plenty for therapeutic spadework. "I'm the daughter of a minor criminal and the granddaughter of a major criminal. Kellan has the case files. I wasn't always an open book but now Chiefheart and I talk about everything."

Travis' jaw set stubbornly. He wasn't one of those men who needed a beard to hide a weak chin. "It's for her own good. Poppy knows more than she should already."

"I have enough on my hands with two and a half kangaroos arriving. Are you going to make this hard for me? Because I won't stop excavating your past until my sister knows everything there is to know. That's how I keep people safe. Even if it annoys my fiancé."

His Adam's apple bobbed. "I'll talk to her."

"Better yet, take her to visit your dad before he dies. He wants to apologize to you."

He swallowed again. "He said that?"

"Not exactly, but he's seen the error of his ways. And I'd hurry if I were you because Percy doesn't think he has long."

"Fine. I'll go as soon as Kellan gives me clearance."

"Asher can drive you down with Poppy. And Camden, too."

Pulling out his phone, he pressed her number and frowned. "Voicemail. Tried her earlier, too. Thought she might be with you."

"She was and we both got our butts kicked by a roo. Try her again when she's had time to shower. And keep trying."

He saluted. "Got it, boss."

"Just so we're clear, you owe me. I'm helping to clean up your brother's mess. What kind of idiot drives around with livestock?"

Finally, he laughed and it was genuine, rather than his usual jeering. "Guess you two had something in common. He was a rescuer without your finesse."

"Exactly. Finesse is my middle name." I pushed myself off the fence and snapped my fingers for Keats. "You also owe me self-defense lessons. The first one was a complete bust because of you posturing with that dude instead of doing your job."

"Brydon Ting. Now, there's an idiot. I don't like that he's been helping Liam train your nephews."

"The boys do all right. Saved me with some skilled moves not long back. I'd like to be able to return the favor."

"When this is done, I'll take over. Brydon's not the right guy for the job. Trust me."

Keats circled back to give his leg another nip. That Travis allowed such a blatant attack proved how far off his game he was.

"I *don't* trust you," I said, as the dog got me moving. "You're still hiding something and not just from Poppy. Is there another secret baby around?"

"Not mine, that's for sure," he called after me. "As for Knox, there could be a dozen. The Wigg genes really pack a wallop."

I flinched as the jeering laugh drifted toward me. "Tell it to someone who cares, Travis. If you're lucky, that's Poppy."

CHAPTER EIGHTEEN

I had planned to spend the rest of the day attempting to win over the new macropod guest but Keats and Percy had other ideas. The cat sat on the hood of the truck until I took a second hint delivered to my pant cuffs.

"Going somewhere?" my father asked as I gathered my things.

"Yeah. Location yet to be determined." I gestured to the pets. "I just take orders."

"You're not going after the jack alone, are you?" Dad's voice was always calm but there was a slight note of concern now.

"Nope. Not after the pummeling I got from his lady." I pulled up my sleeve to show him scratches and bruises. "My hair's going to stink of bog rot for a week."

"Never caught a roo, myself. Wouldn't say no to joining your rescue party."

"You got it. The more the merrier. I'll let you know when they get a drone sighting."

He leaned on the spade he'd probably been using to shape my manure pile into a petite version of the one I'd left. "Probably won't be far from where you found the jill."

"They're not monogamous, though. The males like a harem and cover a lot of ground in the wild finding and fighting for them."

"In the wild, yeah. These roos are pretty much domesticated, I would think. Escaped animals of any kind are more likely to stick together than go it alone. Just my two cents."

Dad didn't freely offer his two cents often. Coins of knowledge had to be picked out of his pocket. "I'll pass that along to Cori. How's the jill doing?"

"Agitated. She'll calm down, but maybe not before she kicks the fence to bits. That's why I'm staying in close range."

"Thanks, Dad." Mostly I called him by his first name to keep a bit of mental distance, but meeting Hoyle had made me realize my childhood could have been far worse. An absentee dad was better than an abusive one. Besides, my other siblings—Daisy in particular—had spent more time with him and benefited from his parenting style. Since she stepped into the matriarch role after he left, that had trickled down to me. Mom had always been flighty, so by nature or nurture, Dad's chill manner had some influence over us.

He watched me drive off and that alone told me he was worried. When Calvin was on the farm he pretty much never stopped moving till he dropped onto his cot in the loft among the barn cats.

"Where are we headed?" I asked my tuxedoed navigator, once we were on the highway. "Waterfield? Fleetborough?"

Keats didn't weigh in right away so I kept going. Sometimes I wondered if he just wanted me to drive around till he saw or smelled something interesting. The approach had paid off a few times but I preferred a more targeted strategy.

"I thought you'd be down in the dumps with a roo still on the loose. It's not like you to joyride when a job's only half done."

The flash of blue eye was fleeting. Perhaps he was of two minds about the search now that he knew more about our formidable foe. The boomer wasn't technically an adversary, but he'd likely act like one when we tried to bring him in. Drawing him away from forest and swamp would level the playing field, which is why the Mafia was putting out food stations baited with the very pellets that exposed Gilroy Leek.

Since the dog didn't offer his usual guidance, I turned into Daisy's neighborhood across town. Keats' happy pant made me wonder if that was his plan all along. The canine puppet-master was adept at hiding the strings.

My sister was at the kitchen counter making a mess instead of cleaning one up when I let myself into the house with the key she gave me when she married. It felt good to know I had a permanent welcome there.

"Didn't you hear me knock?" I asked.

She shook her head and turned a big mound of dough on the counter. "The younger boys are just finishing a guitar jam upstairs and the older boys are making a racket downstairs. Thump thump thump." She pounded the bread with a thump of her own. "Kneading bread is so therapeutic."

"You should try manure."

"No, thanks. We all have our outlets."

I watched her work her fingers into the mass and then flip it and slam it hard enough to send a cloud of flour into the air. Was she creating a mess just to have something to clean up later?

"What's worrying you so much that you need to blow up a dust storm? I thought everything had settled down here."

"Ivy, you have no idea what it's like to be a parent. I haven't had an hour's peace since twin one made his early arrival into the world." Catching my eye, she gave me a wan smile. "It's always something. I imagine you'll find out soon enough."

"Hope so." I walked around the counter to stand out of reach of flying flour. My overalls were fresh out of the wash. "Do you ever regret having so many?"

"Every day. And never." The dough went over with another thump. "I was raised to be a parent, remember? Can't imagine a different or better job. But it's tiring. Hardly a day passes without a challenge that wasn't in the manual."

Perching on the kitchen table, I crossed my arms. "You got a manual?"

"Created my own. More of a 'what not to do,' based on our own parents." She punched the dough hard. "I was barely thirteen when Dad left. He wasn't always around even before that, but still managed to balance Mom out." She pretended to make a set of scales with each floury hand and let the left fall to the counter. "Boom. The real lessons began."

Something twisted in my belly. Guilt, probably. "I'm sorry. You got weighed down early and it hasn't let up."

"There were a few easy years, when you guys were older. Roger and I were dating and I thought he would be…"

"More present?" I suggested, trying to ignore Keats' pokes in my shin. My big sis needed to talk and he could be patient.

Daisy's sigh blew a few tendrils of hair off her forehead. There was plenty of gray now, along with some lines, but she was still the fairest of the Galloway Girls. Her features were classic and when she smiled, her hazel eyes sparkled. "I guess. But maybe it's always this way. That the woman carries most of the load."

"Like a kangaroo," I said. "Imagine lugging that load around."

"I don't need to imagine, having carried twins twice." She smiled more sincerely, although there was no sparkle. "You caught me on a bad day, Ivy. Most of the time I wouldn't change a thing. And you'll say the same in a few years. Or twenty."

"At least they're nearly out of the nest." I pushed myself upright, knowing she was making a mental note of where my butt touched the table to scour it later. "You won't know what to do with yourself when the boys leave." Keats circled to move me away. The time for sister-bonding had ended. "Oh right, you can look after *my* kids, then. There's no one else I'd trust so completely. You made me what I am, Daisy."

Her eyes did catch a sparkle. "Don't blame that on me. I didn't raise you to be a renegade."

"Must be in the genes, then. Because your boys have that trait, too, and Roger's the opposite. Came through you, sis."

She slapped and shaped the dough into a smooth round and set it gently in a bowl. "I'm doing my best to rein that trait in but the older two are always beating on each other. They want to be your bodyguards."

"Nope. Won't have it. They're born to be mechanics and I'll do everything in my power to make that happen."

"Thank you. I have enough to worry about without thinking of them knee-trapping your attackers."

"Knee-trapping?"

"One of their favorite mixed martial arts techniques. Part of a street-fighting combination. Me, I prefer the spinning sidekick."

"You're training, too?"

"I was." She covered the bowl with a towel and slipped it into the oven to rise. "Until an unexpected move swept my legs out from under me. I'm on a time out."

"Huh." Keats was steadily shifting me to the basement stairs. "I want to learn this five-move street-fighting combo. Sounds as handy as a utility knife. Good for everything from a kangaroo capture to a criminal takedown."

She waved to the stairs. "Go try your luck. Liam and Brydon are here giving a private lesson."

"Ooh... private lessons. Fancy."

"It's new. Lessons for all four boys are being financed by a generous benefactor who wants to keep his grandkids alive."

I stopped with my hand on the doorknob. "Dad? I didn't know

he had opinions about martial arts. Or street-fighting. Or much else besides barn cats."

Daisy laughed. "Try talking to him. Works better if his hands are busy. If you're too direct, he bolts."

"Complete opposite of Mom. No wonder they hit it off. She wore him out, though. Just like two sets of twins stole your spark."

"First, if I'm learning flying scissor kicks, I've got plenty of spark. Second, their flame is still lit."

I gasped. It was one thing for Uncle Sterling to think so and quite another for their firstborn daughter. "Don't joke about that, Daisy."

"I'm not saying anything will happen. Just that some couples seem inevitable. You and Kellan, for example. I knew it when you were teens and always hoped you'd find your way back to each other."

"Don't mention our inevitability in the same breath as the other two," I said, opening the basement door.

"Jilly and Asher then."

"Inevitable. Agreed."

She eyed me slyly. "Poppy and Travis."

My scowl didn't faze her. It never had. "You want Pops to get hitched to a guy like that? He's basically feral."

"So are the Galloways. We just dress it up differently." She used another dishtowel to scrape at her hands and apron, leaving a generous dusting of flour in a half circle on the terra-cotta colored tile. "Travis will make a good dad to Camden if he stays, and his own kids if Poppy forgives him."

I turned my scowl on Keats. "Why did you bring me here and let me think it was my idea?"

He poked my leg to go down and join the lesson, but the twins were already on their way upstairs with Liam and Brydon. All were red-faced, sweaty and obviously played out. Some of them had visible scratches and bruises that were already blooming.

"Hey Aunt Ivy," Sutton said. "You missed a great sparring session. The guys taught us a couple of new moves."

"Great, then you can teach me."

"Proprietary," Liam said, grinning. His scalp was rosy under his sparse hair. Both instructors were about my age and it was probably hard on them to lose their manes so young. "Every teacher has a few signature combos they only share with their best and brightest. Right, Brydon?"

"I guess." Brydon didn't crack a smile as he checked my feet to see if I was wearing boots. He hadn't forgotten our exchange at the dojo. I wished I'd kept my boots on but Daisy would have had a fit. There were obviously different rules for family and martial artists because the instructors wore sneakers. "I hold mine back if I can."

"Makes sense," Sutton said. "What if you meet a former student in a street fight, Liam?"

Liam shrugged. "Not worried, because then I'd know your whole game." He directed a smile at me. "Happy to take you through some moves another time, Ivy. These boys wore me out. I can handle two on one but not twins competing against each other."

"I can attest to that, times two," Daisy said. "Staying for dinner, guys? Homemade bread coming up."

Brydon shook his head. "Tempting, but I gotta skip the carbs."

"I can't either," Liam said, shrugging on his jacket. "Visiting my grandparents." He led the way to the front door and the mellow sensei squealed as he gained an orange fluffy mascot on his shoulder. Percy had been lying in wait among Daisy's glass bird collection on a high shelf. The figurines flew up there when the boys were toddlers and never came down.

Sutton ran over to extract Percy but the hold was probably harder to break than a knee trap. The cat's claws dug deep into heavy denim. "Sorry, sorry," my nephew said. "This cat is always pranking someone."

He set Percy down and the cat looked disgruntled. The ferrets had obviously proven elusive today, sending my feisty feline after bigger prey.

I bent to collect Percy and my sock slipped on the flour. Someone else had stepped in it and tracked it to the front door. Daisy and her rubber gloves would be in paradise.

After their teachers left, the twins vanished before I could press for a demo. "Just give them an hour to recoup," Daisy said. "That's all it takes at their age. By the time you're done, the bread will be ready."

"I never skip the carbs but someone has other ideas." I gestured to Keats, now worrying my cuffs. "He wanted me to get in on that lesson instead of chatting. Guess he needs assurance I can protect him from the buck kangaroo when we find him."

She saw us to the door, picking her way around the flour. "Be careful, Ivy. A kick in the wrong place could put an end to your twin production."

I wasn't sure whether to hit her or hug her and decided on the latter. Daisy deftly sidestepped the embrace.

"Do I really stink that much? You're a hugger, like Asher."

She pointed to her floury apron. "And a clean freak, like Dad. I'm protecting your overalls."

"Dad's a clean freak? Since when?"

"Oh, Ivy." Daisy shook her head. "So sharp about some things and so oblivious about others."

"Isn't that true of everyone?"

She leaned around me and opened the door. "You're still my favorite child. Just so you know."

"But you're kicking me out of the nest, aren't you?" I released the struggling cat onto the porch.

"Just for today. After the family meeting and bread prep, I'm as tired as the boys, only it takes me days, not hours, to bounce back."

Keats drove me down the front stairs to the truck behind puffy

Percy. "Check for two ferrets, will you? Percy's in a mood, so they may be MIA."

"Just what I need," she said. "Another set of twins to worry about."

The door closed with a firm click. With anyone other than Daisy, I'd consider it a slam.

CHAPTER NINETEEN

E dna was in the pen with Hildy Hopper when I got back to the farm. "Docile as a kitten now that she's trapped. Even let me scratch her ears."

"Really? That's awesome." I opened the gate and joined them, making sure to close it quickly to keep the roo in and Keats out. The dog whined, a rare sound.

"Don't worry, Keats," Edna said. "I've got plenty of moves that could lay this roo to waste as required."

I kept a respectful distance from the kangaroo. "What kind of moves?"

Edna came over and joined me, leaning against the fence. "Mixed martial arts with my own twist. Handy with humans and other animals on occasion."

"Your own twist? Do you have signature moves? Liam Turco was just telling me about that."

She gave her perm a modest pat. "It's the secret sauce of self-defense. Anyone can win against a common thug but when you're facing someone with training it's more challenging. We know most of the same moves and expect certain sequences. So, you need to make it your own for the element of surprise."

Keeping my eyes on the roo, I asked, "Can you show me?"

"Then the sauce wouldn't be secret, would it?"

I took the risk of a sideways glance. "I bet you have a dozen signature moves. I only want two."

Edna turned and climbed the fence nimbly, despite an available gate. "Two moves are only enough to get you in trouble, Ivy. You'll give your opponent the idea you've got a full arsenal and run out of ammo in ten seconds."

"Three, then. Edna, please?"

On the other side of the fence, she poked my shoulder. "Why? Are you that upset about getting trounced by this jill?"

"Yeah, I'm upset. That's the only reason I'd ask you to teach me martial arts moves now, when I'm stiff and bruised from a roo drubbing."

"Now? You want a lesson today?"

"No time like the present. You have mats in your basement for that reason, don't you?"

"Full padding in the rec room. Gertie and I like to throw down occasionally. In the end times, we'll eventually run out of bullets and then what are we going to do?"

"Knee traps and scissor sweeps," I said. "Nail those zombies."

She snickered. "Can anyone say with certainty that zombies have knees?"

"I'm quite sure of it. All those movies can't be wrong."

Boots crunched on gravel as she walked away. "I'll show you a triple combo, Ivy. Be aware that I won't go easy on you just because you're bruised and a novice."

"What about my concussion?" I called over my shoulder. "Jilly won't like it if you steal my remaining faculties."

"I'm less worried about Jillian than the dog and cat. They've been known to do worse for less and I want to preserve my good looks."

"That's what a perm's for, isn't it? Too wiry for claws and fangs to get through. You'll still look fine when—"

"If you mention that man's name, I'm coming back to offer you to the roo."

I laughed as her voice faded. She was taking the lane back to her house. It was an invitation. "See you in half an hour!" I called.

"See you on the floor," she replied. "You'll live to regret this."

Her voice was faint now and I finished the repartee in a normal voice. "As long as I live, period."

I looked through the slats of the gate at Keats and his tail came up. He seemed well satisfied that an octogenarian prepper was going to hand me my butt on a platter. On the bright side, she'd probably protect my reproductive organs for pragmatic reasons. Someone would need to repopulate the planet after the apocalypse and there could be worse vessels.

The late-day sun was at the perfect angle to highlight the joey's sweet face. "Hey, little girl, you're adorable. Based on my research, it won't be long till you're out of the pouch. Your fur's still a little sparse." In fact, Rooby's rosy skin tone reminded me of Liam's scalp earlier. It was a shame how the hirsute Wiggs made everyone else look bare. "Give it a month and you'll be fluffed up and ready to pop into the world."

The doe took a tentative hop toward me. My back was still to the fence so I slid along to the gate for ease of exit. "Keats, would you head into the barn and see if Dad needs help?"

I could pretty much feel the dog's blue eye searing a hole through my T-shirt, as well as my ruse. One thing I never did to my wonder dog was banish him, yet that's exactly what I was doing now. If I wanted a chance at scratching the doe's big ears, it was more likely to happen without the dog nearby.

"Sorry, buddy. You can keep watch from the barn door. Promise I'll scream if I need you."

That was a lie, too. I would never offer a canine canapé to this deceptively mild-looking animal. Her water tub was too small to drown him, but she could do fatal damage with her built-in weapons.

Keats trailed off, grumbling of treachery and betrayal, or at least, that's how I heard it. Meanwhile, Hildy hopped to the corner facing the meadow and made her own music. The low, grunting bark wasn't tuneful to my ear, but perhaps it would carry on the wind to her beau in the bush. Hopefully, he was still a good way off. It hadn't occurred to me he would follow her all the way to the farm but it was possible. Maybe I shouldn't have sent Edna home so soon.

I waited till the jill turned around and held my ground with some trepidation as she approached. The carrots in my pocket were a blatant bribe and it looked like she might fall for it.

Sure enough, Hildy hopped over slowly and then nuzzled my pocket. I pulled out a carrot and offered it to her. She began chewing, using her left front paw under my fingers to propel the vegetable into her mouth.

"So it's true," I said, quietly. "Kangaroos really are southpaws."

Hildy was indifferent to the observation. Her attention was wholly on the carrot, which made me hope she was relaxing in the new environment. When she was done, she made soft clucking sounds that were probably directed at Rooby but were soothing for me, too.

She didn't hop away and after a few minutes, I dared to touch her back gently, well away from the joey. The fur was more woolly than soft and through the dense pelt, the clucks felt a little bit like a purr.

"I wish you could talk," I murmured. "I'd really like to know what you saw at Midway Mall the other night. It must have been traumatizing. You've been through a lot this week."

Hildy hopped away again, almost as if she knew we'd moved on to murderous subject matter. In the far corner, she let out the same barking cough. There was a lonesome quality to the sound, at least to my ears. In her country of origin, kangaroos often moved in large mobs. Here, they were hard to find. The Mafia was searching far and wide to locate the right home.

"Ivy?" I heard the voice and didn't answer. "*Ivy*."

Dad probably hadn't used that tone on me since I was three but my nervous system remembered and sat up to take notice like a kangaroo. "What?"

"Your dog is worried sick about you, that's what. He tried to climb the ladder to the loft to get me. I heard the clatter and came down."

"I'm fine." I shook off the vague trance that often fell over me in animal company, especially after a tiring day. "We're fine."

"Can you be fine outside the fence? The sun's going down and the last place you want to be is in a dark pasture with a wild animal."

"She's practically domesticated."

"Didn't sound like it earlier, when she shoved two of my daughters into a swamp."

"I guess she picks her moments." As much as I wanted to believe Hildy was a mild cow or sweet alpaca in a fascinating package, she wasn't regular livestock. I was sure there was more to her than others believed but we could get better acquainted in the morning. "I'm coming."

"I heard you talking to her," he said, as I slipped through the gate he opened. "Did it help?"

"It helped me. Not so sure about her."

Kneeling, I accepted Keats' frenzied greeting. It was almost as dramatic as when I'd recovered him from a dognapper. The very thought made me hug him close. Normally he didn't encourage that, but given the circumstances, he gave me leeway. I ended up on the ground with him in my lap. It was one of those moments where gratitude for what I had washed over me, and I'd learned not to resist.

"Dad, do you know martial arts?" I asked, looking up at him.

"Not per se, but I can get out of a tussle when needed. It's been needed on occasion."

"Do you have a signature move?"

Smiling, he leaned against the fence. "Do I know how to surprise an opponent? Sure. Does it always work? Nope. There's an element of theater in a physical altercation. Not like those wrestling shows I grew up on, but maybe a little showmanship."

"As in sneakery?"

His laugh was more like Asher's than I remembered, which was understandable when Dad didn't laugh that often. "Or fakery. For example, you can try to catch your opponent's eye and feign going for his head. Then, you kick while his hands are up and his midriff is unguarded. And when you get him down by whatever means necessary, you run. The safest move in any altercation is exiting stage right. Otherwise, it might be curtains."

"Got it. Fake out with eyes and hands, then sharp and fast with a kick. Run so you can live to fight another day."

"I'm sure you've heard from others about the wisdom of avoiding a fight in the first place. Make like a kangaroo and flee a dicey situation. Only fight if cornered and whatever you do, try to stay off the ground. Grappling rarely ends well, especially for women."

I walked with him to the barn. "Wouldn't enjoy that with anyone except Kellan and maybe not even then."

"Not even then. Grappling is about holds and submission. Helplessness." Something like a shudder ran over him. "No one wants that."

Keats was all perky again, trotting ahead with his tail up. "How did you learn all this, Dad?"

That was several "Dads" in the course of one day. Was I becoming soft?

"The hard way. We didn't have classes here in my day, but we were born knowing the value of self-defense. So we learned by doing. I broke my hand, ankle and collarbone before I was 12, and that's when the going got tough. By the time I was in my mid-teens, it wasn't just for training anymore. Broke a few more bones, and after that I turned to other modes of self-defense."

I rarely saw my father carry a weapon but I suspected he usually had one handy. While his family enemies had mostly died, been jailed or moved away, there was always the risk of someone rising up like a zombie. Keats turned to shoot me a look with his blue eye and I thought again about Knox Wigg. Did an old enemy of his family rise up? Very possible, but why hadn't they gone after Travis first? Or maybe they did go after Travis and Knox got caught in the middle.

Keats mumbled an order to get a move on it. "Gotta run," I said.

"Oh? Jilly said dinner would be ready soon."

I hadn't checked my texts but for once I wasn't hungry. "I'll grab something at Edna's. We've got a strategy session."

He stopped, framed in the rectangle of light from the double doors. "So, that's what I tell Kellan when he comes looking later?"

"Sure, but I'll tell him first. He'd be a proponent of strategy over street-fighting." I thought about adding an extra "Dad" on top of my answer but he had the merest trace of judgement on his face. Seemed like he was forgetting he was more an honorary parent, at least to the youngest of his kids. "We're going to talk about the boomer rescue."

Edna and I would no doubt do just that in the breaks between kicking each other.

"Ivy, you know I don't often intervene but this situation really stinks in an old, familiar way. And if I'm right, there's no trouble like longstanding grudges. You've encountered those before."

I had, more than once. "The sooner those are stamped out, the better. Kellan and Asher will get to the bottom of it."

"They're making headway. Ash sounded upbeat when he dropped off the Wiggs. If you could just…"

He stopped speaking but it was already one step too far. There were two reasons my father and I got along. One was that he was such a boon to the farm and I trusted him implicitly with my animals. The other was that he didn't lecture, judge or try to smother me. It was something he had over Mom and pretty much everyone in the family. Now he was walking dangerously close to that line. There were plenty of "if you had just" thoughts on my side of the equation but it wasn't the time for lectures or recrimination.

"It's all good, Calvin," I said. "Thanks for keeping an eye on Hildy. You checked the security cameras? Wouldn't put it past Gilroy Leek to attempt roo-napping."

"Then I guess you'd see some street fighting right in your own pasture. I'm not as spry as I used to be but I can grapple that oily zookeeper."

I laughed as I followed the pets to the truck. "You wouldn't. Daisy says you're a clean freak, like her."

"A clean freak? How could I work on a farm and be a clean freak?"

"Just realized that's why you have so many gloves. And you're trying to eradicate my manure pile."

"I wouldn't sleep in the loft if I cared that much about dirt or dust, would I now?"

My nearly unflappable father had a faint hint of a squeak in his voice. It made him sound like a scrappy teen again. "Look, I'm just passing along what your firstborn said. It's a trait, not a flaw."

"Sure feels like one. In hill country we need to be ready to get our hands dirty. Without gloves."

I turned back. "Relax, I won't tell anyone. At least, as long as you keep your cat colony out of the kangaroo pasture. Feline feces can carry a parasite that's deadly for kangaroos."

"You want me to keep track of eight cats, not counting Percy?"

"Please. I know you have more than eight up there. You're a collector, but you too can be cured, like Edna."

Now he flinched. "I don't care for that comparison, Ivy."

The score felt even, so I relented. "Objection sustained. See you later, Dad."

CHAPTER TWENTY

Two hours later, I rubbed my aching shoulder as I pulled out of Edna's lane and onto the highway. "I can't believe she made me wear a helmet. And took a photo. That was humiliating."

Keats gave a pant-laugh. He and Percy had perched on a bench to watch the show and found it riveting. The cat was so drained from the excitement that he dozed off the second we were in the truck.

"Obviously everyone was right about self-defense having a steep learning curve. Especially for someone like me. Asher's the only athlete in the family and I got all the nerd genes."

I hit the left turn signal at the farm's lane. Keats reached out and flipped it back up with his muzzle. It was the first time he'd done that but I was too tired to be amazed. Between fighting a roo and a prepper I was worn out and ready to collapse into bed. Yet his new move suggested the day was not quite over.

"Seriously? I've had enough, buddy. Can't it wait till morning?"

I tried the turn signal again to see if it was a fluke.

It wasn't a fluke.

He nudged the lever again with just enough precision to get the signal to stop.

"Straight ahead it is, then. I suppose you'd ask for the helm if you didn't want to keep eyes, nose and ears free." He ignored me, applying himself to the open window. It was the perfect early summer evening to enjoy an expansive sensory experience. "Normally I just take direction, but if you want to hunt roo, I really need backup, Keats. It's important to acknowledge our limits."

He mumbled something that sounded vaguely soothing, or maybe I just wanted to hear it that way. Tension rose in my throat until the dog pounded the dash to take the turnoff onto a tributary highway. We were heading away from Midway Mall and the dancing paws told me to pick up the pace.

"I'm already over the speed limit. What's the rush?"

His next mumble seemed deliberately unintelligible, or maybe I was too tired to decipher his message.

"Thistledown?" I asked, feeling a spark of hope. Visiting Maud and the pups was always fun, and Thelma, too. They'd be surprised to see us but we'd arrived later before.

We passed the turnoff without canine comment and I started to feel a prickle of unease.

"Fleetborough? Are we dropping in on Sterling? Not ideal. He's all about the recliner and crime shows at this hour."

It wasn't Fleetborough, either. My throat got even tighter as I thought about other local possibilities. The nursing home? Brandi Brownhill? We still didn't know what secrets her shed held.

The paws danced on. We weren't "there" yet.

A few minutes later, the muzzle came over and hit the left turn signal at Waterfield. I was as impressed as I could be in the face of dread. There were several potential destinations here, none appealing. My first guess was Gilroy Leek's private zoo. The pets had investigated thoroughly but I didn't get to take a look. Were there other animals that needed rescuing?

But no, we passed his lane without more than a rude grumble. It was a problem, but one that could wait for another day.

The next option was Lenore Wigg's apartment but that wasn't it, either.

"Oh no," I said. "Tell me we're not going to the campsite."

We were going to the campsite. At dusk. On foot. And alone.

"Keats, I refuse to rassle a roo on my own. Hard pass. If the buck is around we're waiting as long as it takes for Edna and the others to get down here."

His mumbled retort had a sassy note, perhaps to remind me he wouldn't choose to deal with the supersized macropod alone, either.

At least we'd discovered the road earlier and didn't need to take the dirt bike trail in. It was more like a lane but not as rough as I'd expected, given it hadn't been used for decades.

The dog knew exactly where to cut into the bush and it wasn't long at all before we reached the Wigg boys' old refuge. By that time, Percy was up and ready to go. His eager meow prompted me to pick up the phone.

"Hey, Jilly," I said, as I got out of the truck. My voice sounded too perky. I knew it and she knew it.

"Where are you?" There was the usual clang of pots at her end. "And what are you doing that you shouldn't be doing? You missed dinner."

"There's my bestie, always getting straight to the point."

"And there's *my* bestie, always evading it. I know this isn't good, Ivy. My spidey sense is firing hard."

"It's not that bad, Jilly. There's still some light."

She groaned. "You're somewhere in the dark alone, aren't you?"

"Not alone," I scoffed. "You're never alone with a brilliant border collie and intrepid cat. We just popped down for another look at the Wigg brothers' old campsite."

"*Ivy.* You didn't."

Her voice held just as much judgment as my dad's had earlier, but I didn't mind it coming from Jilly. She'd earned the right to judge a hundred times over.

"Wasn't my idea." I put her on speaker as I lowered the tailgate to collect my backpack. "I'm beat and wanted to come home but someone's learned how to work the turn signal."

She was silent. The pots were silent. The water stopped running in the kitchen sink.

Keats gave a mollifying mumble and she answered that. "Keats Galloway, you'd better have a good explanation for this."

He circled my legs without bothering to answer. We had to take the call on the move, apparently.

"Aren't you impressed about the turn signal?" I winced as I slid into the backpack. I'd been stiffer before but not often. "It's only a matter of time before he takes over the driving entirely. He can probably manage the stick shift better than me. Granted, that wouldn't take much."

"I'm waiting." The water and clanging started again. It was safe to proceed. "Spit it out, Ivy."

"If I knew why we're here, I'd tell you." I shut the tailgate, locked the truck and started walking. "I just take orders."

"Not buying it. I mean, I know what Keats is like but some of this comes from you, Ivy. You two feed off each other."

I gave a grudging nod and figured she'd sense it. "Sometimes, unanswered questions start to itch, that's all. I try not to scratch, at least not right away. But then Keats and Percy want to scratch that itch and I can't resist."

"And what questions are you scratching right now?"

I shone the bright flashlight around the vacant campsite. There was no sign of a police presence now. "That's just it. Sometimes I don't even know. I want to take a look at Gilroy Leek's zoo, for example. And I want to poke around Brandi Brownhill's shed and see what she's hiding. I also want to talk to both Lenore and Hoyle Wigg again and find out about old grudges that may have played out at the mall. The campsite was not on my conscious radar at all."

"It's on your subconscious radar. Keats wanted to poke around a bit more this morning."

The dog mumbled an affirmative. "That he did, but I didn't expect to circle back so soon."

"Does that mean you're looking for the buck kangaroo?"

I shuddered at the thought of more. "It's the most obvious explanation but Keats and Percy would probably want backup for that. After what happened with Hildy, they know Roofus will be a handful."

She turned off the water again. "What do *you* think? On your own, without pets in your head."

I laughed. "There isn't much room in my head for my own thoughts, but if I had to guess, I'd say Roofus was near that cliff earlier. Keats wanted to stop and explore, and I just couldn't face it. When Cori went back to check there was nothing."

"So, he could have headed down there?"

"Promise not to freak out?" I asked.

"Of course not, but tell me anyway."

"I think Hildy's calling him to the farm."

She groaned again. "So I can't even go out to water the flowers tomorrow without protection."

"The Mafia's on notice and Edna's flying a thermal drone over the farm tonight. Your petunias will be fine." I chuckled. "Petunia. That's a floral name Mom didn't use if you want to carry on the tradition."

"Pass." Cutlery jangled into the dishwasher. "What are you doing now?"

"Just strolling around with the pets. Seeing what we may have missed."

"Ivy, promise me you'll call in reinforcements at the first sign of that buck."

"That's a promise I can easily make." I took another look at the firepit, now empty, and thought about the two young Wiggs swapping tales over baked beans long ago. "How did dinner go?"

"Better than I feared." The dishwasher clicked closed. "Poppy came and was civil with Travis and nice to Camden."

"Good for her. Do you think Travis will win her over?"

She moved on to handwashing the "delicates." No spots allowed on the inn's glassware. "Poppy and I had a chat while I was cooking. We talked about the complexities of hill country life in general and marriage in particular. Chemistry and connection are the easy part, right? It's all about compromise and communication."

"That's a lot of 'c' words. I think I'm still stuck on 'b.'"

She laughed. "For border collie, your first love."

The dog himself was in the pen where the roos had stayed, but the investigation was brief. "B for how it bothered me when Kellan raised his voice earlier. I try his patience, Jilly, and I worry it will run out."

Glassware tinkled in the dish rack. "Which is why you didn't tell him you're down there tonight."

"Right. He's so grumpy I can't help thinking the stakes are higher than with an ordinary murder."

"*Ordinary murder.*" Jilly mocked me. "There's no such thing."

"True. But something bigger is going on and I don't want to aggravate him for nothing. The pets are nearly done here."

"That's a fat F for communication and compromise, my friend," she said. "If I don't hear the wind blowing through your truck in ten minutes I'll be the one texting him. And you know why? Because I have another marital c-word for you. *Children.* I want to raise ours together."

"I want that, too, so back to b-words for bride."

"Exactly. Let that *be* the goal. Get it?"

We laughed together and I promised to call shortly before clicking off. "You done, boys?"

Keats gave an indifferent mumble. There was nothing of particular interest, but he wasn't fully satisfied. He did another circuit while I shone the light around.

The place had been creepy in daytime and was even more so now. The beam lit up drifting ropes of spiderwebs and bats swooped over the clearing. Bats didn't worry me as they had before spending time in a closet with some at Halloween. I was happy enough to share the night sky with them.

The light kept bouncing back to the fire pit as I thought about those young boys camping for days at a time. It was sad that eating prepper fare in the woods was preferable to being at home with Hoyle Wigg and his bottle. I remembered Travis kidding us about backwoods squirrel stew and realized it may not have been a joke after all. There was a good chance the boys had to forage for meals.

Picturing all that made me glad I'd doled out a bonus "Dad" to my father earlier. Calvin never once hit any of us and he left home to keep us safe. He'd sent money to Mom to help raise us, and when she refused to accept it, found ways around her. It wasn't a great childhood, but seeing how the Wigg brothers had lived gave me a new perspective on my past. While Travis was out here, I was in the library earning a scholarship. While I was complaining about corporate life, he gave up his success in the army to hide out for years. He sacrificed a lot for Knox, and all because of Hoyle's abuse.

Keats was never one to indulge rumination and certainly not tonight. I returned to the present with a yip of pain.

"Stop it. That one will bleed."

He dove at me again and I hustled ahead of him past the livestock pen and into the woods on the other side. I held up the light and found a sliver of a trail that had seen recent use. Broken branches suggested someone broad-shouldered had come through.

A cop, most likely. The damp earth in one area showed a footprint that didn't belong to a police-issue boot, however. I'd seen enough of those to know. It must have been Knox or Camden.

Percy was ahead of us at the edge of the cone of light. This cat knew exactly how to serve as a beacon and I appreciated his talent.

Keats was initially behind me but once he was confident his livestock was moving, he brushed past me and moved ahead. Both pets trotted with quiet deliberation, tails down. Their ears were also back but there was no telltale puff to get my own hackles up.

The path twisted and turned until I wasn't quite sure what direction we were going. There was no moon tonight. That would be too easy.

Eventually we reached an old fence that blocked the path. Percy went over and Keats under. I lifted one boot and my muscles screamed from the punishment in Edna's basement. Flashing the light in both directions, I saw it wasn't so much a fence as a long barricade. I could walk around it, and I did.

The next barricade was a natural one in the form of a stream a few feet too wide to jump over. Keats shuddered as he faced water, his mortal enemy, but Percy the beacon showed us some stones deliberately spaced to allow safe crossing.

"What next?" I asked. "Quicksand? A bunker trap?"

Saying it aloud made me more cautious with my footing. It wouldn't be easy for Edna and Gertie to find me out here. They'd pull it off, I had no doubt, but better safe than sorry. My phone had a full charge, but cell reception in a bunker was always dicey.

I expected another barrier and found it. The Wigg boys had covered the path with piles of sticks that really shouldn't have survived from their childhood. Did Knox take time to refresh them when he was here? Maybe he wanted to show off their backup site to Camden. But the various damp areas in the path only showed one set of prints and Keats' interest in them suggested another owner.

The dog lifted his paw and directed my attention to a long plank propped against a tree. It was mostly concealed, but I figured out how to maneuver it into place to cross the "moat" of branches that likely hid a pit of some sort.

"What next? Spikes?" I grumbled as I crossed gingerly. "Boiling water from a tower? If so, I'm calling it quits, you two."

I couldn't, though. The pets were totally committed to this mission. There was something worth seeing.

Luckily, that was the final challenge. Just a few yards further, we emerged in a clearing. Both pets stopped moving to confirm we'd arrived at the destination. I held the light over my head with both hands and bathed the entire circle in a warm glow. The space was quite large but there wasn't much in it.

One metal chair beside a large fire pit.

One old oil tank propped over the pit on a metal frame that had probably held a mattress before it was jury-rigged.

"It's like a big oven," I said. "Maybe the Wigg boys like to roast dinner on a spit out here. Only I don't see a spit. Or even a grill."

Keats lifted his paw to tell me to take a closer look.

"As you wish. I suppose Knox and Camden could have come back here and had a fire."

There was a piece of heavy metal resting on the oil tank. Pulling work gloves out of my pocket, I lifted it off and exposed a large rectangular cavity cut out of the topside. I shone the light into the tank and saw nothing but ash. There was plenty of it and it hadn't burned completely down.

"That's a little strange, isn't it? The fire's underneath and there's ash inside. I'm not sure quite how this oven works. Travis was bragging about his backwoods cookery. Maybe this is the secret to his success. He could have a reality TV show."

Keats' mumble suggested I take the situation more seriously. His paw was still raised in a point. Whatever I needed to discover, the ash wasn't it. Or at least, all of it.

"Okay, I'll poke around in there."

I didn't need to go far for a poker. A metal rod sat propped against the chair.

By the time I came back, Percy was on top of the oil tank preparing to jump in.

"Percy, don't. You'll be covered in ash and that's a big cleanup job. Just let me do it."

His meow was defiant. This job was worth a night's grooming, it seemed.

The cat jumped inside, making ash rise in a cloud. The cloud only grew as he moved around, claws raking or scraping against the metal bottom.

Soon came a slight sound of metal on metal and he pulled something to the side closest to me. It was a small blob that had a familiar shape. I tried unsuccessfully to pluck it out with my work gloves and ended up swapping them for the nitrile version pilfered from Asher's box.

Meanwhile, Percy went back to work and hooked something with his claw.

A ring.

I took it from him and dropped it into my palm. "Barbecue fumble, I guess."

Dipping into the ash, I pulled out the first object Percy found. "I wonder what this blobby thing is?" And then, "Oh. I see it now."

Unless I was very much mistaken, it was a tooth.

CHAPTER TWENTY-ONE

I wasn't mistaken.

The small object I passed to Kellan when we met at the side of the highway about 20 minutes later was very much a tooth. More specifically, a gold crown. I was glad Jilly had ratted me out, because even that short space of time until my fiancé arrived felt like forever. We'd reversed course through the various traps in record time and I'd left grooves from spinning the tires.

"What are the chances someone bent over an old oil tank oven and a gold tooth fell out?" I asked.

"Nil." Kellan looked at the photos I showed him. His officers had already gone into the woods to investigate. "Especially when combined with the ring."

"So, you're saying someone staged a private cremation? And these are cremains?"

My fiancé frowned but he didn't look shocked. Kellan was an expert at concealing his emotions, but I was generally able to read into eyebrows, furrowed lines and especially shifty eyes. Asher's expression readily revealed all, but Kellan took more work. Happily, I was willing to study his handsome, inscrutable face forever.

"I'm saying when a gold tooth and a wedding ring show up in a makeshift oven, it's going to take a lot of investigating."

"Will there be DNA?" I asked. "If someone was unofficially cremated, I mean."

"Possibly. Even with very high heat in an official crematorium there are—"

"Cremains," I supplied.

He nodded. "Bone, teeth, metals, obviously. We'll run a magnet through the ash and sift very carefully."

"A magnet! Why didn't I think of that? Bet there's one in my go-kit. Edna prepares, as you know."

"You didn't think of it because you're not a police officer," he said, still frowning. "I've reminded you of that often, yet here you are."

His voice had a romance-killing vibe. Not that I expected a glimmer of romance in the general vicinity of an unofficial crematorium.

"I was looking for clues about the buck kangaroo," I said. "He's still missing, in case you were wondering."

"I wasn't. Because I get regular reports from Cori."

"Really?" That surprised me. While their relationship had improved considerably over the past two years, I didn't think they were at the "regular reports" stage.

"It was part of our agreement. I let her fly drones over a crime scene provided she share all the footage."

"Aw, that's great. You're worried about the roo, too."

"I'm worried a two-hundred-pound beast might knock over a child or frail senior."

"Or worse," I said. "Some guy got knocked off his motorbike by a roo and roughed up pretty badly. But it happens less often than you think."

"Untrue, because I don't think of it at all. Nor do I want to. The sooner they get that thing detained, the better." His eyes narrowed. "It had better not be detained on your property very long. Cori promised to have a plan in place by tomorrow."

"Tomorrow? That's a shame. I wanted more time to get to know them. The mama roo seems quite sweet."

"She body-slammed you into a pond, if I remember correctly."

"It's not the first time that's happened. Remember Wilma nearly drowned me."

"And you don't call Wilma sweet."

He had me there. I rarely got near Wilma without a metal poker on a long pole. "Hildy's different. She was just scared and protecting her joey. Wilma is deliberately mean."

"Cori could make a plan for her, too." His lip twitched, knowing full well I'd never part with my fractious sow.

"Wilma's part of the Runaway Farm family, but Hildy and hubs can't stay," I conceded. "They're illegal, but that boundary's been crossed before with the mayor's blessing. The problem is my dad's cat colony. They carry disease that's lethal to macropods."

He stared up at the sky muttering under his breath. It sounded like a prayer of gratitude, but he wasn't normally a pray-in-public kind of guy. It wouldn't fit his chiefly image.

His eyes found mine again. "Explain to me why you're way down in Waterfield looking for a roo last seen in Clover Grove. Alone, no less."

"They can cover a lot of ground fast, as you know, and they're happy taking a highway when available. My thinking was that the buck might come back to familiar territory."

"So, you went to Gilroy Leek's home first and trespassed?"

"No trespassing tonight, I'm happy to say. Unless this forest is privately owned, which I doubt." I paused to let him comment but he let me go on. "Keats wasn't interested in Mr. Leek's home so we kept driving. Then I wondered if the roo came back to its temporary lodging at the Wigg brothers' campsite. One thing led to another and we found their crematorium."

He shook his head. "Highly doubt it's theirs, but I've had officers bring Travis and Camden back in for questioning."

"Travis said you have a suspect in custody. Maybe he's been lighting fires here."

"And maybe you should head on home to be fresh to resume roo rescue tomorrow."

"I should. It's been a long day." Staring at him, I assessed my chances and decided to go for it. "Can I just ask one question?" His lips were already forming "no" when I blurted, "Is anyone missing?"

His hand came up and did the hair churning thing I found so endearing, even though it usually meant he was super stressed. "Ivy, you know I have a stack a mile high of open cases and that's just for Clover Grove. Across hill country, dozens of people have vanished over the decades."

Percy chose that moment to hit Kellan mid back and scale to his shoulder. I couldn't bear to mention the ashy paw prints on his uniform. Especially not given the origins of said ash.

"Well, maybe this will be one case closed," I said. "Or even more."

I thought he might find a modicum of relief in the idea but he didn't. "I don't really want to think about someone lounging in a chair while burning my cold cases."

Percy crossed to his other shoulder for more even distribution of ash. I thought about moving the cat myself but it would mean touching the last vestiges of someone who lived—and likely committed crimes—around here. What little I knew of Kellan's cold cases suggested criminal ties.

"There are so many old grudges in hill country. People almost never let go of them. I don't know how my dad managed to extricate himself from that world."

"By moving away, like Knox did, and not coming back till all the loose ends could be tied up."

Keats nudged my fingertips. "Do you think Knox came back too soon?"

"Possibly. And then, just to make a grand entrance, he stole kangaroos. He could have flown under the radar, delivered Camden to Travis and moved on to another oil rig far away from the land of marsupials."

It was a crumb of information and I jumped on it like Wilma on table scraps. "Is that why Knox brought his son home to Travis? To keep him safe from trouble in Australia?"

Kellan looked like he regretted saying so much. "Probably. Camden seemed to think it was an extraction. The boy's mother encouraged it."

"That's too bad. It seemed like Knox was living a good life there. I figured roo rehab had rehabbed him, but he fell down the criminal rabbit hole again."

"Not necessarily. Knox had no record there. Not a step out of line." He looked up again, probably oblivious to the stars in the clear sky. Cremains trumped constellations. "It's possible the old grudge took a long flight. Or hired someone local to do the job."

I let out a sigh. "How tragic. To clean up your life, discover you have a son and then get cut down while still in your prime. Poor Knox. Poor Camden."

He said what I didn't. "And poor Travis. He sacrificed a lot for his brother."

"But who would go to such lengths to punish Knox? Did he cross people enough here to deserve that?"

Now Kellan sighed. "Deserve is a relative term when it comes to grudges. Maybe they were willing to let bygones be really gone until Camden surfaced. Not long after Knox and his son met, someone took a shot at them at the animal sanctuary." He saw my unanswered question and added, "No roos were hurt in the attempted hit."

"So, that's why Knox came home. To find out who put them in danger."

Kellan lifted Percy off his shoulder and tried to offer him to me. I declined, so he set him down. "It's possible Camden was the target, but he has a spotless record. Model student."

He hadn't shut me down yet, so I forged on. "What about Brandi Brownhill? She was acting suspicious and Percy was sure there was something in her shed."

The cat swished around Kellan's cuffs, spreading more ash. "He was right. She had a stash of stolen water filters in a cavity. High-end."

"Ah, makes sense. She said there's big money in health and wellness."

Kellan bent with hands on thighs to look Keats in the eye. "You led your lady here alone and I do not approve. I'm revoking your deputy status."

The dog didn't approve of his tone and prepared to sanction Kellan's cuffs. Then he stopped, probably avoiding the taste of cremains. He settled for an insolent mumble instead.

"Did you know he can operate turn signals?" I was eager to change the subject. "It's incredible."

"Do you know what would be more incredible? If you three went home and actually stayed there."

Keats replied in a cheeky mumble that promised nothing.

"All over that," I said. "I'm absolutely beat. And beaten up. Edna gave me a self-defense lesson."

When he straightened, there were dusty handprints on his thighs. "Ivy, that's a bad idea."

"Why? Because of my head injury? Don't worry, she made me wear a helmet."

He finally smiled, no doubt picturing it. "I'm worried that you'll overreach."

"Overreach? How?"

"You'll think your flashy new moves are up to combating a crazed killer. It's one thing to grapple in Edna's basement and another to take on a stranger with a vengeful streak. Ask me how I know."

I grinned. "You've grappled with Edna in her basement?"

He blinked a few times, likely trying to dispel a less amusing image. "That's something I'll leave to you. But I've been in my share of combative situations, like any cop. So much can go wrong."

Taking Keats' hint, I started backing to the truck. "Edna and I didn't grapple, so you can let that picture go. Dad told me to avoid grappling at all costs. Once you're on the ground, it's pretty much game over. Feint, kick and run, he said."

"How about you stick to the running part?" Kellan was backing away, too. "Kicks are only going to get you into trouble."

"You underestimate me." I brought my fists up to attract his eyes and then spun and kicked in his direction. It might have been more impressive if I hadn't lost my balance and staggered into the truck. Keats' reverse sneeze suggested he was embarrassed for me.

"Ivy Galloway, that was a sad excuse for a sidekick." Kellan's teeth gleamed from yards away. "But I will *never* underestimate you."

CHAPTER TWENTY-TWO

The phone rang when I was nearly home and I put it on speaker. "Hey, Cori. Do you have a plan for tomorrow?"

"Not tomorrow. Tonight. When it comes to roos, you snooze you lose."

I laughed. When she wasn't being a pest, Cori was funny. The jokes were often at my expense but I could take the hit for humor. "How'd you find him?"

"We pooled our resources with Edna's. In both rescue and prepping, as it turns out, it's important to stay on top of tech developments. In the end, it was a plain ol' critter cam that caught the first shot of the roo, and we sent in more drones. He's circled that strip mall a couple of times. No bait stations in the vicinity so I don't know what he finds so fascinating."

I made a U-turn and headed toward the mall. "Probably looking for Hildy."

There was a weighty pause and I prepared for incoming missiles. "I hate that name, just so you know. You don't get to stick a handle on every animal we rescue."

"I don't see half the animals you rescue. But the ones I meet, I name. Presuming they tell me."

Heavy breathing on her end told me she was assembling gear. "Animals don't tell you their names. I've been rescuing them longer than you've been alive and that never happens."

"Since we're the same age, I presume you were in someone else's body at that point. Someone much taller and nicer. The universe pulled a fast one when it packed you into pint size for your next turn at bat."

"Stop presuming things, Ivy. In particular, stop presuming you're funny, because the only one who thinks so is Kellan."

"Depends on the day. And today he panned me."

"Because you're stepping all over his murder case again?"

I looked down at my black jacket, covered in light gray paw prints that would have been adorable had the ash not come from cremains. The guilty feline had adjourned to the back seat for thorough grooming. "Accidentally, I guess."

"Accidentally on purpose. But I like that about you. Rules are meant to be trampled."

"Not when you're marrying a cop." My laugh sounded rueful. "Hey, that was a roo-ful laugh. Get it?"

There was a metallic clunk, followed by thuds. She was loading her pickup truck. "Stop roo-minating on your murder-blighted romance and get packing."

"It's not blighted. Murder is a hobby we share. Or at least solving crimes. You need to find a hobby and a groom of your own. Get it? Gr-roo-m?"

"My hobby is rescue and it only mixes well with grooming pets." The truck tailgate slammed. "Some of us are meant to be single."

"Poppy would have said the same until recently. If she can find the right guy, you can, too."

"Is he though? The right guy?" She whistled for Clem and a door closed. "Because as much as I like rescue and rehab, Travis seems like a big project."

"Yeah, she's got her work cut out for her. And Poppy's still half-wild herself."

Cori laughed. "Domestication isn't all it's cracked up to be. I like to walk on the wild side myself. Maybe if Travis has another secret brother who rescues, I'll change my stance. But you married ladies seem to walk a constant tightrope."

I turned off the main road and parked in the bush, rather than driving into the mall parking lot. "You're not wrong. And when you're carrying as many animals as I am, it's quite a balancing act."

Her engine roared and she gunned it. "Exactly. One more roo on top and... splat. So, we'll get those off your back ASAP."

Opening the door, I let the pets out and then joined them. "Thanks. Hildy's a sweetheart and the baby's adorable but moving them is for the best."

I expected her to sign off but she was quiet for a moment. "Are you home? I don't hear the motor."

"Not home. I was already on the road so I came directly to the mall. Figured you'd texted Edna and Jilly already."

Cori's sigh surpassed Jilly's in exasperation. "Get back in the truck, Ivy. If you start stumbling around out there you could hurt the roo."

That was where she differed from Jilly. My bestie put *my* welfare first. "How on earth could I hurt a boomer of that size? He could have me for lunch if he weren't vegetarian."

"Keats and Percy will feel compelled to help you and I've seen the blood splatter they leave behind."

"They didn't help with Hildy this afternoon." Keats kept his guilty grumble set to low volume so Cori couldn't hear it.

"They knew there was backup nearby with better tools for the job. But if you try anything brash with this big boomer alone, you know they won't stand by. Is that fair to the pets? Is it fair to the roo? Stand down, Ivy."

"You and your rools." I called the pets back and picked up

Percy. They certainly shouldn't be in the lead and exposed. "Just drive faster, okay? We'll stand right by the studio door. The lights are on so a cop must be back."

"Should have checked my mall cam before I left. I was too excited."

"Well, hurry up and join the party."

"Party of roo, coming right up," she said, and clicked off before I could laugh.

I slipped the phone into my side pocket for easy reach. The front of the mall was lit by a lone, feeble light secured halfway up a pole. It symbolized the hopelessness of the location. None of the ill-fated businesses ever attracted customers by night, or even marauders who'd bother to break in for a few coins and some posies.

Percy was on my shoulder now, and he felt unusually light. That was often the case when he was puffed, and I lifted a hand to check.

Yep. Puffed. An orange dandelion that could almost float away. Eighteen claws digging into my shoulder made his maiden flight unlikely.

"What's wrong?" I asked, reaching down for Keats. The dog's ears weren't within easy reach because they'd flattened. "Uh-oh. Is the roo bruiser back? Maybe we *should* wait in the truck for the others."

That wasn't the only option, however. The front door of the studio was slightly ajar. Light from the back room trickled into the empty main area.

"Should we go in, boys?"

Both pets growled quietly, although Percy's seemed like a roar in my ear.

"I'll take that as a no."

Keats pawed at the door, proof that no sometimes meant yes. We *shouldn't* go in but we could, so we apparently would.

"This is one of those moments when Jilly wants me to count to ten and make better choices. But there must be something here you want to see. Presumably something that will help with the kangaroo capture." I pulled the door open a little more. "Presuming is one of my shortcomings. Cori's not wrong."

Once inside, I thought about shouting a greeting but Keats shot me a look with his blue eye. It felt like a call for silence. When I reached for my flashlight, he poked me. That felt like a call for shadows.

Awesome.

This was also one of the moments I agreed with Jilly about my choices, suspecting it may already be too late.

The dog nudged me toward the wall and then across the room. Our paws and feet were soundless on the mats. About two-thirds of the way, Percy disembarked. I winced as claws flexed and released. He hooked in at shoulder level and climbed the wall mats quickly. Reaching the top, he glanced back with an eerie green stare. There were no ceiling tiles, just bare rafters. The cat walked along the top of the wall like a stealthy secret agent and then stopped. Keats and I followed, knowing Percy had a trick up his furry sleeve. Catching my eye again, the cat got to work, paws raking into the darkness beyond the wall.

Raking. He was just raking. There was no flourish or flash to announce anything dramatic, like another body. It was hard to believe he could outdo the discovery of cremains but he was certainly committed to the endeavor.

After a few moments, Percy hooked something and dragged it out slowly, bit by bit. I had to choke back a scream when I saw what appeared to be a snake. Possibly a dead one, since it wasn't fighting him. After my encounter in the dogcatcher's basement, I was repulsed by writhing reptiles. I wished them no ill but preferred to keep a distance.

Percy was making that impossible by pulling it up and over the wall and dangling it for me to grab. I delayed just long enough for Keats to prod me into doing Percy's bidding.

My fingers tentatively reached out and touched the dangling object.

It wasn't a snake.

It was fabric.

Black fabric.

At the end, as I reeled it in, I saw a monogram stitched in gold.

And that's when the pieces started coming together.

CHAPTER TWENTY-THREE

I was still facing the wall when the back door slammed and footsteps came toward us. Running on instinct, I began stuffing the fabric into the bib of my overalls. It was stiffer than expected and there was no time to roll it all up and stash it properly. My pockets were full, anyway.

"Hello? Oh, it's you, Ivy." The voice behind me confirmed my suspicion but I didn't turn right away. Instead, I tried wedging the long piece of fabric into the waistband of the shorts I always wore under my overalls in case the straps broke. It had happened once and you don't soon forget getting caught with your pants down—on Main Street, no less.

"Hey there," I said, without looking. "Whatcha doing here so late?"

"I could ask the same. We're closed."

"The door was ajar so I stepped inside for a moment. I have a minor wardrobe issue."

There was a long pause. "Is that why you're wriggling around?"

"Yeah, it's a farmer garment 911. You don't want to know."

"You're right, I don't. I only want to know why you're here at this hour dealing with your farmer garment issue."

I did a few more pokes around my waistband, trying to secure Percy's loot. "Came in to avoid the kangaroo. My friends told me the big male is hanging around the mall and we want to trap it. I got trounced by the female earlier, so I'll wait till everyone else arrives."

"And how do they know it's here?" He sounded wary.

"Critter cam. You know, the gadget that shows something getting into your trash bin or eating cereal in your kitchen."

"There's a critter cam on the mall?"

"Sure." I patted my belly, now misshapen under the forgiving denim. "Half a dozen, if I know my friends. Plus, they've been doing flyovers with drones. This roo is restless. He's circled the building at least twice."

"I heard something a few minutes ago. Went out back with a gun but didn't see it."

"Guess I made the right choice to come inside, then."

He laughed, but I thought I detected a hint of menace. The growl deep in Keats' throat agreed. "Not so sure about that."

I glanced up and found Percy had retreated into the rafters. Keats pressed against my leg, ears flat and ruff high. It was a good thing backup was already on the way. Armed backup. Reaching into my side pocket, I pressed Kellan's number. He was probably too far away to help in time, but at least he'd hear what went down. Finally, I gave my belly a last pat and crossed my arms over my midriff to conceal the telltale bulge of hidden plunder.

"Sorry about my overalls. So embarrassing." I pulled in a calming breath and turned to face my potential adversary in the dim light. All I had to do was keep him talking for 10 or 15 minutes, tops. "You can't shoot a kangaroo, Liam. It's illegal."

"Says who?" I couldn't see much of his expression but there was a smirk in his voice. "There's no law against shooting kangaroos in Clover Grove. Especially in self-defense. That beast could have run right at me. It's a monster."

I suspected that was exactly what happened on the night of the murder. "Well, I guess I can't argue with your logic. You're the expert in self-defense."

He took a step toward me. "That's right. I'm the sensei."

I laughed lightly. "And I'm the senseless. At least if you listen to people like Travis Wigg. I try not to, but he does go on."

"Sure does. Can't shut that guy up. I was glad he disappeared for years. No one wanted him to come out of the backwoods."

Since I had nowhere to go but sideways I took a couple of steps, which Liam matched. So did Keats, and I was reasonably sure Percy would do the same from above. "Except for the mayor. And Kellan. And Asher. I have no idea why authorities like Travis so much. He's been nothing but a thorn in my side."

"Full of himself," Liam said. "Always been that way. Humility is a fundamental principle of martial arts so he doesn't deserve that black belt."

For a second, I worried he could see the belt at my neckline or ankle. I didn't want Liam to know I'd found the real murder weapon.

The one with his name stitched right on it.

The one he'd come back inside to hide after killing Knox and was trying to reclaim tonight.

"He doesn't have his belt anymore, remember. It's in police lockup."

"Probably never earned it, anyway. Joined the army and came back with it. No one gets a black belt in two years unless they pay someone off."

"Sounds like Travis. Total fraud. Whereas I bet you worked your butt off to get yours."

"You bet I did. Nearly five years of hard slogging but I got there. Started a studio in Dog Town and never looked back."

My eyes fell to his footwear. The white showed up well enough to confirm my suspicion. "Nice kicks, Liam. Business must be good."

The high-end sneakers very likely matched the footprints in the damp soil near the Wigg campsite, in addition to the one in the flour on Daisy's kitchen floor. The twins had taught me plenty since I came home, including the brand names of coveted footwear. They'd kill for these shoes, and Liam probably had. The gold from his family's private crematorium alone could finance the very best.

"I do okay." He held out a shoe and inspected it. "Time for a new pair. They get dirty so fast."

"They sure do." I jiggled one work boot before taking another few sideways steps toward the door. "Can't wear shoes like that on a farm."

"Guess not." He mirrored my steps again. "You probably should have kept those boots on the farm tonight."

I pointed an index finger at him. "So right. I told myself I should and yet I couldn't and wouldn't. The things I'll do for a kangaroo. Ooh. More rhyming."

Now we'd entered the circle of insipid light from the parking lot and I could see his expression. He glanced out at the road and back to me, giving me a hint as to his state of mind. I was pretty sure I saw the gleam of crazy in his blue eyes.

"Tell me why you're really here, Ivy," he said. "I like your nephews and there's no reason for us to be at odds."

He wanted to know what I knew before deciding what to do. At this point, he wasn't fully committed to snuffing me out but it wouldn't take much. Not with the crazy in his eyes. All I had to do was keep up some fancy footwork for another 10 minutes, tops. Edna should be here by now. She must have waited for a ride from Gertie.

"Just like I said, Liam. I'm here to rescue the kangaroo. I only came inside because the door was open and my dog was so anxious.

Kangaroos hate dogs, you see, because dingos are their only real enemy in the wild. Other than humans, of course. They'll drown dogs if they can."

Keats was so focused he let that slide, but I'd pay for it later.

If there was a later.

Liam smirked and I could see it this time. "I heard about this from your nephews. They say you're the queen of bafflegab."

"The queen? How flattering, but I think the crown goes to my mother." I pressed a humble palm to my chest. "Speaking of family, I met your grandfather."

The smirk vanished instantly. "My grandfather? When? He didn't mention visitors."

"Just yesterday. I was visiting Hoyle Wigg and he didn't want the potted plant I brought him so I gave it to your grandfather. They're neighbors in the nursing home. He's so nice. Told me to call him Pops."

"My granddad is dying in case you didn't notice. Why would you give him a plant that will last longer than he will?"

"So sorry, Liam." I took a couple more steps away. "I didn't think of it that way. No wonder Hoyle turned it down."

"Hoyle's an idiot, like his sons."

"Does your granddad agree? Because he didn't have a bad thing to say. I didn't intrude long, mind you. Just put the plant on the windowsill beside the photo of you and your brother. You two looked like twins."

He stared at me and even with the added light, I couldn't make out what he was thinking. I sensed it wasn't good, though.

"Don't talk about my brother. He's gone. And now I'm losing my Pops, too."

"What happened to Niall? Heard you used to run a studio together." I'd actually seen Niall's name embroidered on the black belt, alongside Liam's and the name of their studio. It was a tradition I knew about from my nephews.

Liam's Adam's apple bobbed. "A long time ago. Before Knox Wigg killed Niall."

"Knox? Seriously? How horrible. When did that happen?"

Liam started pacing. His grief over losing his brother was obviously still raw today. "Around the time Travis shipped Knox overseas. No one knew where he'd gone till a year ago, when Knox got caught on social media boxing a kangaroo to save a dog. My granddad told me to leave it. Said sometimes you have to let sleeping rats lie."

"Rats?" I made some mental leaps. "Did Knox rat your brother out about something?"

The pacing stopped and he crossed his muscular arms. "Knox was hired to drive getaway on a job. Pops took a chance on him, despite knowing Hoyle's erratic history. When Knox was parked waiting, he saw a dog get hit by a car and ran to help."

"Aw, the poor dog. I'd have done the same."

"Would you?" He tilted his head. "Right in the middle of a life and death job? Because that's when my brother ran out and found the getaway car empty. No key. Nothing. So Niall ran, and the guy he robbed ran faster." His fingers came up in the shape of a pistol. "Bang. No more brother. No best friend. No business partner."

I wanted to ask about the injured dog but a poke in the thigh from another dog kept me on track. "And Knox? What happened to him?"

"Cops found him at the vet's office. Knox sang like a bird. There wasn't enough to tie my granddad to the job, thank goodness. He had a thriving business to run."

A thriving business that dropped people into an old oil tank for demolition. At least, more recently.

"That's so tragic, Liam. Things like that have happened in hill country for a century, but I'm sorry it caught up with Niall."

"And now it's caught up with you," he said.

If I hadn't moved, it was distinctly possible—even likely—that I could have kept the conversation going long enough for my friends to arrive. I was the queen of bafflegab, after all.

But I did move.

And when I took those steps, Liam's black belt started slipping out of my pant leg.

CHAPTER TWENTY-FOUR

L iam processed what he was seeing in a second and lunged for the belt. "Where did you find that?"

"The black belt? It just fell out of the ceiling. I tucked it into my overalls for safekeeping, since I don't carry a purse."

"I believe that's mine." He bent to grab the end and started pulling. It was uncomfortable and the elastic of my shorts snapped hard against my flesh as he gave the belt a rude yank. I backed away a few paces as it unspooled from my overalls.

It was uncomfortable in other ways, too. Liam knew I'd found the belt and that it tied him—quite literally—to Knox's murder. He'd already been on the fence about killing me, but this would push him over. The belt he was rolling up neatly could do double duty and then he'd cart me off to the family incinerator.

Choking probably wouldn't be the worst way to go. If nothing else, this superb athlete would be efficient. He had moved fast before and he'd do the same tonight, with the prospect of my friends arriving.

While he was still bent over gathering the belt, I stared at his balding head. Hair didn't want to grow there, unlike on Wigg scalps. Maybe it was infertile ground.

Keats poked me in the thigh again. Harder this time. I was missing something.

Aha. I was missing an opportunity.

An opportunity to overreach.

Or, if I got lucky, reach just far enough to exit stage left.

As Liam straightened, I took a deep breath to center myself, just like Edna told me. Then I caught Liam's eye and raised both fists high. He instantly matched my posture, the long belt unfurling again from his left hand.

Then I ducked, spun and kicked as hard as I could.

My technique felt flawless, and the kick may have landed just right if Liam hadn't reached out and caught my boot with his right hand.

Technique was nothing without speed when facing a skilled opponent. And now my foot was in Liam's possession. I tried to jerk it back but he loosened his grip only long enough to slide up and clamp my calf above the boot. It was a better grip for someone with large hands. A vicelike grip.

I was standing sideways on one leg, desperately trying to keep my balance with flailing arms. "Okay, Liam, you win. Being in the dojo made me cocky. It was stupid of me to even try a sidekick."

"You're a lot of things, Ivy, but not stupid. The twins said you've evaded death plenty, but you stepped in it this time."

He started moving backward slowly while holding my foot up. I had no choice but to hop along when the alternative was to fall over and risk the grappling Dad warned me about. Keats would help. Percy, too. But this man was a killing machine—as fit an enemy as I'd ever encountered. Not to mention the gun.

Backing away slowly, he hopped me to the door leading to the back room. He'd likely done this countless times in class when boys like my nephews overreached. For me, it was all brand new. If I thought I was fit, I wasn't fit for this.

In the doorway, I braced myself on the frame, panting. "Just give me a minute to catch my breath."

"What's the point?" he said. "These are your last breaths."

"Let me enjoy them, then. Since you're going to kill me, can you tell me why you decided to strangle Knox now? You could have killed him years ago."

He levered my leg up till my hamstrings screamed. The muscles were already tight from a very active day. I figured he was going to ignore my question but then he said simply, "For my Pops. He overheard Lenore tell Hoyle that Knox had a son, and it gutted him. Pops lost his son and then his grandson. He wanted Knox to know exactly how a loss like that felt."

"So you hired someone to take out Camden in Australia."

"Yeah. Never send someone to do a job when you can do it better yourself. That's what Pops said when he found out." With the light framing Liam, I could see a mottled flush rising on his neck. He had let his dying grandfather down. "I booked a flight but before I could leave, Knox came here. Drew attention to himself by stealing those roos. Gilroy Leek's zookeeper saw them and called me."

"Sounds like divine justice," I said. "Now you could turn Knox's love for animals against him."

"Something like that."

He tugged on my foot and I held on tighter. Just a few more minutes. A few more questions.

A harder tug made me release the doorframe. No use pulling my shoulders out of the sockets when there was still a chance I could get him in a knee trap.

Not much of a chance, but with Keats and Percy backing me, I had to keep the faith.

The backroom was tiny—exactly four hops long—and the back door was still ajar. He kicked it open and stepped outside.

Liam was going to kill me in the alley, just like he did Knox.

"Did you plan to kill Travis, too?" I asked, clutching the next doorframe. Keats slid past my leg but Liam either didn't notice or didn't care. He must have heard about the dog's skills from my nephews but it didn't faze him. Guess that confidence came with the black belt.

"Travis would have been a bonus," he said. "The kid was the first mark and Knox second. Followed the van up from Brandi's house, never expecting them to land at the mall when I'd only just left. The kid took off in the van so I changed priorities. Hid behind the dumpster while the brothers argued about something I couldn't hear. When Travis went inside, I took my chance and nailed Knox."

"When did the kangaroo nail *you*?" I asked. "I saw scratches on your arm at Daisy's."

"Glancing blow. Barely slowed me down. Then Travis came back and while he got to know loss, I slipped inside."

"Then you threw your belt into the rafters and left by the front door."

"I'd taken his belt earlier, figuring it would come in handy. Subbed them out fast." His shrug only increased the strain on my leg. "No critter cam to prove anything. No Ivy to prove anything."

"Guess I'm on my way to the family incinerator."

The tension on my leg slackened slightly. "What?"

"I found your crematorium earlier. Well, my pets did. I only wish I could leave you some gold teeth to pawn later for new kicks." I parted my lips in a grin—or grimace. "See? Still have all mine."

His grip eased even more as he factored this into the equation. If the police knew about the oil tank oven, it changed everything. It would bring shame on the Turco name, and if the old man survived long enough, he would be charged. Liam's eyes darted from side to side and I knew he was weighing his options. He had a chance to run as far as Australia.

Instead, Liam dug deep and committed to the task. He clamped down harder on my leg and pulled, reminding me of how Cori and Edna had handled Hildy Hopper today. In her case, they steered by her tail. In mine, it was a leg. They were both levers. My grip on the doorframe was failing.

"Let go. It's time, Ivy."

"Time for you to run, Liam. When I told the chief about your oven, he said the only escape from crime is flight. Knox pulled it off and you can, too."

The next words came in short pants as he tugged. "We. Do. Not. Run. Not the Turcos."

I came out the door with the last phrase. Liam would not let his family down again.

"Humility," I said. "You said it's a fundamental principle of martial arts. What about self-control and respect?"

"I make my own principles now." He deliberately twisted my leg to hurt me, and I couldn't help moaning. "And it's family first."

"I get that, but—"

He twisted again and I spun my arms to stay upright. We were on asphalt and gravel. I would surely slip on pebbles and tear some ligaments going down.

This was hopeless. Utterly hopeless. There were no sirens. No lights or engines from the cavalry rolling in. I was toast.

Except... On the top rim of a new dumpster sat a fluffy feline warrior. He was flexing to plummet onto Liam's bald head. Meanwhile, Keats was crouched and waiting. If the three of us could just get this guy down, I could do what Dad said and run like the wind.

And I had an idea.

Pulling in another deep breath, I lifted my hand slightly to signal the boys.

In that brief pause, I heard a familiar noise in the alley that I struggled to identify.

Thrumming.

There was a rhythmic thump creating a vibration that came up my good leg and made my throat tighten.

Liam's eyes widened and he let go of my foot so suddenly that I fell over on my side. Percy yowled and I rolled instantly onto my back. "Keats," I yelled. "Inside!"

I didn't have a chance to see if he obeyed before the kangaroo bounded right over me. As soon as the big buck passed, I propped myself up on my elbow just in time to see Liam get slammed.

The boomer barely slowed down. He hopped past the dumpster and into the darkness.

Liam started clambering to his feet and I raised my hand again. He would be easier for the pets to tackle now.

But someone beat them to it. A man in a lumberjacket with vast amounts of hair hurtled past the dumpster and executed the spinning sidekick that had eluded me earlier. It sent Liam reeling but he gathered himself quickly. He ran toward Travis, who danced back before landing a punch in the bald man's ear. Then he slid his hand around and forced Liam over till he was kissing his own knee. Locking fingers under Liam's knee, Travis rolled over backward, smashing the bald man into the gravel. Both men jumped up like twin Terminators, programmed to avenge their brothers.

Backing up, Travis ran at Liam and did a scissor sweep, taking him down once again.

This master class in mixed martial arts might have gone on for hours had others not wearied of the show.

As soon as Travis was up and clear, an orange rocket shot down from the dumpster to land on the killer's bald head while the tuxedoed warrior dealt the killing blow to Liam's earlobe.

It felt good to hear that man scream. Really good.

And while the pets had him down, there was a bellow. "Dagnabit, Ivy, what in tarnation is wrong with you?"

I let Jilly and Poppy pull me to my feet and wobbled between them. "Tie him up, Edna."

She stomped over to the fallen man and dismissed Percy, Keats and Travis. "Tie him up, Edna," she repeated. "Always the same old thing without so much as a please. Meanwhile, Travis here is more interested in testosterone theater."

"Watch out for the boomer," I called. "He bodychecked Liam and went into the woods."

Cori came up with her phone in gloved hand. "Critter cam five has him. The roo's coming in hot out front. Someone hold off the cops." She looked at me. "You've got the most clout."

"Me? My cloutometer is at zero. Lower. Trust me, if I ask Kellan to delay an arrest for animal rescue, he'll ask for the rings back."

"He won't," Jilly said, half-hugging me. "Kellan is a gentleman, so he'll let you keep the rings. But he might decide to marry Cori instead."

"We were just talking about that earlier," I said.

"Talking about me marrying Chief Uppity?" Cori flipped an orange flare my way. "No, we were not. He's far too tall. And, you know, uppity."

Poppy squeezed me much harder than Jilly. It didn't feel like a hug but a shoulder strangle. "Stop joking around and get this guy arrested," she said.

"Joking around is my way of dealing with stress. I was very nearly murdered, Poppy."

"So, what else is new? And when we came around the corner, Travis was saving your life. He deserves to see Knox's killer in cuffs."

"He had help. Do you think Travis pierced Liam's earlobe and raked over his scalp?"

She shuddered. "I hope not. But let's just get this guy behind bars."

"This guy is going nowhere," Edna said, getting up off her knees. She had secured his hands and feet, and looped them together, too. He couldn't roll out of this alley if he tried, but it didn't look like he planned to go anywhere.

Cori snapped gloved fingers with her free hand while watching the camera feed on her phone. "The buck roo is back in the woods, people. Based on his pattern, I'm guessing he'll circle round the front again. Let's be ready this time."

"Gertie, will you and Minnie do the honors while the rest of us capture the kangaroo?" Edna asked.

"My pleasure, old friend. Good luck with the boomer."

Edna held out her hand, palm up, to demand my phone. "No luck required. We have all the skills we need."

"Why *my* phone?" I asked, surrendering it reluctantly.

"Because his Royal Chiefness will answer it, if only to tear a strip off you."

She wasn't wrong, but when Kellan's voice came out over the speaker, worry was first on the agenda. "You're okay? Travis says you're okay."

Figured Travis would be first in with the news. "We're fine and—"

"That's enough bonding." Edna pulled the phone away. "Chief, we need you to stand down on the police presence. We have a very good chance of apprehending a second fugitive here, but a half dozen cop cars will send him hopping again."

My fiancé let out a huffy grunt that made Cori wink at me and mouth, "Uppity."

"Miss Evans, I'm not delaying the due process of law while you coax a macropod into a van."

"If only it were that easy, Chief. This is more a matter of roping and grappling. Do you know what it's like to grapple?"

The pause was so long I knew he was having a flashback to our discussion earlier. "I won't be decoyed from the matter at hand, Miss Evans. The police are coming in immediately."

She handed the phone to me. "Work your wiles."

Jilly actually snorted with laughter and I smiled, too. "Fresh out of wiles, Edna. Best I can do is ask nicely. Chief Harper, will you please come on foot with a minimal complement so we can work our rescue magic?"

His grumble sounded a lot like Keats, but I could sense him yielding. "Is Mr. Turco as secure as Travis says?"

"Trussed up thoroughly, and Minnie's on duty. Deputies Percy and Keats are here, too. Neither is inclined to abandon the trophy."

"Ears and scalp?" he asked.

"Substantial lacerations. Bring the first aid kit."

Edna smirked. "Do that, Chief, because this RN is off duty. Come in through the woods, too. You might flush out the roo."

Louder grumbling at the other end made Keats pant-laugh for the first time in what felt like forever. It had been a very tense evening.

After Kellan clicked off, I felt the strength whoosh out of me. Jilly valiantly supported me alone when Poppy left to go over to Travis. He was pacing on the far side of the dumpster, no doubt grieving his brother. I would leave it to Kellan to share the details of Liam's confession.

"Sit down, Ivy," Jilly said. "I'll stay here with you. There are plenty of volunteers. Everyone likes night rescues but us."

"Can we go around the front and watch from there?"

Jilly looked over at Travis and called, "Mr. Wigg? My best friend needs a hand to get back to the truck."

"Another one? I offered hands and feet to serve earlier." His white teeth flashed as he came our way, with Poppy trailing behind. "Aren't you glad I came to help with the rescue?"

"Very. Those were impressive moves. Although I was hoping for more grappling."

Laughing, he swept me out of Jilly's arms and right off my feet. Despite my protests, he carried me around the side of the building and when we reached the front Kellan was walking up the driveway with Asher.

My brother just shook his head at me, squeezed his wife's arm, and continued around the back.

Kellan accepted delivery of an exhausted fiancée. Hugging me, he turned to the crowd in front of the mall. "Do you want to watch from here? Best seat in the house."

I wrapped my arms around his neck, tensing as the roo emerged once more from the bush. He was hopping slowly now, almost as if he hoped to be caught.

Edna didn't wait to be asked twice. She let her rope fly and lassoed the roo in one try. Maybe the buck was as tired as I was because the struggle was brief and almost perfunctory. The crew had him subdued and in Bridget's van in no time at all. When he was secure, Jilly left us to take a closer look.

"Poor guy wants to come in," I said. "Clover Grove wildlife is too much for him."

"For all of us," Kellan said. "Can I set you down?"

I nodded. "Cori? Can you wait till I get home to reunite Hildy and Roofus?"

Her gloves got busy again. "Roofus? You're presuming."

"Roofus and Hildy. Don't ask me how I know, but I just roo."

Another flip of orange fingers was all the satisfaction I got.

With my boots on the ground, I leaned against Kellan and asked, "Did you hear everything?"

"Most of it, yeah. We were already on the way back but I set a new record for speed."

I straightened quickly. "But you left officers there, right? At the oven?"

Affection and annoyance did their familiar dance across his features. "Did I graduate cop school yesterday? Of course there are people there. I pulled officers from all over, because the job is that big."

"You found more cremains?"

"Plenty. And metal detectors suggest there's more buried in the vicinity. I'll head down to talk to Carmen Turco soon. The staff put him in isolation for me so he won't know what's coming."

I thought about my brief visit to the old man. "Check under his rosebushes, Kellan. Carmen credited his gardening success to excellent fertilizer."

He winced. "Will do. This is an important find, Ivy. Likely to answer a lot of questions. The police have been watching Carmen for decades but never got anything to stick. He's the first person we looked into after Knox died but his nose seemed clean. It's a relief to catch him."

"Just in time, before he passes." I bent to brush off my overalls. "Maybe we should head down there now. Carmen could die before you read him his rights."

"You're not going anywhere but home to Rooby Roo and Hildy Hopper." He looked pleased to remember their names. "I'll visit the nursing home as soon as Liam's detained. I'm less worried the old man will die than that someone will kill him first. When word gets out about their long-gone family members, Liam will be glad he's behind bars. But there are plenty of people the Turcos wronged waiting in prison, too."

"Are they serial killers?" I asked.

"Probably more like organized crime. Small scale, but too big by far."

"Mafia without the rescuing animals part?"

He pushed me away a little. "Speaking of your Mafia... Travis had me on speaker when you were trying to fob me off on Cori Hogan."

I laughed. "That will never happen."

"You bet it won't. If you jilt me at the altar I'll die old and alone. And by alone, I mean no pets. Forget about fifty head of livestock."

"That's right. It's just fifty head, not including the roos." It was past 70 but there was no need for specifics. "We're just one big happy family."

He pulled me back in for a hug and then jumped. Someone had clearly left his trophy in Asher's capable handcuffs and come to cut loose on some pant cuffs.

"Deputy, stand down," Kellan said, peering at him over my shoulder. "Good job tonight, and you're promoted again. But don't let it go to your head."

Keats let out a string of humblebrags while Percy ascended Mt. Kellan from the rear. "See, you're not too tall for Percy or me," I said. "Don't let Cori get you down."

"It's 'uppity' I took objection to. I put up with a lot from them. And you."

Since my lever leg was too sore to rise on tiptoe, I pulled his face down and kissed him. It was about as romantic as it could get, based on the setting and circumstances.

"Get a room," Cori yelled out the window as she drove past us slowly. "Presume no one wants to see this, Ivy."

I didn't stop kissing Kellan but I did give my fingers a workout in Cori's direction behind his back. Without the orange flares of her gloves, it lacked panache, but her laughter told me I'd scored a home run.

CHAPTER TWENTY-FIVE

Jilly drove home.

She'd never driven my truck before and I'd been under the impression that she couldn't drive stick. Tonight, she backed out of the parking spot and headed toward the farm with relative ease. There were stutters here and there but nothing compared to my dismal vehicular performance in our early days in Clover Grove.

I stared at the side of her head until she said, "What?"

"What? You're working that clutch like it's a ballroom dance and you're acting like nothing happened? Jilly, I've given you whiplash in this truck dozens of times and you've never let on you know how to handle it."

Her lips curved into a sly smile. "I never said I couldn't and you didn't ask."

"I didn't ask tonight, either. My right leg still works. Mostly."

"You didn't ask but Keats did. It's not often he dares to puncture my jeans but he herded me around to the driver's side. You were too busy kissing Kellan to notice."

"I was also making rude gestures at Cori, so I was distracted for a moment." I continued to stare at her. "How did Keats know you can drive the truck?"

She was gripping the wheel pretty tight but managed to cast a chilly look at the passenger on my lap. "The odd time I've had a grocery emergency while you were out with Kellan. Keats and I had a deal that he could ride along if he didn't blab. Until tonight, he kept his word. I guess he thinks you're more disabled than you do."

"Or he just wants a smoother ride, which he's definitely getting. Jilly Blackwood Galloway, I am shocked and I no longer shock easily. If you could hide this so long and well, what else aren't you telling me?"

She shrugged. "Hard to say. Some things I bury so deep I don't even know that I know. When the timing is right—or someone throws me to the proverbial dogs—I tell you first. Even Asher doesn't know I drive stick. I prefer being a passenger."

"Ouch, would you mind?" I adjusted the pets on my lap. "You'll leave claw marks."

"There are always claw marks on my legs," she said. "Often my arms and midriff, too."

"And still you'd rather ride shotgun?"

"Yep. All those years leading my own firm made me appreciate when others pilot the ship." She smiled for real. "I only drive in the kitchen."

Leaning back, I tried to relax and enjoy the experience of surrendering the wheel. I always loved it when Kellan drove me around on dates but I preferred to pilot my own ship the rest of the time. Jilly probably knew that, too, and was willing to put up with my hack skills. I let her steer the kitchen and she let me steer outside. It was another reason we were besties.

"So if you'll sidestep the truth about driving, are you also sidestepping the kangaroo prophesy?"

She shook her head. "No baby yet, although I think I'm finally ready. Wouldn't it be nice to reproduce the kangaroo way? Goodbye labor, hello pouch."

"There are downsides. They have to carry the baby until it's basically independent. Daisy's twins aren't even independent yet. Imagine hauling them around in your pouch."

We both laughed and shuddered at the same time.

"Janelle's not always right, you know. She twists things to suit her so-called visions. So, Camden might be the prophesied baby, and Poppy the new mom."

My right hand ran over Keats and my left Percy. "Interesting theory. Do you think Travis and Pops will stay together after all this?"

"Probably. There's that inevitability thing you and Daisy talked about. He kept a lot from Poppy but I'm sure she has secrets as well. It's what they do now that matters."

"I feel bad for him. He's in his forties and been a bystander in his own life for nearly half of it." Keats mumbled something and I nodded. "And maybe I identify with that. I didn't truly feel like a participant in my life until we rescued Keats."

"Same. That was a turning point, wasn't it?" She released the wheel and touched the dog. "Thanks, buddy."

"Oh, look, Keats, Jilly can drive with one hand, too. Is there no end to the revelations?"

She geared down smoothly as we reached the lane into Runaway Inn. "There is something else I should mention. Hoping it doesn't happen, but it might."

"What is it?" There was a note of alarm in my voice. "Is Asher taking a promotion?"

The thought of them leaving still sent a bolt of panic through me, although I wouldn't hold them back. It wouldn't be long before Kellan was a permanent fixture at the farm.

Hopefully.

"Not that. We're staying as long as you'll have us. But

someone's threatening to visit." She navigated the lane with one hand on her throat. "My mother."

"Your mom? That's awesome. She didn't make it to the wedding."

"That was for the best, trust me. She's a very difficult woman."

"And Dahlia isn't?"

Her hand returned to the stick shift. "Your mom is difficult in a manageable way. Mine is not."

I laughed. "We'll see about that. It's time she met your husband and saw the new life you've created."

"She doesn't approve of the new life we've created and didn't want to see it. I have no idea what's bringing her here now. It's something. Mom always has an agenda."

"It'll be fine. You have an amazing kitchen, expert chef and hospitality skills, and a fabulous support network. What could go wrong?"

"So much, Ivy. So much." Keats reached out and poked her arm with his muzzle with a comforting mumble. "I appreciate the kind sentiments, Keats, but you were blessed with a wonderful mom."

"Annie doesn't really want anything to do with him unless they're working a job," I pointed out. "She's a genius but a paws-off mother."

Jilly pulled up beside the barn, parked and handed me the keys. She hadn't stalled once. My best friend never failed to impress. "Thanks for standing behind me, Ivy."

"Like you always stand behind me. It's a given. I'm here for you through the apocalypse and beyond."

"There's only one major thing we disagree on," she said, looking pointedly at the large group surrounding the kangaroo pasture. "Your overloaded ark. What's next?"

Keats' mumble suggested he agreed with Jilly but I talked over him. "I'm feeling penguins. Two of them. Like you'd find on the top of a wedding cake. Or maybe a zebra."

"Stick with the wedding cake. Tomorrow, no matter what, you and I are sitting down and making plans for the big event. Asher said they're going to be slammed with work."

"You got it. I'd better marry that man before Cori steals him."

"As if." She opened the door and let the pets shoot past her. "Let's go watch another happily ever after."

We linked arms as we walked to the pasture together. Looking up at our luxurious home, my heart filled with joy. "I do love a happy ending."

CHAPTER TWENTY-SIX

I turned down the luxury of the inn that night in favor of sleeping in the barn. It wasn't the first time and it wouldn't be the last, but it was certainly the most uncomfortable. I ached all over from my martial arts experiment and the encounter with Liam. Bolts of pain shot up my right leg at regular intervals, making me wonder if it would ever work properly again. Jilly might need to take over as chief driver, rescuer and crimefighter.

No matter how restlessly I turned on the bed of hay, Percy stayed anchored on my chest or hip. He spent hours grooming his gorgeous fluff and I tried not to think about breathing in cremains. I couldn't help but muse over the identities of the people who'd ended up in that oven. The next few weeks or even months would be hard slogging for Kellan, but perhaps he'd have answers to some of the many mysteries in our region.

Keats came back from his rounds just after three a.m. and prodded my leg. I'd left the door open so that he could watch over the kangaroos. Their reunion had been uneventful. Roofus hopped in like he owned the place and took over the feeding station. However, I caught the pair grooming each other just before I called it a night. The Mafia promised to regroup with a plan in a few days, when the adventurous macropods had recovered from their furlough.

"Something wrong?" I asked, gently dislodging Percy as I sat up.

The dog's mumble was neutral. It was something different, not necessarily wrong.

I didn't always respond to neutral but I couldn't sleep anyway.

Outside, I saw a shadowy figure standing beside the kangaroo pen. Since Keats wasn't alarmed, I guessed it was my dad keeping watch. Edna would likely be doing the same with her night vision goggles. She didn't seem to need much sleep anymore.

Roo security turned out to be taller and hairier than either of my suspects.

"Hey," Travis said, when I joined him. "You couldn't sleep either?"

"Nope. Forgot to bring painkillers down from the house. This martial arts stuff is for the young and flexible."

"Tell me about it." Reaching into his pocket, he pulled out a bottle of pills and handed them to me. "I'm too old for it, too. It felt great at the time, though."

"I bet it did. It's all you can do to avenge Knox."

"It's all I need to do. I didn't want that life back then and I don't want it now."

Hearing that gave me relief. Part of me worried Travis would go over to the dark side after what happened. I still didn't know him that well. How could I, when Poppy didn't even know him?

"Travis, I'm so sorry about Knox. I assume Kellan told you what Liam said?"

I saw his beard bob up and down. "Yeah. I missed two decades of my brother's life because he saved a dog when he was on tap to commit a crime."

"You didn't know that already?"

"That's the worst part. He told me about the dog. Said it was a sign to get out of a bad situation, but I didn't believe him. Figured he was just stupid and careless. You don't walk away from a promise to someone like Carmen Turco without repercussions."

"I saw what happened to the people who crossed him. You were right to ship Knox off to Australia. He had a decent life there. He couldn't have had that here."

He crossed his arms across the fencepost and rested his head on them. "I keep wondering what else I could have done. What if I'd gone to Carmen and talked man-to-man? Would Knox still be alive?"

"I don't know much about how men like Carmen operate, but if it's like the movies, he'd have expected something in return. Something big. Like a favor that would have tied you to him forever."

"Probably." His voice was muffled by flannel sleeves. "It's enough like the movies for me to know that. Maybe I should have done it. For Knox."

Keats gave me a nudge toward Travis and I tentatively patted the man's shoulder. "The guy who risked his own life to save a dog wouldn't have wanted that for you. He got himself into the predicament and took responsibility by leaving willingly. You paid a steep price anyway by giving up your army career and living in isolation for ages."

"That wasn't a punishment." His voice was sullen. "It was a relief. I have half a dozen sites across the state and two beyond. Kept rolling in case Carmen decided to come after me."

"A strategy Edna recommends for the end times. Are you going to retreat to the woods now?"

His head shook a negative. "Can't. Solo is safer, but Camden wants to stay in the area."

"Ah, so you're a dad now. Congratulations."

His head came up and I caught a glimmer of teeth. "Thanks. I think. Could have used some ramp-up time. I'm used to a solitary life. A selfish life. But it won't be forever. He's nearly eighteen and can do as he likes."

I pointed to the kangaroos. They were lounging side by side on raised dog beds my dad found in a hurry after learning they liked creature comforts. "That joey is almost ready to tumble into the world but they stick around for ages, sharing the pouch with their younger sibling. The girls normally stay with mom forever and the boys sometimes send grandkids home. Isn't that fascinating?"

His teeth flashed even more. "Probably not as fascinating as you think. What's your point?"

I smiled, too. "Camden probably won't go far. That's my point. I tried to get away from my family and here I am, surrounded by them. And my joeys will stick around too, if I do my job right." Waiting a beat, I added, "Aren't you going to have joeys with Poppy?"

"Dunno. This whole thing rattled me. I don't think I'm good husband material." He slid along the fence away from me. "And *you* don't think I'm good husband material."

"Not that my opinion matters here, but I think you and Poppy might just be inevitable."

"Is that because I saved your life with my spinning sidekick?"

"It was the flying scissor sweep that did it. I thought to myself, that man can protect my sister. Maybe even from herself. She's got some battle scars, too, Travis."

"Nah. She's perfect."

"She is. Like the rest of the Galloways."

We both laughed and he slid back toward me. "The next time we all play softball, I'll pick you for my team."

"Oh? You were that impressed by my athletic prowess behind the strip mall? I wish you'd seen my sidekick. It nearly landed."

"What I saw was someone hopping and talking like it was a coffee date with a killer. All light and airy. No sign of incontinence at all. I guess that's what the overalls are for."

I shoved him. "If that's a compliment, I'm having a hard time seeing it."

"It's a compliment. That was courage under pressure. I underestimated you."

"It's okay. I count on that." I looked up at the stars. "Beautiful night."

He looked up, too. "Best times of my life were under a starry sky with Knox. We hated it at home but we loved our camp life. Early independence."

There was a catch in his voice and I chose my words carefully. "Time to build a new family, Travis. That's what I did." He started to object and I raised my hand. "Yeah, I have my blood family and I'm grateful for them. But my 'found family' is my true family now. Jilly, Edna, Gertie, Buckley, the Thistledown crew, the Rescue Mafia and of course, Kellan. I thought I loved my independence in Boston and I hope I never feel like that again."

"That's risky. Depending on others can make you an easy target."

"Beg to disagree. There's a reason animals gather like a mob of kangaroos. Safety in numbers. Harder to single out. Travis, it's time to herd up."

This time he shoved me. "Are you inviting me into your herd, Ivy?"

I pointed to the dog, who was weaving around our feet. Keats was tying us into the sheepdog love knot. It was wide and loose, not as snug as the one he drew around me with Kellan or my grandparents. Maybe I'd never be close pals with Travis but there was room in my herd for him and maybe even my heart. I used to think compassion was a limited commodity but my heart kept expanding to accommodate new people and the animals in my care.

"Conditionally," I said. "The condition being that I want to learn more about martial arts."

"After tonight? A little knowledge is worse than none at all, Ivy."

"Exactly. So I'll take a large order of knowledge, please."

He tugged on my jacket and walked me back to the barn. "Coming right up. After you get some sleep."

CHAPTER TWENTY-SEVEN

W hen I staggered out of the barn at nine a.m., the kangaroos were gone. My heart stampeded into my throat and adrenaline coursed through my veins, chasing some of the stiffness away. I would find them and someone would pay.

Then I saw the battle flag.

On top of the fencepost Travis had leaned against in the night sat a black glove with an orange middle finger. It was stuffed and positioned just right.

I typed four words into my phone: "Where are my roos?" When she didn't answer right away, I added, "You will pay, Cori Hogan."

The phone rang. "Oooh, someone's cranky? Didn't sleep well? You were certainly snoring hard when I peeked into your barn-room at five."

"You can't just come here and take things." My voice sounded both grating and a little teary. "I didn't even get to say goodbye."

"See, this is why you have so many rescue fails, Ivy. You get attached so fast. Those roos couldn't stay and you know it. There were a dozen cats on your dad's cot in the loft. Imagine if little Rooby got sick."

"You peeped on my dad?"

"Oh, relax. He was already up and helped us board the roos. Probably thought it was for the best, too. Next thing you'd be giving them their own room at the inn." She paused for strategic effect. "Wait, your mom's taken over all of them. Or so your brother says. We had coffee last week."

She had tossed a red herring and I snapped at it hungrily. "You had coffee with my brother?"

"Not like sit down and bond coffee. We grabbed a cup to go and chatted in a private location. The poor guy feels crowded right out of that inn."

"Why are you having illicit coffee meetups with my brother? More importantly, why are you telling me about it?"

"Again, I urge you to relax. It wasn't coffee with Asher your brother, but Asher the cop. We needed some intel for rescue and he's a weaker link than Chief Uppity."

"Cori, I'm tired, sore and grumpy. Stop toying with me and tell me what you did with my roos. I'm coming to say goodbye."

"They're en route to a location so secret even I will never know. If we don't know, Gilroy Leek can't find out and take them back. He has plenty of resources and no heart, Ivy. But the Mafia has a vast network and the perfect pasture for Hoppy and Rooben."

"Hildy Hopper and Roofus Roo," I corrected her. "And little Rooby. Cori, it sounds like you don't even know the people you handed them off to."

"I do. Some by name and others by reputation. The roos are fine and we'll be apprised of their status ongoing. Don't worry." I could imagine her waggling a gloved index finger. "I know you're going to worry, but trust me."

I did trust her. And she was right that I'd only get more attached the longer they stayed. I never wanted Elaine the emu but I would hate to part with her now. "Elaine would have liked the kangaroos. She's probably homesick for Oz."

Cori laughed. "She was hatched in hill country and wants for nothing."

"If you ever steal her in the night, I will have Keats pierce your ears."

"First, it wasn't night, and if your dad helped, it wasn't theft. Second, your dog loves me more than you."

I looked around for said dog and found him pant-laughing. "He finds you mildly entertaining, but that's as far as it goes."

"Fine, we're all good then. Unlike you, I have things to do today. Rescuers never sleep the day away in comfy stalls, Ivy."

"This isn't something I say lightly, Cori, but I hate you. And your gloves."

"I wish I could say that hurts but I packed my feelings in mothballs years ago. Edna says it'll be a boon in the end times." I started to speak but she cut me off. "Are you sure you're ready to be a parent? You sound very juvenile."

I laughed. "I know I do. But the roos were the realization of a dream. Thank goodness I took a few pics of the baby."

"Yes, they grow up too fast. Or so I hear from people who like youngsters."

She didn't say goodbye before hanging up, but my phone was already pinging anyway. What's more, I heard pings in the barn and my father came out, rubbing his head.

There were even more pings behind the barn and Travis appeared, looking quizzical. "What's a Butter Tart 911?"

"You're part of our family's emergency meeting now, too?" I asked.

He walked over to me. "Why so surprised? You welcomed me into the herd only hours ago."

Dad trailed after him. Normally he avoided the meetings but he didn't have an excuse today. "Where is it? Daisy's?"

I had assumed so, but then I saw the vehicles coming up the lane. "Here, I guess. Can't imagine what's so urgent."

People poured into the inn but Dad and I held out as long as we could, loitering by the camelid pasture. Maybe with the new additions of Travis and Camden, they wouldn't notice we were missing.

"Ivy Rose Galloway, get in here," Mom yelled from the porch. She didn't summon Dad but he was snared by the same shrill net.

The last person to arrive was Mandy McCain. She got out of her car and marched up the front steps ahead of me carrying a large cooler.

"Mandy, what gives?" I asked, following.

"Here on official business, Ivy. My lips are sealed."

"Official baker business?" My tired brain started reviewing family birthdays. I couldn't come up with a date for half my siblings.

"Official baker business," Mandy said, walking into the dining room. "This is perfect for a surprise party."

She pulled out a large cake with three tiers. It looked like a wedding cake and I had a sudden fear that the surprise occasion was *my* wedding. Would Kellan arrive in a tux and make it official? It wasn't that I didn't want to be married, but a Butter Tart 911 in my own dining room wasn't at all what I had in mind for the big day. Especially when I looked like I'd slept in a stall and probably still smelled of swamp. In the better or worse department, this was worse.

Then I noticed that all of the many florets on the cake were pink and blue. On top stood two tiny kangaroos, one with a joey in its pouch. Four more kangaroos stood in pairs on the other tiers. Keats gave me a nudge and the pieces fell into place. One look at Daisy as she doffed an apron confirmed it.

"About that kangaroo prophesy," she said. "It's me."

"What's she talking about?" Dad whispered in my ear. "Did she hit her head?"

Mom was speechless, her scarlet lips forming a perfect O. Or was it the back half of a "no"?

"Is there an agenda for the family meeting?" Travis asked. "Because I don't have a clue what's going on."

I winked at Daisy and then Jilly and let the rest of them fumble and guess. It was my big sister's news to break as she liked.

"I don't get it," Asher said. "I didn't leave an important investigation to solve riddles."

Jilly squeezed his forearm till her knuckles whitened and he fell silent.

Wringing the apron in her hands, Daisy finally spelled it out. "I'm having a baby. And when I say a baby, I do mean one."

"A baby? Darling, you're far too—" Mom bit off the word.

"Old? That's what I thought when I went to the doctor. But he's confirmed I'm fitting in another joey just under the line."

"Well, that's wonderful." Mom used the right word but it came out sounding tragic. "Are you sure it's just one?"

"Quite sure. I've had all the tests, due to my age. And I'm over three months along."

Jilly looked at the cake. "Are you keeping the gender a surprise?"

Daisy smiled. "Only Mandy knows. I had the doctor seal the results in an envelope and now all shall be revealed." She checked to make sure Roger and the four boys had joined us. They'd probably arrived late to keep the suspense alive, but none looked exactly thrilled about the news. I wasn't worried. They were all good guys. The baby would have backup at home and beyond.

Mandy handed Daisy a fancy knife and my sister sliced into the cake, right between the kangaroo couple. Then she slid the two sections apart and pink and silver glitter exploded from the center. "It's a girl!"

There was a cheer and I was pretty sure every voice chimed in, even those of the younger twins who were about to be displaced by a princess.

"A girl," Mom said, hugging Daisy. "One girl. That really is wonderful, darling. I've always loved my daughters best."

Now everyone laughed. Asher had been the apple of Mom's eye until Jilly arrived to become the new apple. My best friend would happily yield the throne to a tiny apple. This baby would be adored by all.

I moved in next for a hug, murmuring congratulations into Daisy's ear. "It all starts over, sis. This joey couldn't ask for a better mother."

Daisy pulled Jilly in for a joint hug. "Have babies, you two. Let the cousins grow up together."

Asher overheard that. "Great idea! A new generation. Honey, let's do it. Maybe we'll have twins."

He was so excited by the idea that he missed Jilly's wince. One joey would be plenty for her.

I was relieved Kellan couldn't make it for the big reveal. There was no need to put pressure on him when he was investigating one of the biggest cases of his career.

"Cake?" Mandy said, pulling other treats out of the cooler.

"Cake," I said. "I love a cake breakfast, followed by pie for dessert."

Daisy slipped into the kitchen and came back wielding a shammy in her rubber glove. Sparkles from the glitter bomb were all over the place and would likely embed themselves in cracks in the hardwood floors for years to come.

And they'd make me smile every time I saw them, just like my niece when she joined us.

Jilly grabbed a few bottles of sparkling water and we toasted to the growing family. After clinking Daisy's glass in her rubber glove, I turned to Travis and Camden.

"Welcome to the Galloways, you two," I said. "Glitter bombs to follow."

CHAPTER TWENTY-EIGHT

A few nights later, Kellan managed to uncuff himself from his desk and take me to a pet-free dinner at our favorite restaurant. The Bone Appetit Bistro in Dorset Hills was more kitschy than swanky, but it was the updated version of Hills Hamburgers, the site of most of our high school dates. There were many finer places in Dog Town but we kept coming back out of nostalgia. Our lives were often so complicated now and it was nice not to have to look at the menu.

"Two Doggone Best Burgers," Kellan told the waiter, even before we settled in our favorite booth by the window. He kissed my cheek before sitting down. "How are you feeling?"

"Better. It's going to take a while for my leg to stop locking up but it could have been so much worse."

He shook out his napkin with an unnecessary snap. "You think?"

"Yes, I know. It was foolish to go into that studio before the others arrived. But I didn't know it was Liam inside and I didn't know he was Knox's killer anyway." He continued to stare with his intense dark blue eyes. "Keats and Percy knew, but I didn't. Not until the black belt snaked out of the rafters. And that's when he found me. I was trapped."

"I remember the details from your police report."

His voice had such a chill in it that I did up the buttons on my sweater. "How about we take a moment to celebrate your nailing a criminal kingpin and making him accountable while he's still here to know? And with Liam in jail, there's no one to receive the crown."

"We're working hard to make that so. Organizations like Carmen's tend to reform around the next big player. But we've found enough evidence to cut off a lot of grabby tentacles."

"Good. I'm glad we didn't order the calamari."

Still, no smile. "Ivy, I just think you could have put me ahead of the pets for once, when you knew I was dealing with the crematorium you found."

"The pets found it, Kellan. And I was worried about them being harmed by the kangaroo." I leaned back against the vinyl upholstery. "Is this a business meeting? Because I thought it was a date and wore your favorite sweater."

He looked down to check. "That's not my favorite. My favorite has fewer buttons."

"They're just done up. I could unbutton one if you ease off a little."

He rested his forearms on the table. "What'll it take for two?"

I pretended to think about it. "For two, you need to stop pitting yourself against my pets for the rest of the evening. Say something nice about them and I might even lean forward to reach for the ketchup."

"Deal. Percy's find in the studio was impressive, because we'd looked up there. The belt was hanging from a nail between the walls. And Keats' restraint was admirable. He left the heavy kicking to Travis. Maybe it was more about the unpredictable roo, but still, I like it when he's cautious as well as protective."

"He's not here to refute so we'll let it go." I kept my end of the bargain by reaching for the ketchup long before I needed it. Then I put it back and reached for it again.

Kellan grinned at me. "I'm going to marry you. I knew that sitting right here nearly twenty years ago but I'm doubly sure now."

"Nice," I said. "When? Because the masses are getting restless."

"I thought they'd be aflutter with the baby news and forget about our plans."

"Me too, but oddly, it's intensified the pressure. There's a lot of hype about producing the next generation of cousins."

"Yeah? You ready for that, risk-taker?"

The burgers arrived and I took my time adding ketchup before answering. "Why does hopping after a killer on one leg seem less intimidating than growing and raising a tiny human?"

He pushed the mustard toward me. "That bad, eh? What's got you so spooked?"

I swirled a fry in ketchup. "Daisy. Before I knew she was pregnant again she went on and on about the never-ending responsibility. She also talked a lot about growing up without Dad."

"Obviously she had some complicated feelings about starting over, but you said she seemed happy at the party."

"Very. I guess it was an adjustment, but Daisy will rock it. Literally."

He lifted his burger and bit in. "Everything will be just fine," he said around a mouthful.

I wasn't sure whether that was about Daisy or us, but I went with it. Most of the time I knew it would be fine. "Should we aim for a fall wedding? Maybe check out a couple of venues?"

"Fall's my favorite season. And if you want to hold it right here, I'll be fine with that. After all, it's where we had our first real date. Do you remember?"

"How could I forget? It was the best first date ever." At least until we left the old diner and went to a party. But Kellan didn't need to know everything that happened that night. Looking back, I realized it set me on the trail to becoming who I was now. Somehow, I'd blocked it out for a long time and become an uptight HR professional.

"It was." He took another bite and mumbled, "Quite an adventure."

I looked up quickly. What did Kellan really know about that night? Maybe I hadn't been the only one having a life-changing adventure. Just as I was about to ask him more, the waiter came back with an extra plate of fries. "Compliments of the manager."

Bridget Linsmore ran the place and I waved to her as she tied on her apron. She looked weary. The kangaroo rescue had taken a lot out of all of us.

By the time I looked back at Kellan the moment was gone. We'd have a lifetime to talk about that night.

"How about we hold the wedding at that mill down near Fleetborough?" I suggested. "I drove by it the other day and it'll be so pretty when the leaves change."

"Sounds good to me. Any place but that zoo. You know, the cheesy one that hosts parties?"

"Agree totally. If I wanted that many animals around, we'd host it at the farm."

Of course I wanted that many animals around but he'd volunteered to live among them for the rest of our days. I could give him a break for the wedding.

Setting his burger down, he spun the pretty baubles on my ring finger. "One more button and you can have the zoo."

I laughed. "One more button and Bridget will kick us out. No zoo. We're getting married somewhere tasteful and romantic. We deserve that."

We both leaned across the table and met in the middle. When

we tried this last year, the attempted kiss ended very awkwardly indeed. A sweater I borrowed from Jilly had died for the cause.

Since then, we'd learned a thing or two about love and obstacles. And tonight, the kiss came in for an absolutely perfect landing.

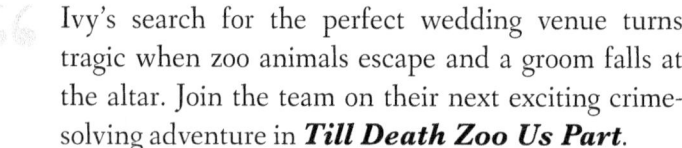

Ivy's search for the perfect wedding venue turns tragic when zoo animals escape and a groom falls at the altar. Join the team on their next exciting crime-solving adventure in ***Till Death Zoo Us Part***.

Interested in hearing more about my writing and my dogs? Join the Ellen Riggs newsletter at ***ellenriggs.com/opt-in***.

RUNAWAY FARM & INN RECIPES

Better than Bingo Pecans

Ingredients

- 1 egg white
- pinch of salt
- 1 cup brown sugar
- 1 tbsp flour

- 1 tbsp vanilla
- 1 cup pecans

Instructions

1. Preheat oven to 325 degrees. Line cookie sheet with aluminum foil and spritz with cooking spray.
2. Add salt to egg white and beat until stiff peaks form.
3. In a separate bowl, combine brown sugar and flour. Slowly add mixture to beaten egg white. Continue mixing until all the brown sugar/flour mixture is well mixed with egg white. Stir in vanilla.
4. Fold in pecans gradually, making sure they are well coated.
5. Use a spoon to transfer pecans one at a time to cookie sheet. (Patience is your friend!)
6. Bake until lightly brown. (Approximately 10-15 minutes, depending on your oven)
7. Let cool until they've hardened a little bit.

(Recipe compliments of Bought-the-Farm reader, Paula Harmon)

More Books by Ellen Riggs

Bought-the-Farm Cozy Mystery Series

- A Dog with Two Tales (Prequel)
- Dogcatcher in the Rye
- Dark Side of the Moo
- A Streak of Bad Cluck
- Till the Cat Lady Sings
- Alpaca Lies

- Twas the Bite Before Christmas
- Swine and Punishment
- The Cat and the Riddle
- Don't Rock the Goat
- Swan with the Wind
- How to Get a Neigh with Murder
- Tweet Revende
- For Love Or Bunny
- Between a Squawk and a Hard Place
- Double Dog Dare
- Deerly Departed
- Think Outside the Fox
- Mouse of Ill Repute
- Bee All and End All
- Sheep with One Eye Open
- Roo the Day
- Till Death Zoo Us Part
- Hit the Road, Quack
- Onc Horse Open Slay
- Beg, Burrow or Steal

Bought-the-Farm Mysteries - Boxed Sets

- Bought the Farm Mysteries - Books 1-3
- Bought the Farm Mysteries - Books 4-6
- Bought the Farm Mysteries - Books 7-9
- Bought the Farm Mysteries - Books 1-10

Dog Town Series

- Ready or Not in Dog Town (The Beginning)
- Bitter and Sweet in Dog Town (Labor Day)
- A Match Made in Dog Town (Thanksgiving)

- Lost and Found in Dog Town (Christmas)
- Calm and Bright in Dog Town (Christmas)
- Tried and True in Dog Town (New Year's)
- Yours and Mine in Dog Town (Valentine's Day)
- Nine Lives in Dog Town (Easter)
- Great and Small in Dog Town (Memorial Day)
- Bold and Blue in Dog Town (Independence Day)
- Better or Worse in Dog Town (Labor Day)

Mystic Mutt Mysteries Paranormal Cozy

- I Want You to Haunt Me (Prequel)
- You Can't Always Get What You Haunt
- Any Way You Haunt It
- I Only Haunt to be with You
- All I Haunt Is You
- Do You Haunt to Know a Secret?
- All I Haunt for Christmas
- I Haunt You Back